Lord Lytton

Pausanias the Spartan

An Unfinished Historical Romance

Lord Lytton

Pausanias the Spartan
An Unfinished Historical Romance

ISBN/EAN: 9783337049447

Printed in Europe, USA, Canada, Australia, Japan

Cover: Foto ©Andreas Hilbeck / pixelio.de

More available books at **www.hansebooks.com**

PAUSANIAS AND CLEONICE.

Page 80.

The Lord Lytton Edition

PAUSANIAS THE SPARTAN

AN UNFINISHED HISTORICAL ROMANCE

BY

THE LATE LORD LYTTON

(EDITED BY HIS SON)

PHILADELPHIA:
J. B. LIPPINCOTT COMPANY.
1888.

TO

THE REV. BENJAMIN HALL KENNEDY, D.D.,

CANON OF ELY, AND REGIUS PROFESSOR OF GREEK IN THE UNI-
VERSITY OF CAMBRIDGE.

MY DEAR DR. KENNEDY,—Revised by your helpful hand,
and corrected by your accurate scholarship, to whom may
these pages be so fitly inscribed as to that one of their author's earliest and most honored friends,* whose generous
assistance has enabled me to place them before the public
in their present form?

It is fully fifteen, if not twenty, years since my father
commenced the composition of an historical romance on
the subject of Pausanias, the Spartan Regent.   Circumstances, which need not here be recorded, compelled him
to lay aside the work thus begun.   But the subject continued to haunt his imagination and occupy his thoughts.
He detected in it singular opportunities for effective ex-

---

* The late Lord Lytton, in his unpublished autobiographical mem-
oirs, describing his contemporaries at Cambridge, speaks of Dr. Kennedy as "a young giant of learning."—L.

1*

ercise of the gifts most peculiar to his genius; and re-
peatedly, in the intervals of other literary labor, he returned
to the task which, though again and again interrupted, was
never abandoned.   To that rare combination of the imaginative and practical faculties which characterized my father's intellect, and received from his life such varied illustration, the story of "Pausanias," indeed, briefly as it is
told by Thucydides and Plutarch, addressed itself with singular force.   The vast conspiracy of the Spartan Regent,
had it been successful, would have changed the whole
course of Grecian history.   To any student of political
phenomena, but more especially to one who, during the
greater part of his life, had been personally engaged in
active politics, the story of such a conspiracy could not
fail to be attractive.   To the student of human nature the
character of Pausanias himself offers sources of the deep-
est interest; and, in the strange career and tragic fate of
the great conspirator, an imagination fascinated by the supernatural must have recognized remarkable elements of
awe and terror.   A few months previous to his death, I
asked my father whether he had abandoned all intention
of finishing his romance of "Pausanias."   He replied, "On
the contrary, I am finishing it now," and entered, with
great animation, into a discussion of the subject and its
capabilities.   This reply to my inquiry surprised and impressed me; for, as you are aware, my father was then engaged in the simultaneous composition of two other and
very different works, "Kenelm Chillingly" and the "Pa-
risians."   It was the last time he ever spoke to me about

"Pausanias;" but from what he then said of it I derived an impression that the book was all but completed, and needing only a few finishing touches to be ready for publication at no distant date.

This impression was confirmed, subsequent to my father's death, by a letter of instructions about his posthumous papers which accompanied his will. In that letter, dated 1856, special allusion is made to "Pausanias" as a work already far advanced toward its conclusion.

You, to whom, in your kind and careful revision of it, this unfinished work has suggested many questions which, alas! I can not answer, as to the probable conduct and fate of its fictitious characters, will readily understand my reluctance to surrender an impression seemingly so well justified. I did not, indeed, cease to cherish it until reiterated and exhaustive search had failed to recover from the "wallet" wherein Time "puts alms for oblivion" more than those few imperfect fragments which, by your valued help, are here arranged in such order as to carry on the narrative of "Pausanias," with no solution of continuity, to the middle of the second volume.

There the manuscript breaks off. Was it ever continued further? I know not. Many circumstances induce me to believe that the conception had long been carefully completed in the mind of its author; but he has left behind him only a very meagre and imperfect indication of the course which, beyond the point where it is broken, his narrative was intended to follow. In presence of this fact, I have had to choose between the total suppression of the fragment, and the publication of it in its present form. My choice has not been made without hesitation; but I trust that, from many points of view, the following pages will be found to justify it.

Judiciously (as I can not but think) for the purposes of his fiction, my father has taken up the story of "Pausanias" at a period subsequent to the battle of Platæa; when the Spartan Regent, as Admiral of the United Greek Fleet in the waters of Byzantium, was at the summit of his power and reputation. Mr. Grote, in his great work, expresses the opinion (which certainly can not be disputed by unbiased readers of Thucydides) that the victory of Platæa was not attributable to any remarkable abilities on the part of Pausanias. But Mr. Grote fairly recognizes as quite exceptional the fame and authority accorded to Pausanias, after the battle, by all the Hellenic States, the influence which his name commanded, and the awe which his character inspired. Not to the mere fact of his birth as a Heracleid, not to the lucky accident (if such it were) of his success at Platæa, and certainly not to his undisputed (but surely by no means uncommon) physical courage, is it possible to attribute the peculiar position which this remarkable man so long occupied in the estimation of his contemporaries. For the little that we know about Pausanias we are mainly dependent upon Athenian writers, who must have been strongly prejudiced against him. Mr. Grote, adopting (as any modern historian needs must do) the narrative so handed down to him, never once pauses to question its estimate of the character of a man who was at one

time the glory, and at another the terror, of all Greece.
Yet in comparing the summary proceedings taken against
Leotychides with the extreme, and seemingly pusillanimous,
deference paid to Pausanias by the Ephors long after they
possessed the most alarming proofs of his treason, Mr.
Grote observes, without attempting to account for the fact,
that Pausanias, though only Regent, was far more powerful than any Spartan King. Why so powerful? Obvious-
ly, because he possessed uncommon force of character; a
force of character strikingly attested by every known incident of his career; and which, when concentrated upon the
conception and execution of vast designs (even if those designs be criminal), must be recognized as the special attribute of genius. Thucydides, Plutarch, Diodorus, Grote,
all these writers ascribe solely to the administrative incapacity of Pausanias that offensive arrogance which characterized his command at Byzantium, and apparently cost
Sparta the loss of her maritime hegemony. But here is
precisely one of those problems in public policy and personal conduct which the historian bequeaths to the imaginative writer, and which needs, for its solution, a profound
knowledge rather of human nature than of books. For,
dealing with such a problem, my father, in addition to the
intuitive penetration of character and motive which is common to every great romance-writer, certainly possessed two
qualifications special to himself : the habit of dealing *prac-
tically* with political questions, and experience in the active management of men. His explanation of the policy
of Pausanias at Byzantium, if it be not (as I think it is)

1*

the right one, is at least the only one yet offered. I venture to think that, historically, it merits attention; as, from
the imaginative point of view, it is undoubtedly felicitous.
By elevating our estimate of Pausanias as a statesman, it
increases our interest in him as a man.

The author of "Pausanias" does not merely tell us that
his hero, when in conference with the Spartan commission-
ers, displayed "great natural powers which, rightly trained,
might have made him not less renowned in council than in
war," but he gives us, though briefly, the arguments used by
Pausanias. He presents to us the image, always interest-
ing, of a man who grasps firmly the clear conception of a
definite but difficult policy, for success in which he is dependent on the conscious or involuntary co-operation of
men impenetrable to that conception, and possessed of a
collective authority even greater than his own. To retain
Sparta temporarily at the head of Greece was an ambition
quite consistent with the more criminal designs of Pausanias; and his whole conduct at Byzantium is rendered
more intelligible than it appears in history, when he points
out that "for Sparta to maintain her ascendency two things
are needful: first, to continue the war by land; secondly,
to disgust the Ionians with their sojourn at Byzantium, to
send them with their ships back to their own havens, and
so leave Hellas under the sole guardianship of the Spartans
and their Peloponnesian allies." And who has not learned,
in a later school, the wisdom of the Spartan commission-
ers? Do not their utterances sound familiar to us? "Increase of dominion is waste of life and treasure. Sparta

is content to hold her own. What care we who leads the
Greeks into blows? The fewer blows, the better. Brave
men fight if they must: wise men never fight if they can
help it." Of this scene and some others in the first volume
of the present fragment (notably the scene in which the Regent confronts the allied chiefs, and defends himself against
the charge of connivance at the escape of the Persian prisoners), I should have been tempted to say that they could
not have been written without personal experience of political life, if the interview between Wallenstein and the
Swedish embassadors in Schiller's great trilogy did not re-
cur to my recollection as I write. The language of the embassadors in that interview is a perfect manual of practical
diplomacy; and yet in practical diplomacy Schiller had no
personal experience. There are, indeed, no limits to the
creative power of genius. But it is perhaps the practical
politician who will be most interested by the chapters in
which Pausanias explains his policy, or defends his position.

In publishing a romance which its author has left unfinished, I may perhaps be allowed to indicate briefly what I
believe to have been the general scope of its design, and the
probable progress of its narrative.

The "domestic interest" of that narrative is supplied by
the story of Cleonice: a story which, briefly told by Plutarch, suggests one of the most tragic situations it is possible to conceive. The pathos and terror of this dark, weird
episode in a life which history herself invests with all the
character of romance, long haunted the imagination of Byron, and elicited from Goethe one of the most whimsical

illustrations of the astonishing absurdity into which criticism sometimes tumbles, when it "o'erleaps itself and falls o' the other."

Writing of Manfred and its author, he says: "There are, properly speaking, two females whose phantoms forever haunt him; and which, in this piece also, perform principal parts. One under the name of Astarte, the other without form or actual presence, and merely a voice. Of the horrid occurrence which took place with the former, the following is related: When a bold and enterprising young man, he won the affections of a Florentine lady. Her husband discovered the amour, and murdered his wife. But the murderer was the same night found dead in the street, and there was no one to whom any suspicion could be attached. Lord Byron removed from Florence, and *these spirits haunted him all his life after.* This romantic incident is rendered highly probable by innumerable allusions to it in his poems; as, for instance, when turning his sad contemplations inward, he applies to himself the fatal history of the King of Sparta. It is as follows: Pausanias, a Lacedæmonian general, acquires glory by the important victory at Platæa; but afterward forfeits the confidence of his countrymen by his arrogance, obstinacy, and secret intrigues with the common enemy. This man draws upon himself the heavy guilt of innocent blood, which attends him to his end; for, while commanding the fleet of the allied Greeks in the Black Sea, he is inflamed with a violent passion for a Byzantine maiden. After long resistance, he at length obtains her from her parents, and she is to be delivered up to

him at night. She modestly desires the servant to put out
the lamp, and, while groping her way in the dark, she over-
turns it. Pausanias is awakened from his sleep: appre-
hensive of an attack from murderers, he seizes his sword
and destroys his mistress. The horrid sight never leaves
him. Her shade pursues him unceasingly; and in vain he
implores aid of the gods and the exorcising priests. That
poet must have a lacerated heart who selects such a scene
from antiquity, appropriates it to himself, and burdens his
tragic image with it."*

It is extremely characteristic of Byron that, instead of
resenting this charge of murder, he was so pleased by the
criticism in which it occurs that he afterward dedicated
"The Deformed Transformed" to Goethe. Mr. Grote re-
peats the story above alluded to, with all the sanction of
his grave authority, and even mentions the name of the
young lady; apparently for the sake of adding a few black
strokes to his character of Pausanias. But the supernatural part of the legend was, of course, beneath the notice of
a nineteenth-century critic; and he passes it by. This
part of the story is, however, essential to the psychological
interest of it. For whether it be that Pausanias supposed
himself, or that contemporary gossips supposed him, to be
haunted by the phantom of the woman he had loved and
slain, the fact in either case affords a lurid glimpse into
the inner life of the man; just as, although Goethe's mur-
der-story about Byron is ludicrously untrue, yet the fact

---

* Moore's "Life and Letters of Lord Byron," p. 723.

that such a story was circulated, and could be seriously repeated by such a man as Goethe without being resented by
Byron himself, offers significant illustration, both of what
Byron was, and of what he appeared to his contemporaries.
Grote also assigns the death of Cleonice to that period
in the life of Pausanias when he was in the command of
the allies at Byzantium, and refers to it as one of the numerous outrages whereby Pausanias abused and disgraced
the authority confided to him. Plutarch, however, who
tells the story in greater detail, distinctly fixes the date of
its catastrophe subsequent to the return of the Regent to
Byzantium, as a solitary volunteer, in the trireme of Her-
mione. The following is his account of the affair:

" It is related that Pausanias, when at Byzantium, sought,
with criminal purpose, the love of a young lady of good
family, named Cleonice. The parents, yielding to fear or
necessity, suffered him to carry away their daughter. Before entering his chamber, she requested that the light
might be extinguished, and, in darkness and silence, she
approached the couch of Pausanias, who was already asleep.
In so doing, she accidentally upset the lamp. Pausanias,
suddenly aroused from slumber, and supposing that some
enemy was about to assassinate him, seized his sword,
which lay by his bedside, and with it struck the maiden
to the ground. She died of her wound; and from that
moment repose was banished from the life of Pausanias.
A spectre appeared to him every night in his sleep, and
repeated to him, in reproachful tones, this hexameter
verse:

" ' Whither I wait thee, march, and receive the doom thou deservest:
Sooner or later, but ever, to man crime bringeth disaster.'

The allies, scandalized by this misdeed, concerted with
Cimon, and besieged Pausanias in Byzantium; but he succeeded in escaping. Continually troubled by the phantom,
he took refuge, it is said, at Heraclea, in that temple
where the souls of the dead are evoked. He appealed to
Cleonice, and conjured her to mitigate his torment. She
appeared to him, and told him that on his return to Sparta
he would attain the end of his sufferings; indicating, as it
would seem, by these enigmatic words, the death which
there awaited him. This" (adds Plutarch) "is a story told
by most of the historians."*

I feel, no doubt, that this version of the story, or at
least the general outline of it, would have been followed
by the romance, had my father lived to complete it. Some
modification of its details would doubtless have been necessary for the purposes of fiction. But that the Cleonice of
the novel is destined to die by the hand of her lover is
clearly indicated. To me it seems that considerable skill
and judgment are shown in the pains taken, at the very
opening of the book, to prepare the mind of the reader
for an incident which would have been intolerably painful,
and must have prematurely ended the whole narrative interest, had the character of Cleonice been drawn otherwise.
than as we find it in this first portion of the book. From
the outset she appears before us under the shadow of a

* Plutarch, "Life of Cimon."

tragic fatality. Of that fatality she is herself intuitively
conscious, and with it her whole being is in harmony.   No
sooner do we recognize her real character than we perceive
that, for such a character, there can be no fit or satisfactory
issue from the difficulties of her position, in any conceivable combination of earthly circumstances.   But she is not
of the earth, earthly.   Her thoughts already habitually
hover on the dim frontier of some vague spiritual region
in which her love seeks refuge from the hopeless realities
of her life; and, recognizing this betimes, we are prepared
to see above the hand of her ill-fated lover, when it strikes
her down in the dark, the merciful and releasing hand of
her natural destiny.

But, assuming the author to have adopted Plutarch's
chronology, and deferred the death of Cleonice till the return of Pausanias to Byzantium (the latest date to which
he could possibly have deferred it), this catastrophe must
still have occurred somewhere in the course, or at the close,
of his second volume.   There would, in that case, have
still remained about nine years (and those the most event-
ful) of his hero's career to be narrated.   The premature
removal of the heroine from the narrative, so early in the
course of it, would therefore, at first sight, appear to be a
serious defect in the conception of this romance.   Here it
is, however, that the credulous gossip of the old biographer
comes to the rescue of the modern artist.   I apprehend
that the Cleonice of the novel would, after her death, have
been still sensibly present to the reader's imagination
throughout the rest of the romance.   She would then

have moved through it like a fate, re-appearing in the most solemn moments of the story, and at all times apparent, even when unseen, in her visible influence upon the fierce and passionate character, the sombre and turbulent career, of her guilty lover. In short, we may fairly suppose that, in all the closing scenes of the tragedy, Cleonice would have still figured and acted as one of those supernatural agencies which my father, following the example of his great predecessor, Scott, did not scruple to introduce into the composition of historical romance.*

Without the explanation here suggested, those metaphysical conversations between Cleonice, Alcman, and Pausanias, which occupy the opening chapters of Book II., might be deemed superfluous. But, in fact, they are essential to the preparation of the catastrophe; and that catastrophe, if reached, would undoubtedly have revealed to any reflective reader their important connection with the narrative which they now appear to retard somewhat unduly.

Quite apart from the unfinished manuscript of this story of Pausanias, and in another portion of my father's papers which have no reference to this story, I have discovered the following, undated, memorandum of the destined contents of the second and third volumes of the work.

PAUSANIAS.

VOL. II.

---

* " Harold."

2*   B

Pausanias with Pharnabazes—On the point of success—Xerxes' daughter—Interview with Cleonice—Recalled. 60.

Sparta—Alcman with his family. 60.

Cleonice—Antagoras—Yields to suit of marriage. 60.

Pausanias suddenly re-appears, as a volunteer—Scenes. 60.

VOL. III.

Pausanias removes Cleonice, etc.—Conspiracy against him—Up to Cleonice's death. 100.

His expulsion from Byzantium—His despair—His journey into Thrace—Scythians, etc. ?

Heraclea—Ghost. 60.

His return—to Colonæ. ?

Antagoras resolved on revenge—Communicates with Sparta. ?

The * * *—Conference with Alcman—Pausanias depends on Helots, and money. 40.

His return—to death. 120.

This is the only indication I can find of the intended conclusion of the story. Meagre though it be, however, it sufficiently suggests the manner in which the author of the romance intended to deal with the circumstances of Cleonice's death as related by Plutarch. With her forcible removal by Pausanias, or her willing flight with him from the house of her father, it would probably have been difficult to reconcile the general sentiment of the romance, in connection with any circumstances less conceivable than those which are indicated in the memorandum. But, in such circumstances, the step taken by Pausanias might have had no worse motive than the rescue of the woman who loved him from forced union with another; and Cleonice's assent to that step might have been quite compatible with the purity and heroism of her character. In this manner, moreover, a strong motive is prepared for that sentiment of revenge on the part of Antagoras whereby the dramatic interest of the story might be greatly heightened in the subsequent chapters. The intended introduction of the supernatural element is also clearly indicated. But, apart from this, fine opportunities for psychological analysis would doubtless have occurred in tracing the gradual deterioration of such a character as that of Pausanias when, deprived of the guardian influence of a hope passionate, but not impure, its craving for fierce excitement must have been stimulated by remorseful memories and impotent despairs. Indeed, the imperfect manuscript now printed contains only the exposition of a tragedy. All the most striking effects, all the strongest dramatic situations, have been reserved for the pages of the manuscript which, alas! are either lost or unwritten.

Who can doubt, for instance, how effectually, in the closing scenes of this tragedy, the grim image of Alithea might have assumed the place assigned to it by history? All that we now see is the preparation made for its effective presentation in the foreground of such later scenes, by the chapter in the second volume describing the meeting between Lysander and the stern mother of his Spartan chief. In Lysander himself, moreover, we have the germ of a singularly dramatic situation. How would Lysander act in the final struggle which his character and fate are already preparing for him, between patriotism and friendship, his fidelity to Pausanias, and his devotion to Sparta? Is Lysander's father intended for that Ephor who, in the last moment, made the sign that warned Pausanias to take refuge in the temple which became his living tomb? Probably. Would Themistocles, who was so seriously compromised in the conspiracy of Pausanias, have appeared and played a part in those scenes on which the curtain must remain unlifted? Possibly. Is Alcman the Helot who revealed to the Ephors the gigantic plots of his master just when those plots were on the eve of execution? There is much in the relations between Pausanias and the Mothon, as they are described in the opening chapters of the romance, which favors, and indeed renders almost irresistible, such a supposition. But then, on the other hand, what genius on the part of the author could reconcile us to the perpetration by his hero of a crime so mean, so cowardly, as that personal perfidy to which history ascribes the revelation of the Regent's far more excusable treasons, and their terrible punishment?

These questions must remain unanswered. The magician can wave his wand no more. The circle is broken, the spells are scattered, the secret lost. The images which he evoked, and which he alone could animate, remain before us incomplete, semi-articulate, unable to satisfy the curiosity they inspire. A group of fragments, in many places broken, you have helped me to restore. With what reverent and kindly care, with what disciplined judgment and felicitous suggestion, you have accomplished the difficult task so generously undertaken, let me here most gratefully attest. Beneath the sculptor's name allow me to inscribe upon the pedestal your own, and accept this sincere assurance of the inherited esteem and personal regard with which I am, my dear Dr. Kennedy,

Your obliged and faithful

LYTTON.

CINTRA, *July 5th*, 1875.

BOOK I.

PAUSANIAS, THE SPARTAN.

CHAPTER I.

On one of the quays which bordered the unrivaled harbor of Byzantium, more than twenty-three centuries before the date at which this narrative is begun, stood two Athenians. In the waters of the haven rode the vessels of the Grecian fleet. So deep was the basin, in which the tides are scarcely felt,* that the prows of some of the ships touched the quays, and the setting sun glittered upon the smooth and waxen surfaces of the prows, rich with diversified colors and wrought gilding. To the extreme right of the fleet, and nearly opposite the place upon which the Athenians stood, was a vessel still more profusely ornamented than the rest. On the prow were elaborately carved the heads of the twin deities of the Laconian mariner, Castor and Pollux; in the centre of the deck was a wooden edifice or pavilion, having a gilded roof and shaded by purple awnings, an imitation of the luxurious galleys of the Barbarian; while the parasemon, or flag, as it idly waved

---

* Gibbon, ch. 17.

in the faint breeze of the gentle evening, exhibited the terrible serpent, which, if it was the fabulous type of demigods and heroes, might also be regarded as an emblem of the wily but stern policy of the Spartan State. Such was the galley of the commander of the armament, which (after the reduction of Cyprus) had but lately wrested from the yoke of Persia that link between her European and Asiatic domains, that key of the Bosporus—"the Golden Horn" of Byzantine.*

High above all other Greeks (Themistocles alone excepted) soared the fame of that renowned chief, Pausanias, Regent of Sparta, and General of the allied troops at the victorious battle-field of Platæa. The spot on which the Athenians stood was lonely, and now unoccupied, save by themselves and the sentries stationed at some distance on either hand. The larger proportion of the crews in the various vessels were on shore; but on the decks idly reclined small groups of sailors, and the murmur of their voices stole, indistinguishably blended, upon the translucent air. Behind rose, one above the other, the Seven Hills, on which long afterward the Emperor Constantine built a second Rome; and over these heights, even then, buildings were scattered of various forms and dates; here the pil-

---

* "The harbor of Constantinople, which may be considered as an arm of the Bosporus, obtained in a very remote period the denomination of the Golden Horn. The curve which it describes might be compared to the horn of a stag, or, as it should seem, with more propriety, to that of an ox."—Gib., ch. 17; Strab., l. x.

lared temples of the Greek colonists, to whom Byzantium owed its origin, there the light roofs and painted domes which the Eastern conquerors had introduced.

One of the Athenians was a man in the meridian of manhood, of a calm, sedate, but somewhat haughty aspect; the other was in the full bloom of youth, of lofty stature, and with a certain majesty of bearing; down his shoulders flowed a profusion of long curled hair,* divided in the centre of the forehead, and connected with golden clasps, in which was wrought the emblem of the Athenian nobles— the Grasshopper—a fashion not yet obsolete, as it had become in the days of Thucydides. Still, to an observer, there was something heavy in the ordinary expression of the handsome countenance. His dress differed from the earlier fashion of the Ionians; it dispensed with those loose linen garments which had something of effeminacy in their folds, and was confined to the simple and statue-like grace that characterized the Dorian garb. Yet the clasp that fastened the chlamys upon the right shoulder, leaving the arm free, was of pure gold and exquisite workmanship, and the materials of the simple vesture were of a quality that betokened wealth and rank in the wearer.

"Yes, Cimon," said the elder of the Athenians, "yonder galley itself affords sufficient testimony of the change that has come over the haughty Spartan. It is difficult, indeed, to recognize in this luxurious satrap, who affects the dress, the manners, the very insolence of the Barbarian, that Pau-

---

* Ion *apud* Plut.

sanias who, after the glorious day of Platæa, ordered the slaves to prepare in the tent of Mardonius such a banquet as would have been served to the Persian, while his own Spartan broth and bread were set beside it, in order that he might utter to the chiefs of Greece that noble pleasantry, 'Behold the folly of the Persians, who forsook such splendor to plunder such poverty.' "*

"Shame upon his degeneracy, and thrice shame!" said the young Cimon, sternly. "I love the Spartans so well that I blush for whatever degrades them. And all Sparta is dwarfed by the effeminacy of her chief."

"Softly, Cimon," said Aristides, with a sober smile. "Whatever surprise we may feel at the corruption of Pausanias, he is not one who will allow us to feel contempt. Through all the voluptuous softness acquired by intercourse with these Barbarians, the strong nature of the descendant of the demi-god still breaks forth. Even at the distaff I recognize Alcides, whether for evil or for good. Pausanias is one on whom our most anxious gaze must be duly bent. But in this change of his I rejoice; the gods are at work for Athens. See you not that, day after day, while Pausanias disgusts the allies with the Spartans themselves, he throws them more and more into the arms of Athens? Let his madness go on, and ere long the violet-crowned city will become the queen of the seas."

"Such was my own hope," said Cimon, his face assuming a new expression, brightened with all the intelligence of am-

---

* Herod., ix. 82.

bition and pride; "but I did not dare own it to myself till you spoke. Several officers of Ionia and the Isles have already openly and loudly proclaimed to me their wish to exchange the Spartan ascendency for the Athenian."

"And with all your love for Sparta," said Aristides, looking steadfastly and searchingly at his comrade; "you would not, then, hesitate to rob her of a glory which you might bestow on your own Athens?"

"Ah, am I not Athenian?" answered Cimon, with a deep passion in his voice. "Though my great father perished a victim to the injustice of a faction—though he who had saved Athens from the Mede died in the Athenian dungeon —still, fatherless, I see in Athens but a mother; and if her voice sounded harshly in my boyish years, in manhood I have feasted on her smiles. Yes, I honor Sparta, but I love Athens. You have my answer."

"You speak well," said Aristides, with warmth; "you are worthy of the destinies for which I foresee that the son of Miltiades is reserved. Be wary, be cautious; above all, be smooth, and blend with men of every state and grade. I would wish that the allies themselves should draw the contrast between the insolence of the Spartan chief and the courtesy of the Athenians. What said you to the Ionian officers?"

"I said that Athens held there was no difference between to command and to obey, except so far as was best for the interests of Greece; that, as on the field of Platæa, when the Tegeans asserted precedence over the Athenians, we, the Athenian army, at once exclaimed, through your
3*

voice, Aristides, 'We come here to fight the Barbarian, not to dispute among ourselves; place us where you will'*— even so now, while the allies give the command to Sparta, Sparta we will obey. But if we were thought by the Grecian States the fittest leaders, our answer would be the same that we gave at Platæa, 'Not we, but Greece be consulted: place us where you will!'"

"O wise Cimon!" exclaimed Aristides, "I have no caution to bestow on you. You do by intuition that which I attempt by experience. But hark! What music sounds in the distance? The airs that Lydia borrowed from the East?"

"And for which," said Cimon, sarcastically, "Pausanias hath abandoned the Dorian flute."

Soft, airy, and voluptuous were indeed the sounds which now, from the streets leading upward from the quay, floated along the delicious air. The sailors rose, listening and eager, from the decks; there was once more bustle, life, and animation on board the fleet. From several of the vessels the trumpets woke a sonorous signal-note. In a few minutes the quays, before so deserted, swarmed with the Grecian mariners, who emerged hastily, whether from various houses in the haven, or from the encampment which stretched along it, and hurried to their respective ships. On board the galley of Pausanias there was more especial animation; not only mariners, but slaves, evidently from the Eastern markets, were seen jostling each other, and

---

* Plut., in Vit. Arist.

heard talking, quick and loud, in foreign tongues. Rich carpets were unfurled and laid across the deck, while trembling and hasty hands smoothed into yet more graceful folds the curtains that shaded the gay pavilion in the centre. The Athenians looked on, the one with thoughtful composure, the other with a bitter smile, while these preparations announced the unexpected, and not undreaded, approach of the great Pausanias.

"Ho, noble Cimon!" cried a young man who, hurrying toward one of the vessels, caught sight of the Athenians and paused. "You are the very person whom I most desired to see. Aristides too!—we are fortunate."

The speaker was a young man of slighter make and lower stature than the Athenians, but well shaped, and with features the partial effeminacy of which was elevated by an expression of great vivacity and intelligence. The steed trained for Elis never bore in its proportions the evidence of blood and rare breeding more visibly than the dark brilliant eye of this young man; his broad, low, transparent brow, expanded nostril, and sensitive lip revealed the passionate and somewhat arrogant character of the vivacious Greek of the Ægean Isles.

"Antagoras," replied Cimon, laying his hand with frank and somewhat blunt cordiality on the Greek's shoulder, "like the grape of your own Chios, you can not fail to be welcome at all times. But why would you seek us now?"

"Because I will no longer endure the insolence of this rude Spartan. Will you believe it, Cimon — will you believe it, Aristides? Pausanias has actually dared to sen-

tence to blows, to stripes, one of my own men — a free
Chian — nay, a Decadarchus.*   I have but this instant
heard it.   And the offense—gods! the *offense!*—was that
he ventured to contest with a Laconian, an underling in
the Spartan army, which one of the two had the fair right
to a wine-cask!   Shall this be borne, Cimon?"

"Stripes to a Greek!" said Cimon, and the color mounted to his brow.   "Thinks Pausanias that the Ionian race
are already his Helots?"

"Be calm," said Aristides; "Pausanias approaches.   I
will accost him."

"But listen still!" exclaimed Antagoras, eagerly, pluck-
ing the gown of the Athenian, as the latter turned away.
"When Pausanias heard of the contest between my soldier
and his Laconian, what said he, think you?   'Prior claim;
learn henceforth that, where the Spartans are to be found,
the Spartans in all matters have the prior claim.'"

"We will see to it," returned Aristides, calmly; "but
keep by my side."

And now the music sounded loud and near, and suddenly, as the procession approached, the character of that
music altered.   The Lydian measures ceased, those who had
attuned them gave way to musicians of loftier aspect and
simpler garb; in whom might be recognized, not indeed
the genuine Spartans, but their free, if subordinate, countrymen of Laconia; and a minstrel, who walked beside
them, broke out into a song, partially adapted from the

---

* Leader of ten men.

bold and lively strain of Alcæus, the first two lines in each stanza ringing much to that chime, the two latter reduced into briefer compass, as, with allowance for the differing laws of national rhythm, we thus seek to render the verse:

SONG.

Multitudes, backward! Way for the Dorian!
Way for the Lord of rocky Laconia!
    Heaven to Hercules opened
        Way on the earth for his son.

Steel and fate, blunted, break on his fortitude;
Two evils only never endureth he—
    Death by a wound in retreating,
        Life with a blot on his name.

Rocky his birthplace; rocks are immutable;
So are his laws, and so shall his glory be.
    Time is the Victor of Nations,
        Sparta the Victor of Time.

Watch o'er him heedful on the wide ocean,
Brothers of Helen, luminous guiding stars;
    Dangerous to Truth are the fickle,
        Dangerous to Sparta the seas.

Multitudes, backward! Way for the Conqueror!
Way for the footstep half the world fled before;
    Nothing that Phœbus can shine on
        Needs so much space as Renown.

Behind the musicians came ten Spartans, selected from the celebrated three hundred who claimed the right to be stationed around the king in battle. Tall, stalwart, sheathed in armor, their shields slung at their backs, their crests of plumage or horse - hair waving over their strong and stern features, these hardy warriors betrayed to the keen eye of Aristides their sullen discontent at the part assigned to them in the luxurious procession; their brows were knit, their lips contracted, and each of them who caught the glance of the Athenians turned his eyes, as half in shame, half in anger, to the ground.

Coming now upon the quay, opposite to the galley of Pausanias, from which was suspended a ladder of silken cords, the procession halted, and, opening on either side, left space in the midst for the commander.

"He comes," whispered Antagoras to Cimon. "By Hercules! I pray you survey him well. Is it the conqueror of Mardonius, or the ghost of Mardonius himself?"

The question of the Chian seemed not extravagant to the blunt son of Miltiades, as his eyes now rested on Pausanias.

The pure Spartan race boasted, perhaps, the most superb models of masculine beauty which the land blessed by Apollo could afford. The laws that regulated marriage insured a healthful and vigorous progeny. Gymnastic discipline from early boyhood gave ease to the limbs, iron to the muscle, grace to the whole frame. Every Spartan, being born to command, being noble by his birth, lord of the Laconians, Master of the Helots, superior in the eyes of Greece to all other Greeks, was at once a Republican and an Aristocrat. Schooled in the arts that compose the presence, and give calmness and majesty to the bearing, he

combined with the mere physical advantages of activity
and strength a conscious and yet natural dignity of mien.
Amidst the Greeks assembled at the Olympian contests,
others showed richer garments, more sumptuous chariots,
rarer steeds; but no state could vie with Sparta in the thews
and sinews, the aspect and the majesty, of the men. Nor
were the royal race, the descendants of Hercules, in external appearance unworthy of their countrymen and of
their fabled origin.

Sculptor and painter would have vainly tasked their
imaginative minds to invent a nobler ideal for the effigies
of a hero than that which the Victor of Platæa offered to
their inspiration. As he now paused amidst the group, he
towered high above them all, even above Cimon himself.
But in his stature there was nothing of the cumbrous bulk
and stolid heaviness which often destroy the beauty of vast
strength. Severe and early training, long habits of rigid
abstemiousness, the toils of war, and, more than all, perhaps, the constant play of a restless, anxious, aspiring temper, had left, undisfigured by superfluous flesh, the grand
proportions of a frame, the very spareness of which had at
once the strength and the beauty of one of those hardy
victors in the wrestling or boxing match, whose agility and
force are modeled by discipline to the purest forms of
grace. Without that exact and chiseled harmony of countenance which characterized perhaps the Ionic rather than
the Doric race, the features of the royal Spartan were noble
and commanding. His complexion was sunburned, almost to Oriental swarthiness, and the raven's plume had no

darker gloss than that of his long hair, which (contrary to
the Spartan custom), flowing on either side, mingled with
the closer curls of the beard.   To a scrutinizing gaze, the
more dignified and prepossessing effect of this exterior
would perhaps have been counterbalanced by an eye, bright
indeed and penetrating, but restless and suspicious, by a
certain ineffable mixture of arrogant pride and profound
melancholy in the general expression of the countenance,
ill according with that frank and serene aspect which best
becomes the face of one who would lead mankind.   About
him altogether—the countenance, the form, the bearing—
there was that which woke a vague, profound, and singular
interest, an interest somewhat mingled with awe, but not
altogether uncalculated to produce that affection which belongs to admiration, save when the sudden frown or disdainful lip repelled the gentler impulse, and tended rather
to excite fear, or to irritate pride, or to wound self-love.

But if the form and features of Pausanias were eminently those of the purest race of Greece, the dress which he
assumed was no less characteristic of the Barbarian.   He
wore, not the garb of the noble Persian race, which, close
and simple, was but a little less manly than that of the
Greeks, but the flowing and gorgeous garments of the
Mede.   His long gown, which swept the earth, was covered with flowers wrought in golden tissue.   Instead of the
Spartan hat, the high Median cap or tiara crowned his perfumed and lustrous hair, while (what of all was most hate-
ful to Grecian eyes) he wore, though otherwise unarmed,
the curved cimeter and short dirk that were the national

weapons of the Barbarian. And as it was not customary, nor indeed legitimate, for the Greeks to wear weapons on peaceful occasions and with their ordinary costume, so this departure from the common practice had not only in itself something offensive to the jealous eyes of his comrades, but was rendered yet more obnoxious by the adoption of the very arms of the East.

By the side of Pausanias was a man whose dark beard was already sown with gray. This man, named Gongylus, though a Greek—a native of Eretria, in Euboea—was in high command under the great Persian king. At the time of the Barbarian invasion under Datis and Artaphernes, he had deserted the cause of Greece, and had been rewarded with the lordship of four towns in Æolis. Few among the apostate Greeks were more deeply instructed in the language and manners of the Persians; and the intimate and sudden friendship that had grown up between him and the Spartan was regarded by the Greeks with the most bitter and angry suspicion. As if to show his contempt for the natural jealousy of his countrymen, Pausanias, however, had just given to the Eretrian the government of Byzantium itself, and with the command of the citadel had intrusted to him the custody of the Persian prisoners captured in that port. Among these were men of the highest rank and influence at the court of Xerxes; and it was more than rumored that of late Pausanias had visited and conferred with them, through the interpretation of Gongylus, far more frequently than became the General of the Greeks. Gongylus had one of those countenances which are ob-

4

served when many of more striking semblance are overlooked. But the features were sharp and the visage lean, the
eyes vivid and sparkling as those of the lynx, and the dark
pupil seemed yet more dark from the extreme whiteness of
the ball, from which it lessened or dilated with the impulse
of the spirit which gave it fire. There was in that eye
all the subtle craft, the plotting and restless malignity,
which usually characterized those Greek renegades who
prostituted their native energies to the rich service of the
Barbarian; and the lips, narrow and thin, wore that everlasting smile which to the credulous disguises wile, and to
the experienced betrays it. Small, spare, and prematurely
bent, the Eretrian supported himself by a staff, upon which
now leaning, he glanced, quickly and pryingly, around, till
his eyes rested upon the Athenians, with the young Chian
standing in their rear.

"The Athenian Captains are here to do you homage,
Pausanias," said he, in a whisper, as he touched with his
small lean fingers the arm of the Spartan.

Pausanias turned and muttered to himself, and at that
instant Aristides approached.

"If it please you, Pausanias, Cimon and myself, the leaders of the Athenians, would crave a hearing upon certain
matters."

"Son of Lysimachus, say on."

"Your pardon, Pausanias," returned the Athenian, lowering his voice, and with a smile—"this is too crowded a
council-hall; may we attend you on board your galley?"

"Not so," answered the Spartan, haughtily; "the morning to affairs, the evening to recreation. We shall sail in the bay to see the moon rise, and if we indulge in consultations, it will be over our wine-cups. It is a good custom."

"It is a Persian one," said Cimon, bluntly.

"It is permitted to us," returned the Spartan, coldly, "to borrow from those we conquer. But enough of this. I have no secrets with the Athenians. No matter_if the whole city hear what you would address to Pausanias."

"It is to complain," said Aristides with calm emphasis, but still in an under-tone.

"Ay, I doubt it not: the Athenians are eloquent in grumbling."

"It was not found so at Platæa," returned Cimon.

"Son of Miltiades," said Pausanias, loftily, "your wit outruns your experience. But my time is short. To the matter!"

"If you will have it so, I will speak," said Aristides, raising his voice. "Before your own Spartans, our comrades in arms, I proclaim our causes of complaint. Firstly, then, I demand release and compensation to seven Athenians, free-born and citizens, whom your orders have condemned to the unworthy punishment of standing all day in the open sun with the weight of iron anchors on their shoulders."

"The mutinous knaves!" exclaimed the Spartan. "They introduced into the camp the insolence of their own Agora, and were publicly heard in the streets inveighing against myself as a favorer of the Persians."

"It was easy to confute the charge; it was tyrannical to

punish words in men whose deeds had raised you to the command of Greece."

"*Their* deeds! Ye gods, give me patience! By the help of Juno the Protectress, it was this brain and this arm that— But I will not justify myself by imitating the Athenian fashion of wordy boasting. Pass on to your next complaint."

"You have placed slaves — yes, Helots — around the springs, to drive away with scourges the soldiers that come for water."

"Not so, but merely to prevent others from filling their vases until the Spartans are supplied."

"And by what right— ?" began Cimon, but Aristides checked him with a gesture, and proceeded.

"That precedence is not warranted by custom, nor by the terms of our alliance; and the springs, O Pausanias, are bounteous enough to provide for all. I proceed. You have formally sentenced citizens and soldiers to the scourge. Nay, this very day you have extended the sentence to one in actual command among the Chians. Is it not so, Antagoras?"

"It is," said the young Chian, coming forward boldly; "and in the name of my countrymen I demand justice."

"And I also, Uliades of Samos," said a thick-set and burly Greek who had joined the group unobserved, "*I* demand justice. What, by the gods! Are we to be all equals in the day of battle? 'My good sir, march here;' and, 'My dear sir, just run into that breach;' and yet when we have won the victory and should share the glory, is one state, nay, one man, to seize the whole, and deal out iron anchors and tough cowhides to his companions? No, Spar-

tans, this is not your view of the case; you suffer in the
eyes of Greece by this misconduct.   To Sparta itself I appeal."

"And what, most patient sir," said Pausanias, with calm
sarcasm, though his eye shot fire, and the upper lip, on which
no Spartan suffered the beard to grow, slightly quivered
—"what is *your* contribution to the catalogue of complaints?"

"Jest not, Pausanias; you will find me in earnest," answered Uliades, doggedly, and encouraged by the evident
effect that his eloquence had produced upon the Spartans
themselves.   "I have met with a grievous wrong, and all
Greece shall hear of it, if it be not redressed.   My own
brother, who at Mycale slew four Persians with his own
hand, headed a detachment for forage.   He and his men
were met by a company of mixed Laconians and Helots,
their forage taken from them, they themselves assaulted,
and my brother, a man who has moneys and maintains forty slaves of his own, struck thrice across the face by a ras-
cally Helot.   Now, Pausanias, your answer!"

"You have prepared a notable scene for the commander
of your forces, son of Lysimachus," said the Spartan, ad-
dressing himself to Aristides.   "Far be it from me to affect
the Agamemnon, but your friends are less modest in imitating the venerable model of Thersites.   Enough" (and,
changing the tone of his voice, the chief stamped his foot
vehemently to the ground): "we owe no account to our
inferiors; we render no explanation save to Sparta and her
Ephors."

4*

"So be it, then," said Aristides, gravely; "we have our answer, and you will hear of our appeal."

Pausanias changed color. "How?" said he, with a slight hesitation in his tone. "Mean you to threaten me—Me—with carrying the busy tales of your disaffection to the Spartan government?"

"Time will show. Farewell, Pausanias. We will detain you no longer from your pastime."

"But," began Uliades.

"Hush," said the Athenian, laying his hand on the Samian's shoulder. "We will confer anon."

Pausanias paused a moment, irresolute and in thought. His eyes glanced toward his own countrymen, who, true to their rigid discipline, neither spake nor moved, but whose countenances were sullen and overcast, and at that moment his pride was shaken, and his heart misgave him. Gongylus watched his countenance, and, once more laying his hand on his arm, said, in a whisper,

"He who seeks to rule never goes back."

"Tush! you know not the Spartans."

"But I know Human Nature; it is the same everywhere. You can not yield to this insolence; to-morrow, of your own accord, send for these men separately and pacify them."

"You are right. Now to the vessel!"

With this, leaning on the shoulder of the Persian, and with a slight wave of his hand toward the Athenians—he did not deign even that gesture to the island officers—Pausanias advanced to the vessel, and, slowly ascending, disappeared within his pavilion. The Spartans and the musicians followed; then, spare and swarthy, some half score of Egyptian sailors; last came a small party of Laconians and Helots, who, standing at some distance behind Pausanias, had not hitherto been observed. The former were but slightly armed; the latter had forsaken their customary rude and savage garb, and wore long gowns and gay tunics, somewhat in the fashion of the Lydians. With these last there was one of a mien and aspect that strongly differed from the lowering and ferocious cast of countenance common to the Helot race. He was of the ordinary stature, and his frame was not characterized by any appearance of unusual strength; but he trod the earth with a firm step and an erect crest, as if the curse of the slave had not yet destroyed the inborn dignity of the human being. There were a certain delicacy and refinement, rather of thought than beauty, in his clear, sharp, and singularly intelligent features. In contradistinction from the free-born Spartans, his hair was short, and curled close above a broad and manly forehead; and his large eyes of dark blue looked full and bold upon the Athenians with something, if not of defiance, at least of pride in their gaze, as he stalked by them to the vessel.

"A sturdy fellow for a Helot," muttered Cimon.

"And merits well his freedom," said the son of Lysimachus. "I remember him well. He is Alcman, the foster-brother of Pausanias, whom he attended at Platæa. Not a Spartan that day bore himself more bravely."

"No doubt they will put him to death when he goes back to Sparta," said Antagoras. "When a Helot is brave, the Ephors clap the black mark against his name, and at the next crypteia he suddenly disappears."

"Pausanias may share the same fate as his Helot, for all I care," quoth Uliades. "Well, Athenians, what say you to the answer we have received?"

"That Sparta shall hear of it," answered Aristides.

"Ah, but is that all? Recollect the Ionians have the majority in the fleet; let us not wait for the slow Ephors. Let us at once throw off this insufferable yoke, and proclaim Athens the Mistress of the Seas. What say you, Cimon?"

"Let Aristides answer."

"Yonder lie the Athenian vessels," said Aristides. "Those who put themselves voluntarily under our protection we will not reject. But remember we assert no claim; we yield but to the general wish."

"Enough; I understand you," said Antagoras.

"Not quite," returned the Athenian, with a smile. "The breach between you and Pausanias is begun, but it is not yet wide enough. You yourselves must do that which will annul all power in the Spartan, and then if ye come to Athens ye will find her as bold against the Doric despot as against the Barbarian foe."

"But speak more plainly. What would ye have us do?" asked Uliades, rubbing his chin in great perplexity.

"Nay, nay, I have already said enough. Fare ye well, fellow-countrymen," and, leaning lightly on the shoulder of Cimon, the Athenian passed on.

Meanwhile, the splendid galley of Pausanias slowly put forth into the farther waters of the bay. The oars of the rowers broke the surface into countless phosphoric sparkles; and the sound they made, as they dashed amidst the gentle waters, seemed to keep time with the song and the instruments on the deck. The Ionians gazed in silence as the stately vessel, now shooting far ahead of the rest, swept into the centre of the bay. And the moon, just rising, shone full upon the glittering prow, and streaked the rippling billows over which it had bounded, with a light, as it were, of glory.

Antagoras sighed.

"What think you of?" asked the rough Samian.

"Peace," replied Antagoras. "In this hour, when the fair face of Artemis recalls the old legends of Endymion, is it not permitted to man to remember that before the iron age came the golden, before war reigned love?"

"Tush!" said Uliades. "Time enough to think of love when we have satisfied vengeance. Let us summon our friends, and hold council on the Spartan's insults."

"Whither goes now the Spartan?" murmured Antagoras abstractedly, as he suffered his companion to lead him away. Then, halting abruptly, he struck his clenched hand on his breast.

"O Aphrodite!" he cried; "this night—this night I will seek thy temple. Hear my vows—soothe my jealousy!"

"Ah," grunted Uliades, "if, as men say, thou lovest a fair Byzantine, Aphrodite will have sharp work to cure thee of jealousy, unless she first makes thee blind."

Antagoras smiled faintly, and the two Ionians moved on slowly and in silence. In a few minutes more the quays were deserted, and nothing but the blended murmur, spreading wide and indistinct throughout the camp, and a noisier but occasional burst of merriment from those resorts of obscener pleasure which were profusely scattered along the haven, mingled with the whispers of "the far resounding sea."

CHAPTER II.

On a couch, beneath his voluptuous awning, reclined
Pausanias. The curtains, drawn aside, gave to view the
moonlit ocean and the dim shadows of the shore, with the
dark woods beyond, relieved by the distant lights of the
city. On one side of the Spartan was a small table, that
supported goblets and vases of that exquisite wine which
Maronea proffered to the thirst of the Byzantine; and those
cooling and delicious fruits which the orchards around the
city supplied as amply as the fabled gardens of the Hes-
perides, were heaped on the other side. Toward the foot
of the couch, propped upon cushions piled on the floor, sat
Gongylus, conversing in a low, earnest voice, and fixing his
eyes steadfastly on the Spartan. The habits of the Eretrian's life, which had brought him in constant contact
with the Persians, had infected his very language with the
luxuriant extravagance of the East. And the thoughts he
uttered made his language but too musical to the ears of
the listening Spartan.

"And fair as these climes may seem to you, and rich as
are the gardens and granaries of Byzantium, yet to me who
have stood on the terraces of Babylon and looked upon
groves covering with blossom and fruit the very fortresses

and walls of that queen of nations—to me, who have roved
amidst the vast delights of Susa, through palaces whose
very porticoes might inclose the limits of a Grecian city—
who have stood, awed and dazzled, in the courts of that
wonder of the world, that crown of the East, the marble
magnificence of Persepolis—to me, Pausanias, who have
been thus admitted into the very heart of Persian glories,
this city of Byzantium appears but a village of artisans and
fishermen.   The very foliage of its forests, pale and sickly,
the very moonlight upon these waters, cold and smileless
—ah, if thou couldst but see!   But pardon me, I weary
thee ?"

"Not so," said the Spartan, who, raised upon his elbow,
listened to the words of Gongylus with deep attention.
"Proceed."

"Ah, if thou couldst but see the fair regions which the
great king has apportioned to thy countryman, Demaratus.
And if a domain that would satiate the ambition of the
most craving of your earlier tyrants fall to Demaratus,
what would be the splendid satrapy in which the conqueror
of Platæa might plant his throne ?"

"In truth, my renown and my power are greater than
those ever possessed by Demaratus," said the Spartan, musingly.

"Yet," pursued Gongylus, "it is not so much the mere
extent of the territories which the grateful Xerxes could
proffer to the brave Pausanias—it is not their extent so
much that might tempt desire, neither is it their stately
forests, nor the fertile meadows, nor the ocean-like rivers,

which the gods of the East have given to the race of Cyrus.
There, free from the strange constraints which our austere
customs and solemn deities impose upon the Greeks, the
beneficent Ormuzd scatters ever-varying delights upon the
paths of men.   All that art can invent, all that the marts
of the universe can afford of the rare and voluptuous, are
lavished upon abodes the splendor of which even our idle
dreams of Olympus never shadowed forth.   There, instead
of the harsh and imperious helpmate to whom the joyless
Spartan confines his reluctant love, all the beauties of every
clime contend for the smile of their lord.   And wherever
are turned the change-loving eyes of Passion, the Aphrodite
of our poets, such as the Cytherean and the Cyprian fable
her, seems to recline on the lotus leaf or to rise from the
unruffled ocean of delight.   Instead of the gloomy brows
and the harsh tones of rivals envious of your fame, hosts
of friends aspiring only to be followers will catch gladness
from your smile or sorrow from your frown.   There, no
jarring contests with little men, who deem themselves the
equals of the great, no jealous Ephor is found, to load the
commonest acts of life with fetters of iron custom.   Talk
of liberty !   Liberty in Sparta is but one eternal servitude ;
you can not move, or eat, or sleep, save as the law directs.
Your very children are wrested from you just in the age
when their voices sound most sweet.   Ye are not men ;
ye are machines.   Call you this liberty, Pausanias?   I, a
Greek, have known both Grecian liberty and Persian royalty.   Better be chieftain to a king than servant to a
mob!   But in Eretria, at least, pleasure was not denied.

In Sparta the very Graces preside over discipline and war only."

"Your fire falls upon flax," said Pausanias, rising, and with passionate emotion. "And if you, the Greek of a happier state, you who know but by report the unnatural bondage to which the Spartans are subjected, can weary of the very name of Greek, what must be the feelings of one who from the cradle upward has been starved out of the genial desires of life? Even in earliest youth, while yet all other lands and customs were unknown, when it was duly poured into my ears that to be born a Spartan constituted the glory and the bliss of earth, my soul sickened at the lesson, and my reason revolted against the lie. Often when my whole body was lacerated with stripes, disdaining to groan, I yet yearned to strike, and I cursed my savage tutors who denied pleasure even to childhood with all the madness of impotent revenge. My mother herself (sweet name elsewhere) had no kindness in her face. She was the pride of the matronage of Sparta, because of all our women Alithea was the most unsexed. When I went forth to my first crypteia, to watch, amidst the wintry dreariness of the mountains, upon the movements of the wretched Helots, to spy upon their sufferings, to take account of their groans, and if one more manly than the rest dared to mingle curses with his groans, to mark *him* for slaughter, as a wolf that threatened danger to the fold; to lurk, an assassin, about his home, to dog his walks, to fall on him unawares, to strike him from behind, to filch away his life, to bury him in the ravines, so that murder might leave no trace;

when upon this initiating campaign, the virgin trials of our
youth, I first set forth, my mother drew near, and girding
me herself with my grandsire's sword, 'Go forth,' she said,
'as the young hound to the chase, to wind, to double, to
leap on the prey, and to taste of blood. See, the sword
is bright; show me the stains at thy return.'"

"Is it, then, true, as the Greeks generally declare," interrupted Gongylus, "that in these campaigns, or crypteias,
the sole aim and object is the massacre of Helots?"

"Not so," replied Pausanias; "savage though the custom, it smells not so foully of the shambles. The avowed
object is to harden the nerves of our youth. Barefooted,
unattended, through cold and storm, performing ourselves
the most menial offices necessary to life, we wander for a
certain season daily and nightly through the rugged territories of Laconia.* We go as boys—we come back as
men.† The avowed object, I say, is inurement to hardship,
but with this is connected the secret end of keeping watch
on these half-tamed and bull-like herds of men whom we
call the Helots. If any be dangerous, we mark him for the
knife. One of them had thrice been a ringleader in revolt.
He was wary as well as fierce. He had escaped in three
succeeding crypteias. To me, as one of the Heraclidæ, was
assigned the honor of tracking and destroying him. For
three days and three nights I dogged his footsteps (for he

---

* Plat. Leg. i., p. 633. See also Müller's "Dorians," vol. ii.,
p. 41.

† Pueros puberes—neque prius in urbem redire quam viri
facti essent.—*Justin*, iii., 3.

had caught the scent of the pursuers and fled), through forest and defile, through valley and crag, stealthily and relentlessly. I followed him close. At. last, one evening, having lost sight of all my comrades, I came suddenly upon him as I emerged from a wood. It was a broad patch of waste land, through which rushed a stream swollen by the rains, and plunging with a sullen roar down a deep and gloomy precipice, that to the right and left bounded the waste, the stream in front, the wood in the rear. He was reclining by the stream, at which, with the hollow of his hand, he quenched his thirst. I paused to gaze upon him, and as I did so he turned and saw me. He rose and fixed his eyes on mine, and we examined each other in silence. The Helots are rarely of tall stature, but this was a giant. His dress, that of his tribe, of rude sheep-skins, and his cap, made from the hide of a dog, increased the savage rudeness of his appearance. I rejoiced that he saw me, and that, as we were alone, I might fight him fairly. It would have been terrible to slay the wretch if I had caught him in his sleep."

"Proceed," said Gongylus, with interest, for so little was known of Sparta by the rest of the Greeks, especially outside the Peloponnesus, that these details gratified his natural spirit of gossiping inquisitiveness.

"'Stand!' said I, and he moved not. I approached him slowly. 'Thou art a Spartan,' said he, in a deep and harsh voice, 'and thou comest for my blood. Go, boy, go; thou art not mellowed to thy prime, and thy comrades are far away. The shears of the Fatal deities hover over the thread, not of my life, but of thine.' I was struck, Gongylus, by this address, for it was neither desperate nor dastardly, as I had anticipated; nevertheless, it beseemed not a Spartan to fly from a Helot, and I drew the sword which my mother had girded on. The Helot watched my movements, and seized a rude and knotted club that lay on the ground beside him.

"'Wretch,' said I, 'darest thou attack face to face a descendant of the Heraclidæ? In me behold Pausanias, the son of Cleombrotus.'

"'Be it so; in the city one is the god-born, the other the man-enslaved. On the mountains we are equals.'

"'Knowest thou not,' said I, 'that if the gods condemned me to die by thy hand, not only thou, but thy whole house, thy wife and thy children, would be sacrificed to my ghost?'

"'The earth can hide the Spartan's bones as secretly as the Helot's,' answered my strange foe. 'Begone, young and unfleshed in slaughter as you are; why make war upon me? My death can give you neither gold nor glory. I have never harmed thee or thine. How much of the air and sun does this form take from the descendant of the Heraclidæ?'

"'Thrice hast thou raised revolt among the Helots; thrice at thy voice have they risen in bloody, though fruitless, strife against their masters.'

"'Not at my voice, but at that of the two deities who are the war-gods of slaves—Persecution and Despair.'*

---

* When Themistocles sought to extort tribute from the An-
5*

"Impatient of this parley, I tarried no longer. I sprung upon the Helot. He evaded my sword, and I soon found that all my agility and skill were requisite to save me from the massive weapon, one blow of which would have sufficed to crush me. But the Helot seemed to stand on the defensive, and continued to back toward the wood from which I had emerged. Fearful lest he would escape me, I pressed hard on his footsteps. My blood grew warm; my fury got the better of my prudence. My foot stumbled; I recovered in an instant, and, looking up, beheld the terrible club suspended over my head; it might have fallen, but the stroke of death was withheld. I misinterpreted the merciful delay; the lifted arm left the body of my enemy exposed. I struck him on the side; the thick hide blunted the stroke, but it drew blood. Afraid to draw back within the reach of his weapon, I threw myself on him, and grappled to his throat. We rolled on the earth together; it was but a moment's struggle. Strong as I was even in boyhood, the Helot would have been a match for Alcides. A shade passed over my eyes; my breath heaved short. The slave was kneeling on my breast, and, dropping the club, he drew a short knife from his girdle. I gazed upon him grim and mute. I was conquered, and I cared not for the rest.

"The blood from his side, as he bent over me, trickled down upon my face.

---

drians, he said, "I bring with me two powerful gods—Persuasion and Force." "And on our side," was the answer, "are two deities not less powerful—Poverty and Despair!"

"'And this blood,' said the Helot, 'you shed in the very moment when I spared your life: such is the honor of a Spartan. Do you not deserve to die?'

"'Yes, for I am subdued, and by a slave. Strike!'

"'There,' said the Helot, in a melancholy and altered tone, 'there speaks the soul of the Dorian, the fatal spirit to which the gods have rendered up our wretched race. We are doomed—doomed—and one victim will not expiate our curse. Rise, return to Sparta, and forget that thou art innocent of murder.'

"He lifted his knee from my breast, and I rose, ashamed and humbled.

"At that instant I heard the crashing of the leaves in the wood, for the air was exceedingly still. I knew that my companions were at hand. 'Fly,' I cried; 'fly. If they come I can not save thee, royal though I be. Fly.'

"'And *wouldest* thou save me!' said the Helot in surprise.

"'Ay, with my own life. Canst thou doubt it? Lose not a moment. Fly. Yet stay;' and I tore off a part of the woolen vest that I wore. 'Place this at thy side; stanch the blood, that it may not track thee. Now, begone!'

"The Helot looked hard at me, and I thought there were tears in his rude eyes; then, catching up the club with as much ease as I this staff, he sped with inconceivable rapidity, despite his wound, toward the precipice on the right, and disappeared amidst the thick brambles that clothed the gorge. In a few moments three of my com-

panions approached. They found me exhausted, and panting rather with excitement than fatigue. Their quick eyes
detected the blood upon the ground. I gave them no time
to pause and examine. 'He has escaped me—he has fled,'
I cried; 'follow,' and I led them to the opposite part of
the precipice from that which the Helot had taken. Heading the search, I pretended to catch a glimpse of the goat-
skin ever and anon through the trees, and I stayed not
the pursuit till night grew dark, and I judged the victim
was far away."

"And he escaped?"

"He did. The crypteia ended. Three other Helots
were slain, but not by me. We returned to Sparta, and
my mother was comforted for my misfortune in not having slain my foe by seeing the stains on my grandsire's
sword. I will tell thee a secret, Gongylus"—and here Pausanias lowered his voice, and looked anxiously toward him
—"since that day I have not hated the Helot race. Nay,
it may be that I have loved them better than the Dorian."

"I do not wonder at it. But has not your wounded
giant yet met with his death?"

"No, I never related what had passed between us to any
one save my father. He was gentle for a Spartan, and he
rested not till Gylippus—so was the Helot named—obtained
exemption from the black list. He dared not, however, attribute his intercession to the true cause. It happened,
fortunately, that Gylippus was related to my own foster-
brother, Alcman, brother to my nurse; and Alcman is celebrated in Sparta, not only for courage in war, but for arts

in peace. He is a poet, and his strains please the Dorian ear, for they are stern and simple, and they breathe of war. Alcman's merits won forgiveness for the offenses of Gylippus. May the gods be kind to his race !"

"Your Alcman seems one of no common intelligence, and your gentleness to him does not astonish me, though it seems often to raise a frown on the brows of your Spartans."

"We have lain on the same bosom," said Pausanias, touchingly, "and his mother was kinder to me than my own. You must know that to those Helots who have been our foster-brothers, and whom we distinguish by the name of Mothons, our stern law relaxes. They have no rights of citizenship, it is true, but they cease to be slaves;* nay, sometimes they attain not only to entire emancipation, but to distinction. Alcman has bound his fate to mine. But to return, Gongylus. I tell thee that it is not thy descriptions of pomp and dominion that allure me, though I am not above the love of power; neither is it thy glowing promises, though blood too wild for a Dorian runs riot in my veins: but it is my deep loathing, my inexpressible disgust for Sparta and her laws, my horror at the thought of wearing away life in those sullen customs, amidst that joyless round of tyrannic duties, in my rapture at the hope of escape, of life in a land which the eye of the Ephor never pierces; this it is, and this alone, O Persian, that makes me

---

* The appellation of Mothons was not confined to the Helots who claimed the connection of foster-brothers, but was given also to household slaves.

(the words must out) a traitor to my country—one who dreams of becoming a dependent on her foe."

"Nay," said Gongylus, eagerly; for here Pausanias moved uneasily, and the color mounted to his brow. "Nay, speak not of dependence. Consider the proposals that you can alone condescend to offer to the great king. Can the conqueror of Platæa, with millions for his subjects, hold himself dependent, even on the sovereign of the East? How, hereafter, will the memories of our sterile Greece and your rocky Sparta fade from your mind; or be remembered only as a state of thralldom and bondage, which your riper manhood has outgrown!"

"I will try to think so, at least," said Pausanias, gloomily. "And, come what may, I am not one to recede. I have thrown my shield into a fearful peril; but I will win it back or perish. Enough of this, Gongylus. Night advances. I will attend the appointment you have made. Take the boat, and within an hour I will meet you with the prisoners at the spot agreed on, near the Temple of Aphrodite. All things are prepared?"

"All," said Gongylus, rising, with a gleam of malignant joy on his dark face. "I leave thee, kingly slave of the rocky Sparta, to prepare the way for thee, as Satrap of half the East."

So saying, he quit the awning, and motioned three Egyptian sailors who lay on the deck without. A boat was lowered, and the sound of its oars woke Pausanias from the reverie into which the parting words of the Eretrian had plunged his mind.

CHAPTER III.

WITH a slow and thoughtful step, Pausanias passed on to the outer deck. The moon was up, and the vessel scarcely seemed to stir, so gently did it glide along the sparkling waters. They were still within the bay, and the shores rose, white and distinct, to his view. A group of Spartans, reclining by the side of the ship, were gazing listlessly on the waters. The Regent paused beside them.

"Ye weary of the ocean, methinks," said he. "We Dorians have not the merchant tastes of the Ionians."*

"Son of Cleombrotus," said one of the group, a Spartan whose rank and services entitled him to more than ordinary familiarity with the chief, "it is not the ocean itself that we should dread; it is the contagion of those who, living on the element, seem to share in its ebb and flow. The Ionians are never three hours in the same mind."

"For that reason," said Pausanias, fixing his eyes steadfastly on the Spartan, "for that reason I have judged it advisable to adopt a rough manner with these innovators, to draw with a broad chalk the line between them and the Spartans, and to teach those who never knew discipline the

---

* No Spartan served as a sailor, or indeed condescended to any trade or calling but that of war.

stern duties of obedience.   Think you I have done wisely?"

The Spartan, who had risen when Pausanias addressed him, drew his chief a little aside from the rest.

"Pausanias," said he, "the hard Naxian stone best tames and tempers the fine steel;* but the steel may break if the workman be not skillful.   These Athenians are grown insolent since Marathon, and their soft kindred of Asia have relighted the fires they took of old from the Cecropian Prytaneum.   Their sail is more numerous than ours; on the sea they find the courage they lose on land.   Better be gentle with those wayward allies, for the Spartan greyhound shows not his teeth but to bite."

"Perhaps you are right.   I will consider these things, and appease the mutineers.   But it goes hard with my pride, Thrasyllus, to make equals of this soft-tongued race. Why, these Ionians, do they not enjoy themselves in perpetual holidays?—spend days at the banquet?—ransack earth and sea for dainties and for perfumes?—and shall they be the equals of us men, who, from the age of seven to that of sixty, are wisely taught to make life so barren and toilsome that we may well have no fear of death?   I hate these sleek and merry feast-givers; they are a perpetual insult to our solemn existence."

There was a strange mixture of irony and passion in the Spartan's voice as he thus spoke, and Thrasyllus looked at him in grave surprise.

---

* Pind., Isth., v. (vi.), 73.

"There is nothing to envy in the woman-like debaucheries of the Ionian," said he, after a pause.

"Envy! no; we only hate them, Thrasyllus. Yon Eretrian tells me rare things of the East. Time may come when we shall sup on the black broth in Susa."

"The gods forbid! Sparta never invades. Life with us is too precious, for we are few. Pausanias, I would we were well quit of Byzantium. I do not suspect you, not I; but there are those who look with vexed eyes on those garments, and I, who love you, fear the sharp jealousies of the Ephors, to whose ears the birds carry all tidings."

"My poor Thrasyllus," said Pausanias, laughing scornfully, "think you that I wear these robes, or mimic the Median manners, for love of the Mede? No, no! But there are arts which save countries as well as those of war. This Gongylus is in the confidence of Xerxes. I desire to establish a peace for Greece upon everlasting foundations. Reflect; Persia hath millions yet left. Another invasion may find a different fortune; and, even at the best, Sparta gains nothing by these wars. Athens triumphs, not Lacedæmon. I would, I say, establish a peace with Persia. I would that Sparta, not Athens, should have that honor. Hence these flatteries to the Persian—trivial to us who render them, sweet and powerful to those who receive. Remember these words hereafter, if the Ephors make question of my discretion. And now, Thrasyllus, return to our friends, and satisfy them as to the conduct of Pausanias."

Quitting Thrasyllus, the Regent now joined a young Spartan who stood alone by the prow in a musing attitude.

6

"Lysander, my friend, my only friend, my best-loved Lysander," said Pausanias, placing his hand on the Spartan's shoulder. "And why so sad?"

"How many leagues are we from Sparta?" answered Lysander, mournfully.

"And canst thou sigh for the black broth, my friend? Come, how often hast thou said, 'Where Pausanias is, *there* is Sparta!'"

"Forgive me, I am ungrateful," said Lysander, with warmth. "My benefactor, my guardian, my hero, forgive me if I have added to your own countless causes of anxiety. Wherever you are, there is life, and there glory. When I was just born, sickly and feeble, I was exposed on Taygetus. You, then a boy, heard my faint cry, and took on me that compassion which my parents had forsworn. You bore me to your father's roof, you interceded for my life. You prevailed even on your stern mother. I was saved; and the gods smiled upon the infant whom the son of the humane Hercules protected. I grew up strong and hardy, and belied the signs of my birth. My parents then owned me; but still you were my fosterer, my savior, my more than father. As I grew up, placed under your care, I imbibed my first lessons of war. By your side I fought, and from your example I won glory. Yes, Pausanias, even here, amidst luxuries which revolt me more than the Parthian bow and the Persian sword, even amidst the faces of the stranger, I still feel thy presence my home, thyself my Sparta."

The proud Pausanias was touched, and his voice trembled as he replied, "Brother in arms and in love, whatever service fate may have allowed me to render unto thee, thy high nature and thy cheering affection have more than paid me back. Often in our lonely rambles amidst the dark oaks of the sacred Scotitas,* or by the wayward waters of Tiasa,† when I have poured into thy faithful breast my impatient loathing, my ineffable distaste for the iron life, the countless and wearisome tyrannies of custom which surround the Spartans, often have I found a consoling refuge in thy divine contentment, thy cheerful wisdom. Thou lovest Sparta; why is she not worthier of thy love? Allowed only to be half men, in war we are demi-gods; in peace, slaves. Thou wouldst interrupt me. Be silent. I am in a willful mood; thou canst not comprehend me, and I often marvel at thee. Still we are friends, such friends as the Dorian discipline, which makes friendship necessary in order to endure life, alone can form. Come, take up thy staff and mantle. Thou shalt be my companion ashore. I seek one whom alone in the world I love better than thee. To - morrow to stern duties once more. Alcman shall row us across the bay; and as we glide along, if thou wilt praise Sparta, I will listen to thee as the Ionians listen to their tale-tellers. Ho! Alcman, stop the rowers, and lower the boat."

The orders were obeyed, and a second boat soon darted toward the same part of the bay as that to which the one that bore Gongylus had directed its course. Thrasyllus

---

* Paus., Lac., x.　　　　　　　　† *Ibid.*, c. xviii.

and his companions watched the boat that bore Pausanias and his two comrades, as it bounded, arrow-like, over the glassy sea.

" Whither goes Pausanias?" asked one of the Spartans.

" Back to Byzantium on business," replied Thrasyllus.

" And we?"

" Are to cruise in the bay till his return."

" Pausanias is changed."

" Sparta will restore him to what he was. Nothing thrives out of Sparta. Even man spoils."

" True, sleep is the sole constant friend, the same in all climates."

CHAPTER IV.

On the shore to the right of the port of Byzantium were at that time thickly scattered the villas or suburban retreats of the wealthier and more luxurious citizens. Byzantium was originally colonized by the Megarians, a Dorian race kindred with that of Sparta; and the old features of the pure and antique Hellas were still preserved in the dialect,* as well as in the forms, of the descendants of the colonists; in their favorite deities and rites and traditions; even in the names of places, transferred from the sterile Megara to that fertile coast; in the rigid and Helot-like slavery to which the native Bithynians were subjected; and in the attachment of their masters to the oligarchic principles of government. Nor was it till long after the present date that democracy in its most corrupt and licentious form was introduced among them. But like all the Dorian colonies, when once they departed from the severe and masculine mode of life inherited from their ancestors, the reaction was rapid, the degeneracy complete. Even then the Byzantines, intermingled with the foreign merchants and traders that thronged their haven, and womanized by the soft contagion of the

---

* "The Byzantine dialect was in the time of Philip, as we know from the decree in Demosthenes, rich in Dorisms."—Mül-ler *on the Doric Dialect.*

6*   E

East, were voluptuous, timid, and prone to every excess save
that of valor. The higher class were exceedingly wealthy,
and gave to their vices or their pleasures a splendor and refinement of which the elder states of Greece were as yet unconscious. At a later period, indeed, we are informed that
the Byzantine citizens had their habitual residence in the
public hostels, and let their houses—not even taking the
trouble to remove their wives—to the strangers who crowded
their gay capital. And when their general found it necessary to demand their aid on the ramparts, he could only se-
cure their attendance by ordering the taverns and cook-
shops to be removed to the place of duty. Not yet so far
sunk in sloth and debauch, the Byzantines were nevertheless
hosts eminently dangerous to the austerer manners of their
Greek visitors. The people, the women, the delicious wine,
the balm of the subduing climate, served to tempt the senses
and relax the mind. Like all the Dorians, when freed from
primitive restraint, the higher class, that is, the descendants
of the colonists, were in themselves an agreeable, jovial race.
They had that strong bias to humor, to jest, to satire, which
in their ancestral Megara gave birth to the Grecian comedy,
and which lurked even beneath the pithy aphorisms and
rude merry-makings of the severe Spartan.

Such were the people with whom of late Pausanias had
familiarly mixed, and with whose manners he contrasted, far
too favorably for his honor and his peace, the habits of his
countrymen.

It was in one of the villas we have described, the favorite
abode of the rich Diagoras, and in an apartment connected

with those more private recesses of the house appropriated
to the females, that two persons were seated by a window
which commanded a wide view of the glittering sea below.
One of these was an old man in a long robe that reached to
his feet, with a bald head, and a beard in which some dark
hairs yet withstood the encroachments of the gray. In his
well-cut features and large eyes were remains of the beauty
that characterized his race; but the mouth was full and wide,
the forehead low though broad, the cheeks swollen, the chin
double, and the whole form corpulent and unwieldy. Still
there was a jolly, sleek good-humor about the aspect of the
man that prepossessed you in his favor. This personage,
who was no less than Diagoras himself, was reclining lazily
upon a kind of narrow sofa cunningly inlaid with ivory,
and studying new combinations in that scientific game which
Palamedes is said to have invented at the siege of Troy.

His companion was of a very different appearance. She
was a girl who to the eye of a Northern stranger might have
seemed about eighteen, though she was probably much younger, of a countenance so remarkable for intelligence that it
was easy to see that her mind had outgrown her years.
Beautiful she certainly was, yet scarcely of that beauty from
which the Greek sculptor would have drawn his models.
The features were not strictly regular, and yet so harmo-
niously did each blend with each, that to have amended one
would have spoiled the whole. There was in the fullness
and depth of the large but genial eye, with its sweeping
fringe, and straight, slightly chiseled brow, more of Asia than
of Greece. The lips, of the freshest red, were somewhat full

and pouting, and dimples without number lay scattered round them—lurking-places for the loves. Her complexion was clear, though dark; and the purest and most virgin bloom mantled, now paler, now richer, through the soft surface. At the time we speak of she was leaning against the open door with her arms crossed on her bosom, and her face turned toward the Byzantine. Her robe, of a deep yellow, so trying to the fair women of the North, became well the glowing colors of her beauty—the damask cheek, the purple hair. Like those of the Ionians, the sleeves of the robe, long and loose, descended to her hands, which were marvelously small and delicate. Long ear-rings, which terminated in a kind of berry, studded with precious stones, then common only with the women of the East; a broad collar, or necklace, of the smaragdus, or emerald; and large clasps, medallion-like, where the swan-like throat joined the graceful shoulder, gave to her dress an appearance of opulence and splendor that betokened how much the ladies of Byzantium had borrowed from the fashions of the Oriental world. Nothing could exceed the lightness of her form, rounded, it is true, but slight and girlish; and the high instep, with the slender foot, so well set off by the embroidered sandal, would have suited such dances as those in which the huntress nymphs of Delos moved around Diana. The natural expression of her face, if countenance so mobile and changeful had one expression more predominant than another, appeared to be irresistibly arch and joyous, as of one full of youth and conscious of her beauty; yet, if a cloud came over the face, nothing could equal the thoughtful and deep sadness of the dark abstracted eyes, as if some touch of higher and more animated emotion — such as belongs to pride, or courage, or intellect—vibrated on the heart. The color rose, the form dilated, the lip quivered, the eye flashed light, and the mirthful expression heightened almost into the sublime. Yet, lovely as Cleonice was deemed at Byzantium, lovelier still as she would have appeared in modern eyes, she failed in what the Greeks generally, but especially the Spartans, deemed an essential of beauty—in height of stature. Accustomed to look upon the virgin but as the future mother of a race of warriors, the Spartans saw beauty only in those proportions which promised a robust and stately progeny ; and the reader may remember the well-known story of the opprobrious reproaches, even, it is said, accompanied with stripes, which the Ephors addressed to a Spartan king for presuming to make choice of a wife below the ordinary stature. Cleonice was small and delicate, rather like the Peri of the Persian than the sturdy Grace of the Dorian. But her beauty was her least charm. She had all that feminine fascination of manner, wayward, varying, inexpressible, yet irresistible, which seizes hold of the imagination as well as the senses, and which has so often made willing slaves of the proud rulers of the world. In fact, Cleonice, the daughter of Diagoras, had enjoyed those advantages of womanly education wholly unknown at that time to the free-born ladies of Greece proper, but which gave to the women of some of the Isles and Ionian cities their celebrity in ancient story. Her mother was of Miletus, famed for the intellectual cultivation of the sex no less

than for their beauty—of Milctus, the birthplace of Aspasia
—of Miletus, from which those remarkable women who, under the name of Hetæræ, exercised afterward so signal an
influence over the mind and manners of Athens, chiefly derived their origin, and who seem to have inspired an affection, which in depth, constancy, and fervor approached to
the more chivalrous passion of the North. Such an education consisted not only in the feminine and household arts
honored universally throughout Greece, but in a kind of
spontaneous and luxuriant cultivation of all that captivates
the fancy and enlivens the leisure. If there were something
pedantic in their affectation of philosophy, it was so graced
and vivified by a brilliancy of conversation, a charm of
manner carried almost to a science, a womanly facility of
softening all that comes within their circle, of suiting yet
refining each complexity and discord of character admitted
to their intercourse, that it had at least nothing masculine
or harsh. Wisdom, taken lightly or easily, seemed but another shape of poetry. The matrons of Athens, who could
often neither read nor write—ignorant, vain, tawdry, and
not always faithful, if we may trust to such scandal as has
reached the modern time—must have seemed insipid beside
these brilliant strangers; and while certainly wanting their
power to retain love, must have had but a doubtful superiority in the qualifications that insure esteem. But we are
not to suppose that the Hetæræ (that mysterious and important class peculiar to a certain state of society, and whose
appellation we can not render by any proper word in modern language) monopolized all the graces of their country-

women. In the same cities were many of unblemished virtue and repute who possessed equal cultivation and attraction, but whom a more decorous life has concealed from the equivocal admiration of posterity; though the numerous female disciples of Pythagoras throw some light on their capacity and intellect. Among such as these had been the mother of Cleonice, not long since dead, and her daughter inherited and equaled her accomplishments, while her virgin youth, her inborn playfulness of manner, her pure guilelessness, which the secluded habits of the unmarried women at Byzantium preserved from all contagion, gave to qualities and gifts so little published abroad the effect, as it were, of a happy and wondrous inspiration rather than of elaborate culture.

Such was the fair creature whom Diagoras, looking up from his pastime, thus addressed:

"And so, perverse one, thou canst not love this great hero, a proper person truly, and a mighty warrior, who will eat you an army of Persians at a meal. These Spartan fighting-cocks want no garlic, I warrant you.* And yet you can't love him, you little rogue."

"Why, my father," said Cleonice, with an arch smile and a slight blush, "even if I did look kindly on Pausanias, would it not be to my own sorrow? What Spartan—above all, what royal Spartan—may marry with a foreigner, and a Byzantine?"

---

* Fighting-cocks were fed with garlic, to make them more fierce. The learned reader will remember how Theorus advised Dicæopolis to keep clear of the Thracians with garlic in their mouths.—See the *Acharnians of Aristophanes*.

"I did not precisely talk of marriage—a very happy state, doubtless, to those who dislike too quiet a life, and a very honorable one, for war is honor itself; but I did not speak of that, Cleonice. I would only say that this man of might loves thee—that he is rich, rich, rich. Pretty pickings at Platæa; and we have known losses, my child, sad losses. And if you do not love him, why, you can but smile and talk as if you did, and when the Spartan goes home, you will lose a tormentor and gain a dowry."

"My father, for shame!"

"Who talks of shame? You women are always so sharp at finding oracles in oak-leaves, that one doesn't wonder Apollo makes choice of your sex for his priests. But listen to me, girl, seriously," and here Diagoras with a great effort raised himself on his elbow, and, lowering his voice, spoke with evident earnestness. "Pausanias has life and death, and, what is worse, wealth or poverty, in his hands; he can raise or ruin us with a nod of his head, this black-curled Jupiter. They tell me that he is fierce, irascible, haughty; and what slighted lover is not revengeful? For my sake, Cleonice, for your poor father's sake, show no scorn, no repugnance; be gentle, play with him, draw not down the thunder-bolt, even if you turn from the golden shower."

While Diagoras spoke, the girl listened with downcast eyes and flushed cheeks, and there was an expression of such shame and sadness on her countenance, that even the Byzantine, pausing and looking up for a reply, was startled by it.

"My child," said he, hesitatingly and absorbed, "do not misconceive me. Cursed be the hour when the Spartan saw thee; but since the Fates have so served us, let us not make bad worse. I love thee, Cleonice, more dearly than the apple of my eye; it is for *thee* I fear, for thee I speak. Alas! it is not dishonor I recommend; it is force I would shun."

"Force!" said the girl, drawing up her form with sudden animation. "Fear not that. It is not Pausanias I dread; it is—"

"What then?"

"No matter; talk of this no more. Shall I sing to thee?"

"But Pausanias will visit us this very night."

"I know it. Hark!" and, with her finger to her lip, her ear bent downward, her cheek varying from pale to red, from red to pale, the maiden stole beyond the window to a kind of platform or terrace that overhung the sea. There, the faint breeze stirring her long hair, and the moonlight full upon her face, she stood, as stood that immortal priestess who looked along the starry Hellespont for the young Leander; and her ear had not deceived her. The oars were dashing in the waves below, and dark and rapid the boat bounded on toward the rocky shore. She gazed long and steadfastly on the dim and shadowy forms which that slender raft contained, and her eye detected among the three the loftier form of her haughty wooer. Presently the thick foliage that clothed the descent shut the boat, nearing the strand, from her view; but she now heard below,

mellowed and softened in the still and fragrant air, the
sound of the cithara and the melodious song of the Mothon, thus imperfectly rendered from the language of immortal melody:

SONG.

Carry a sword in the myrtle bough,
Ye who would honor the tyrant-slayer;
I, in the leaves of the myrtle bough,
Carry a tyrant to slay myself.

I pluck'd the branch with a hasty hand,
But Love was lurking amidst the leaves;
His bow is bent and his shaft is poised,
And I must perish or pass the bough.

Maiden, I come with a gift to thee;
Maiden, I come with a myrtle wreath;
Over thy forehead, or round thy breast,
Bind, I implore thee, my myrtle wreath.*

From hand to hand by the banquet lights
On with the myrtle bough passes song;
From hand to hand by the silent stars
What with the myrtle wreath passes?   Love.

I bear the god in a myrtle wreath,
Under the stars let him pass to thee;
Empty his quiver and bind his wings,
Then pass the myrtle wreath back to me.

Cleonice listened breathlessly to the words, and sighed
heavily as they ceased.   Then, as the foliage rustled below,
she turned quickly into the chamber and seated herself at
a little distance from Diagoras; to all appearance calm, in-

---

* Garlands were twined round the neck, or placed upon the
bosom (ὑποθυμίαδες).   See the quotations from Alcæus, Sappho,
and Anacreon, in Athenæus, book xiii., c. 17.

different, and composed. Was it nature, or the arts of Miletus, that taught the young beauty the hereditary artifices of the sex?

"So it is he, then?" said Diagoras, with a fidgety and nervous trepidation. "Well, he chooses strange hours to visit us. But he is right; his visits can not be too private. Cleonice, you look provokingly at your case."

Cleonice made no reply, but shifted her position so that the light from the lamp did not fall upon her face, while her father, hurrying to the threshold of his hall to receive his illustrious visitor, soon re-appeared with the Spartan Regent, talking as he entered with the volubility of one of the parasites of Alciphron and Athenæus.

"This is most kind, most affable. Cleonice said you would come, Pausanias, though I began to distrust you. The hours seem long to those who expect pleasure."

"And, Cleonice, _you_ knew that I should come," said Pausanias, approaching the fair Byzantine; but his step was timid, and there was no pride now in his anxious eye and bended brow.

"You said you would come to-night," said Cleonice, calmly, "and Spartans, according to proverbs, speak the truth."

"When it is to their advantage, yes,"* said Pausanias,

---

* So said Thucydides of the Spartans, many years afterward. "They give evidence of honor among themselves; but with respect to others, they consider honorable whatever pleases them, and just whatever is to their advantage."—See _Thucyd._, lib. v.

with a slight curl of his lips; and, as if the girl's compliment to his countrymen had roused his spleen and changed his thoughts, he seated himself moodily by Cleonice, and remained silent.

The Byzantine stole an arch glance at the Spartan, as he thus sat, from the corner of her eyes, and said, after a pause,

"You Spartans ought to speak the truth more than other people, for you say much less. We too have our proverb at Byzantium, and one which implies that it requires some wit to tell fibs."

"Child, child!" exclaimed Diagoras, holding up his hand reprovingly, and directing a terrified look at the Spartan. To his great relief, Pausanias smiled, and replied,

"Fair maiden, we Dorians are said to have a wit peculiar to ourselves, but I confess that it is of a nature that is but little attractive to your sex. The Athenians are blander wooers."

"Do you ever attempt to woo in Lacedæmon, then? Ah, but the maidens there, perhaps, are not difficult to please."

"The girl puts me in a cold sweat!" muttered Diagoras, wiping his brow. And this time Pausanias did not smile; he colored, and answered, gravely,

"And is it, then, a vain hope for a Spartan to please a Byzantine?"

"You puzzle me. That is an enigma; put it to the oracle."

The Spartan raised his eyes toward Cleonice, and, as she

saw the inquiring, perplexed look that his features assumed, the ruby lips broke into so wicked a smile, and the eyes that met his had so much laughter in them, that Pausanias was fairly bewitched out of his own displeasure.

"Ah, cruel one!" said he, lowering his voice, "I am not so proud of being Spartan that the thought should console me for thy mockery."

"Not proud of being Spartan! say not so," exclaimed Cleonice. "Who ever speaks of Greece and places not Sparta at her head? Who ever speaks of freedom and forgets Thermopylæ? Who ever burns for glory, and sighs not for the fame of Pausanias and Platæa? Ah, yes, even in jest say not that you are not proud to be a Spartan!"

"The little fool!" cried Diagoras, chuckling, and mightily delighted; "she is quite mad about Sparta—no wonder!"

Pausanias, surprised and moved by the burst of the fair Byzantine, gazed at her admiringly, and thought within himself how harshly the same sentiment would have sounded on the lips of a tall Spartan virgin; but when Cleonice heard the approving interlocution of Diagoras, her enthusiasm vanished from her face, and, putting out her lips poutingly, she said, "Nay, father, I repeat only what others say of the Spartans. They are admirable heroes; but from the little I have seen, they are—"

"What?" said Pausanias, eagerly, and leaning nearer to Cleonice.

"Proud, dictatorial, and stern as companions."

Pausanias once more drew back.

"There it is again!" groaned Diagoras. "I feel exactly

7*

as if I were playing at odd and even with a lion; she does
it to vex me.   I shall retaliate, and creep away."

"Cleonice," said Pausanias, with suppressed emotion,
"you trifle with me, and I bear it."

"You are condescending.   How would you avenge your-
self?"

"How!"

"You would not beat me; you would not make me bear
an anchor on the shoulders, as they say you do your soldiers.   Shame on you!   *You* bear with me!   True, what
help for you?"

"Maiden," said the Spartan, rising in great anger, "for
him who loves and is slighted there is a revenge you have
not mentioned."

"For him who *loves!*   No, Spartan; for him who shuns
disgrace and courts the fame dear to gods and men, there
is no revenge upon women.   Blush for your threat."

"You madden, but subdue me," said the Spartan, as he
turned away.   He then first perceived that Diagoras had
gone—that they were alone.   His contempt for the father
awoke suspicion of the daughter.   Again he approached,
and said: "Cleonice, I know but little of the fables of
poets, yet is it an old maxim often sung and ever belied,
that love scorned becomes hate.   There are moments when
I think I hate thee."

"And yet thou hast never loved me," said Cleonice; and
there was something soft and tender in the tone of her
voice, and the rough Spartan was again subdued.

"I never loved thee!   What, then, is love?   Is not thine

image always before me?—amidst schemes, amidst perils of which thy very dreams have never presented equal perplexity or phantoms so uncertain, I am occupied but with thee. Surely, as upon the hyacinth is written the exclamation of woe, so on this heart is graven thy name. Cleonice, you who know not what it is to love, you affect to deny or to question mine."

"And what," said Cleonice, blushing deeply, and with tears in her eyes, "what result can come from such a love? You may not wed with the stranger. And yet, Pausanias, yet you know that all other love dishonors the virgin even of Byzantium. You are silent; you turn away. Ah, do not let them wrong you. My father fears your power. If you love me, you are powerless; your power has passed to me. Is it not so? I, a weak girl, can rule, command, irritate, mock you, if I will. You may fly me, but not control."

"Do not tempt me too far, Cleonice," said the Spartan, with a faint smile.

"Nay, I will be merciful henceforth; and you, Pausanias, come here no more. Awake to the true sense of what is due to your divine ancestry—your great name. Is it not told of you that, after the fall of Mardonius, you nobly dismissed to her country, unscathed and honored, the captive Coan lady?* Will you reverse at Byzantium the fame acquired at Platæa? Pausanias, spare us; appeal not to my father's fear, still less to his love of gold."

---

* Herod., ix.

"I can not, I can not fly thee," said the Spartan, with great emotion. "You know not how stormy, how inexorable are the passions which burst forth after a whole youth of restraint. When Nature breaks the barriers, she rushes headlong on her course. I am no gentle wooer; where in Sparta should I learn the art? But, if I love thee not as these mincing Ionians, who come with offerings of flowers and song, I do love thee with all that fervor of which the old Dorian legends tell. I could brave, like the Thracian, the dark gates of Hades, were thy embrace my reward. Command me as thou wilt—make me thy slave in all things, even as Hercules was to Omphale; but tell me only that I may win thy love at last. Fear not. Why fear me? In my wildest moments a look from thee can control me. I ask but love for love. Without thy love thy beauty were valueless. Bid me not despair."

Cleonice turned pale, and the large tears that had gathered in her eyes fell slowly down her cheeks; but she did not withdraw her hand from his clasp, or avert her countenance from his eyes.

"I do not fear thee," said she, in a very low voice. "I told my father so; but—but—" (and here she drew back her hand and averted her face), "I fear myself."

"Ah, no, no," cried the delighted Spartan, detaining her, "do not fear to trust to thine own heart. Talk not of dishonor. There are" (and here the Spartan drew himself up, and his voice took a deeper swell)—"there are those on earth who hold themselves above the miserable judgments of the vulgar herd—who can emancipate themselves from

those galling chains of custom and of country which helot-
ize affection, genius, Nature herself. What is dishonor here
may be glory elsewhere; and this hand, outstretched toward a mightier sceptre than Greek ever wielded yet, may
dispense, not shame and sorrow, but glory and golden afflu-
ence to those I love."

"You amaze me, Pausanias. *Now* I fear you. What
mean these mysterious boasts? Have you the dark ambition to restore in your own person that race of tyrants
whom your country hath helped to sweep away? Can you
hope to change the laws of Sparta, and reign there, your
will the state?"

"Cleonice, we touch upon matters that should not disturb the ears of women. Forgive me if I have been roused
from myself."

"At Miletus—so have I heard my mother say—there
were women worthy to be the confidants of men."

"But they were women who loved. Cleonice, I should
rejoice in an hour when I might pour every thought into
thy bosom."

At this moment there was heard on the strand below a
single note from the Mothon's instrument, low, but pro-
longed; it ceased, and was again renewed. The royal conspirator started and breathed hard.

"It is the signal," he muttered; "they wait me. Cleonice," he said aloud, and with much earnestness in his voice,
"I had hoped, ere we parted, to have drawn from your lips
those assurances which would give me energy for the present and hope in the future. Ah, turn not from me because

4*   F my speech is plain and my manner rugged.   What, Cleonice, what if I could defy the laws of Sparta; what if, instead of that gloomy soil, I could bear thee to lands where heaven and man alike smile benignant on love?   Might I not hope then?"

"Do nothing to sully your fame."

"Is it, then, dear to thee?"

"It is a part of thee," said Cleonice, falteringly; and as if she had said too much, she covered her face with her hands.

Emboldened by this emotion, the Spartan gave way to his passion and his joy.   He clasped her in his arms—his first embrace—and kissed, with wild fervor, the crimsoned forehead, the veiling hands.   Then, as he tore himself away, he cast his right arm aloft.

"O Hercules!" he cried, in solemn and kindling adjuration, "my ancestor and my divine guardian, it was not by confining thy labors to one spot of earth that thou wert borne from thy throne of fire to the seats of the gods. Like thee I will spread the influence of my arms to nations whose glory shall be my name; and as thy sons, my fathers, expelled from Sparta, returned thither with sword and spear to defeat usurpers and to found the long dynasty of the Heracleids, even so may it be mine to visit that dread abode of torturers and spies, and to build up in the halls of the Atridæ a power worthier of the lineage of the demigod.   Again the signal!   Fear not, Cleonice, I will not tarnish my fame, but I will exchange the envy of abhorring rivals for the obedience of a world.   One kiss more!   Farewell!"

Ere Cleonice recovered herself, Pausanias was gone, his wild and uncomprehended boasts still ringing in her ear. She sighed heavily, and turned toward the opening that admitted to the terraces.   There she stood watching for the parting of her lover's boat.   It was midnight; the air, laden with the perfumes of a thousand fragrant shrubs and flowers that bloom along that coast in the rich luxuriance of nature, was hushed and breathless.   In its stillness every sound was audible, the rustling of a leaf, the ripple of a wave.   She heard the murmur of whispered voices below, and in a few moments she recognized, emerging from the foliage, the form of Pausanias; but he was not alone. Who were his companions?   In the deep lustre of that shining and splendid atmosphere she could see sufficient of the outline of their figures to observe that they were not dressed in the Grecian garb; their long robes betrayed the Persian.

They seemed conversing familiarly and eagerly as they passed along the smooth sands, till a curve in the wooded shore hid them from her view.

"Why do I love him so," said the girl, mechanically, "and yet wrestle against that love?   Dark forebodings tell me that Aphrodite smiles not on our vows.   Woe is me! What will be the end?"

CHAPTER V.

On quitting Cleonice, Pausanias hastily traversed the long passage that communicated with a square peristyle or colonnade, which again led, on the one hand, to the more public parts of the villa, and, on the other, through a small door left ajar, conducted by a back entrance, to the garden and the sea-shore. Pursuing the latter path, the Spartan bounded down the descent and came upon an opening in the foliage, in which Lysander was seated beside the boat that had been drawn partially on the strand.

"Alone? Where is Alcman?"

"Yonder; you heard his signal?"

"I heard it."

"Pausanias, they who seek you are Persians. Beware!"

"Of what? murder? I am warned."

"Murder to your good name. There are no arms against appearances."

"But I may trust thee?" said the Regent, quickly; "and of Alcman's faith I am convinced."

"Why trust to any man what it were wisdom to reveal to the whole Grecian Council? To parley secretly with the foe is half a treason to our friends."

"Lysander," replied Pausanias, coldly, "you have much to learn before you can be wholly Spartan. Tarry here yet a while."

"What shall I do with this boy?" muttered the conspirator as he strode on. "I know that he will not betray me, yet can I hope for his aid? I love him so well that I would fain he shared my fortunes. Perhaps by little and little I may lead him on. Meanwhile, his race and his name are so well accredited in Sparta, his father himself an Ephor, that his presence allays suspicion. Well, here are my Persians."

A little apart from the Mothon, who, resting his cithara on a fragment of rock, appeared to be absorbed in reflection, stood the men of the East. There were two of them; one of tall stature and noble presence, in the prime of life; the other more advanced in years, of a coarser make, a yet darker complexion, and of a sullen and gloomy countenance. They were not dressed alike; the taller, a Persian of pure blood, wore a short tunic that reached only to the knees; and the dress fitted to his shape without a single fold. On his round cap or bonnet glittered a string of those rare pearls, especially and immemorially prized in the East, which formed the favorite and characteristic ornament of the illustrious tribe of the Pasargadæ. The other, who was a Mede, differed scarcely in his dress from Pausanias himself, except that he was profusely covered with ornaments; his arms were decorated with bracelets, he wore earrings, and a broad collar of unpolished stones in a kind of filigree was suspended from his throat. Behind the Orientals stood Gongylus, leaning both hands on his staff, and watching the approach of Pausanias with the same icy smile and glittering eye with which he listened to the pas-

8

sionate invectives or flattered the dark ambition of the Spartan. The Orientals saluted Pausanias with a lofty gravity, and Gongylus, drawing near, said: "Son of Cleombrotus, the illustrious Ariamanes, kinsman to Xerxes, and of the house of the Achæmenids, is so far versed in the Grecian tongue that I need not proffer my offices as interpreter. In Datis the Mede, brother to the most renowned of the Magi, you behold a warrior worthy to assist the arms even of Pausanias."

"I greet ye in our Spartan phrase, 'The beautiful to the good,'" said Pausanias, regarding the Barbarians with an earnest gaze. "And I requested Gongylus to lead ye hither in order that I might confer with ye more at ease, than in the confinement to which I regret ye are still sentenced. Not in prisons should be held the conversations of brave men."

"I know," said Ariamanes (the statelier of the Barbarians), in the Greek tongue, which he spoke intelligibly indeed, but with slowness and hesitation, "I know that I am with that hero who refused to dishonor the corpse of Mardonius; and even though a captive, I converse without shame with my victor."

"Rested it with me alone, your captivity should cease," replied Pausanias. "War, that has made me acquainted with the valor of the Persians, has also enlightened me as to their character. Your king has ever been humane to such of the Greeks as have sought a refuge near his throne. I would but imitate his clemency."

"Had the great Darius less esteemed the Greeks, he

would never have invaded Greece. From the wanderers whom misfortune drove to his realms, he learned to wonder at the arts, the genius, the energies of the people of Hellas. He desired less to win their territories than to gain such subjects. Too vast, alas! was the work he bequeathed to Xerxes."

"He should not have trusted to force alone," returned Pausanias. "Greece may be won, but by the arts of her sons, not by the arms of the stranger. A Greek only can subdue Greece. By such profound knowledge of the factions, the interests, the envies, and the jealousies of each state as a Greek alone can possess, the mistaken chain that binds them might be easily severed; some bought, some intimidated, and the few that hold out subdued amidst the apathy of the rest."

"You speak wisely, right hand of Hellas," answered the Persian, who had listened to these remarks with deep attention. "Yet had we in our armies your countryman, the brave Demaratus."

"But, if I have heard rightly, ye too often disdained his counsel. Had he been listened to, there had been neither a Salamis nor a Platæa.* Yet Demaratus himself had been

---

* After the action at Thermopylæ, Demaratus advised Xerxes to send three hundred vessels to the Laconian coast, and seize the island of Cythera, which commanded Sparta. "The profound experience of Demaratus in the selfish and exclusive policy of his countrymen made him argue that if this were done the fear of Sparta for herself would prevent her joining the forces of the rest of Greece, and leave the latter a more easy prey to the invader."—*Athens: its Rise and Fall.* This advice

too long a stranger to Greece, and he knew little of any state save that of Sparta. Lives he still?"

"Surely yes, in honor and renown; little less than the son of Darius himself."

"And what reward would Xerxes bestow on one of greater influence than Demaratus; on one who has hitherto conquered every foe, and now beholds before him the conquest of Greece herself?"

"If such a man were found," answered the Persian, "let his thought run loose, let his imagination rove, let him seek only how to find a fitting estimate of the gratitude of the king and the vastness of the service."

Pausanias shaded his brow with his hand, and mused a few moments; then lifting his eyes to the Persian's watchful but composed countenance, he said, with a slight smile:

"Hard is it, O Persian, when the choice is actually before him, for a man to renounce his country. There have been hours within this very day when my desires swept afar from Sparta, from all Hellas, and rested on the tranquil pomp of Oriental satrapies. But now, rude and stern parent though Sparta be to me, I feel still that I am her son; and, while we speak, a throne in stormy Hellas seems the fitting object of a Greek's ambition. In a word, then, I would rise, and yet raise my country. I would have at

---

was overruled by Achæmenes. So, again, had the advice of Artemisia, the Carian princess, been taken—to delay the naval engagement of Salamis, and rather to sail to the Peloponnesus —the Greeks, failing of provisions and divided among themselves, would probably have dispersed.

my will a force that may suffice to overthrow in Sparta its
grim and unnatural laws, to found amidst its rocks that
single throne which the son of a demi-god should ascend.
From that throne I would spread my empire over the whole
of Greece, Corinth and Athens being my tributaries. So
that, though men now, and posterity hereafter, may say,
'Pausanias overthrew the Spartan government,' they shall
add, 'but Pausanias annexed to the Spartan sceptre the
realm of Greece. Pausanias was a tyrant, but not a traitor.'
How, O Persian, can these designs accord with the policy
of the Persian king?"

"Not without the authority of my master can I answer
thee," replied Ariamanes, "so that my answer may be as
the king's signet to his decree. But so much at least I
say that it is not the custom of the Persians to interfere
with the institutions of those states with which they are
connected. Thou desirest to make a monarchy of Greece,
with Sparta for its head. Be it so; the king my master
will aid thee so to scheme and so to reign, provided thou
dost but concede to him a vase of the water from thy
fountains, a fragment of earth from thy gardens."

"In other words," said Pausanias, thoughtfully, but with
a slight color on his brow, "if I hold my dominions tributary to the king?"

"The dominions that by the king's aid thou wilt have
conquered. Is that a hard law?"

"To a Greek and a Spartan the very mimicry of alle-
giance to the foreigner is hard."

The Persian smiled. "Yet, if I understand thee aright,
8*

O Chief, even kings in Sparta are but subjects to their people. Slave to a crowd at home, or tributary to a throne abroad; slave every hour, or tributary for earth and water once a year, which is the freer lot?"

"Thou canst not understand our Grecian notions," replied Pausanias, "nor have I leisure to explain them. But though I may subdue Sparta to myself as to its native sovereign, I will not, even by a type, subdue the land of the Heracleid to the Barbarian."

Ariamanes looked grave; the difficulty raised was serious. And here the craft of Gongylus interposed.

"This may be adjusted, Ariamanes, as befits both parties. Let Pausanias rule in Sparta as he lists, and Sparta stand free of tribute. But for all other states and cities that Pausanias, aided by the great king, shall conquer, let the vase be filled, and the earth be Grecian. Let him but render tribute for those lands which the Persians submit to his sceptre. So shall the pride of the Spartan be appeased, and the claims of the king be satisfied."

"Shall it be so?" said Pausanias.

"Instruct me so to propose to my master, and I will do my best to content him with the exception to the wonted rights of the Persian diadem. And then," continued Ariamanes, "then, Pausanias, Conqueror of Mardonius, Captain at Platæa, thou art indeed a man with whom the lord of Asia may treat as an equal. Greeks before thee have offered to render Greece to the king my master; but they were exiles and fugitives, they had nothing to risk or lose; thou hast fame, and command, and power, and riches, and all—"

"But for a throne," interrupted Gongylus.

"It does not matter what may be my motives," returned the Spartan, gloomily, "and were I to tell them, you might not comprehend. But so much by way of explanation. You too have held command?"

"I have."

"If you knew that, when power became to you so sweet that it was as necessary to life itself as food and drink, it would then be snatched from you forever, and you would serve as a soldier in the very ranks you had commanded as a leader; if you knew that, no matter what your services, your superiority, your desires, this shameful fall was inexorably doomed, might you not see humiliation in power itself, obscurity in renown, gloom in the present, despair in the future? And would it not seem to you nobler even to desert the camp than to sink into a subaltern?"

"Such a prospect has in our country made out of good subjects fierce rebels," observed the Persian.

"Ay, ay, I doubt it not," said Pausanias, laughing bitterly. "Well, then, such will be my lot, if I pluck not out a fairer one from the Fatal Urn. As Regent of Sparta, while my nephew is beardless, I am general of her armies, and I have the sway and functions of her king. When he arrives at the customary age, I am a subject, a citizen, a nothing, a miserable fool of memories gnawing my heart away amidst joyless customs and stern austerities, with the recollection of the glories of Platæa and the delights of Byzantium. Persian, I am filled from the crown to the sole with the desire of power, with the tastes of pleasure. I

have that within me which before my time has made heroes
and traitors, raised demi-gods to heaven, or chained the
lofty Titans to the rocks of Hades. Something I may yet
be; I know not what. But as the man never returns to the
boy, so never, never, never once more, can I be again the
Spartan subject. Enough; such as I am, I can fulfill what
I have said to thee. Will thy king accept me as his ally,
and ratify the terms I have proposed?"

"I feel well-nigh assured of it," answered the Persian;
"for since thou hast spoken thus boldly, I will answer thee
in the same strain. Know, then, that we of the pure race
of Persia, we the sons of those who overthrew the Mede,
and extended the race of the mountain tribe, from the
Scythian to the Arab, from Egypt to Ind, we at least
feel that no sacrifice were too great to redeem the disgrace we have suffered at the hands of thy countrymen;
and the world itself were too small an empire, too confined a breathing-place, for the son of Darius, if this
nook of earth were still left without the pale of his dominion."

"This nook of earth? Ay, but Sparta itself must own
no lord but me."

"It is agreed."

"If I release thee, wilt thou bear these offers to the king,
traveling day and night till thou restest at the foot of his
throne?"

"I should carry tidings too grateful to suffer me to loiter
by the road."

"And Datis, he comprehends us not; but his eyes glitter

fiercely on me. It is easy to see that thy comrade loves not the Greek."

"For that reason he will aid us well. Though but a Mede, and not admitted to the privileges of the Pasargadæ, his relationship to the most powerful and learned of our Magi, and his own services in war, have won him such influence with both priests and soldiers that I would fain have him as my companion. I will answer for his fidelity to our joint object."

"Enough; ye are both free. Gongylus, you will now conduct our friends to the place where the steeds await them. You will then privately return to the citadel, and give to their pretended escape the probable appearances we devised. Be quick, while it is yet night. One word more. Persian, our success depends upon thy speed. It is while the Greeks are yet at Byzantium, while I yet am in command, that we should strike the blow. If the king consent, through Gongylus thou wilt have means to advise me. A Persian army must march at once to the Phrygian confines, instructed to yield command to me when the hour comes to assume it. Delay not that aid by such vast and profitless recruits as swelled the pomp, but embarrassed the arms, of Xerxes. Armies too large rot by their own unwieldiness into decay. A band of fifty thousand, composed solely of the Medes and Persians, will more than suffice. With such an army, if my command be undisputed, I will win a second Platæa, but against the Greek."

"Your suggestions shall be law. May Ormuzd favor the bold!"

"Away, Gongylus! You know the rest."

Pausanias followed with thoughtful eyes the receding forms of Gongylus and the Barbarians. "I have passed forever," he muttered, "the pillars of Hercules. I must go on or perish. If I fall, I die execrated and abhorred; if I succeed, the sound of the choral flutes will drown the hootings. Be it as it may, I do not and will not repent. If the wolf gnaw my entrails, none shall hear me groan." He turned and met the eyes of Alcman, fixed on him so intently, so exultingly, that, wondering at their strange expression, he drew back and said, haughtily, "You imitate Medusa, but I am stone already."

"Nay," said the Mothon, in a voice of great humility, "if you are of stone, it is like the divine one which, when borne before armies, secures their victory. Blame me not that I gazed on you with triumph and hope. For, while you conferred with the Persian, methought the murmurs that reached my ear sounded thus: 'When Pausanias shall rise, Sparta shall bend low, and the Helot shall break his chains.'"

"They do not hate me, these Helots?"

"You are the only Spartan they love."

"Were my life in danger from the Ephors—"

"The Helots would rise to a man."

"Did I plant my standard on Taygetus, though all Sparta encamped against it—"

"All the slaves would cut their way to thy side. O Pausanias, think how much nobler it were to reign over tens of thousands who become freemen at thy word, than to be but the equal of ten thousand tyrants."

"The Helots fight well, when well led," said Pausanias, as if to himself. "Launch the boat."

"Pardon me, Pausanias, but is it prudent any longer to trust Lysander? He is the pattern of the Spartan youth, and Sparta is his mistress. He loves her too well not to blab to her every secret."

"O Sparta, Sparta! wilt thou not leave me one friend?" exclaimed Pausanias. "No, Alcman, I will not separate myself from Lysander till I despair of his alliance. To your oars! Be quick!"

At the sound of the Mothon's tread upon the pebbles, Lysander, who had hitherto remained motionless, reclining by the boat, rose and advanced toward Pausanias. There was in his countenance, as the moon shining on it cast over his statue-like features a pale and marble hue, so much of anxiety, of affection, of fear, so much of the evident, unmistakable solicitude of friendship, that Pausanias, who, like most men envied and unloved, was susceptible even of the semblance of attachment, muttered to himself, "No, thou wilt not desert me, nor I thee."

"My friend, my Pausanias," said Lysander, as he approached, "I have had fears — I have seen omens. Undertake nothing, I beseech thee, which thou hast meditated this night."

"And what hast thou seen?" said Pausanias, with a slight change of countenance.

"I was praying the gods for thee and Sparta, when a star shot suddenly from the heavens. Pausanias, this is the eighth year, the year in which on moonless nights the Ephors watch the heavens."

"And if a star fall, they judge their kings," interrupted Pausanias (with a curl of his haughty lip), "to have offended the gods, and suspend them from their office till acquitted by an oracle at Delphi, or a priest at Olympia. A wise superstition. But, Lysander, the night is not moonless, and the omen is therefore naught."

Lysander shook his head mournfully, and followed his chieftain to the boat, in gloomy silence.

BOOK II.

CHAPTER I.

At noon the next day, not only the vessels in the harbor presented the same appearance of inactivity and desertion which had characterized the preceding evening, but the camp itself seemed forsaken. Pausanias had quit his ship for the citadel, in which he took up his lodgment when on shore; and most of the officers and sailors of the squadron were dispersed among the taverns and wine-shops, for which, even at that day, Byzantium was celebrated.

It was in one of the lowest and most popular of these latter resorts, and in a large and rude chamber, or rather outhouse, separated from the rest of the building, that a number of the Laconian Helots were assembled. Some of these were employed as sailors, others were the military attendants on the Regent and the Spartans who accompanied him.

At the time we speak of, these unhappy beings were in the full excitement of that wild and melancholy gayety which is almost peculiar to slaves in their hours of recreation, and in which reaction of wretchedness modern writers have discovered the indulgence of a native humor. Some of them were drinking deep, wrangling, jesting, laughing in loud discord over their cups. At another table rose the deep voice of a singer, chanting one of those antique airs

known but to these degraded sons of the Homeric Achæan,
and probably in its origin going beyond the date of the
Tale of Troy; a song of gross and rustic buffoonery, but
ever and anon charged with some image or thought worthy
of that language of the universal Muses.   His companions
listened with a rude delight to the rough voice and homely sounds, and now and then interrupted the wassailers at
the other tables by cries for silence, which none regarded.
Here and there, with intense and fierce anxiety on their
faces, small groups were playing at dice; for gambling is
the passion of slaves.   And many of these men, to whom
wealth could bring no comfort, had secretly amassed large
hoards at the plunder of Platæa, from which they had sold
to the traders of Ægina gold at the price of brass.   The
appearance of the rioters was startling and melancholy.
They were mostly stunted and undersized, as are generally
the progeny of the sons of woe; lean and gaunt with early
hardship, the spine of the back curved and bowed by habitual degradation; but with the hard-knit sinews and prominent muscles which are produced by labor and the mountain air; and under shaggy and lowering brows sparkled
many a fierce, perfidious, and malignant eye; while, as
mirth, or gaming, or song, aroused smiles in the various
groups, the rude features spoke of passions easily released
from the sullen bondage of servitude, and revealed the nature of the animals which thralldom had failed to tame.
Here and there, however, were to be seen forms, unlike the
rest, of stately stature, of fair proportions, wearing the divine lineaments of Grecian beauty.   From some of these a

higher nature spoke out, not in mirth, that last mockery of supreme woe, but in an expression of stern, grave, and disdainful melancholy; others, on the contrary, surpassed the rest in vehemence, clamor, and exuberant extravagance of emotion, as if their nobler physical development only served to entitle them to that base superiority. For health and vigor can make an aristocracy even among Helots. The garments of these merry-makers increased the peculiar effect of their general appearance. The Helots in military excursions naturally relinquished the rough sheep-skin dress that characterized their countrymen at home, the serfs of the soil. The sailors had thrown off, for coolness, the leathern jerkins they habitually wore, and, with their bare arms and breasts, looked as if of a race that yet shivered, primitive and unredeemed, on the outskirts of civilization.

Strangely contrasted with their rougher comrades were those who, placed occasionally about the person of the Regent, were indulged with the loose and clean robes of gay colors worn by the Asiatic slaves; and these ever and anon glanced at their finery with an air of conscious triumph. Altogether, it was a sight that might well have appalled, by its solemn lessons of human change, the poet who would have beheld in that imbruted flock the descendants of the race over whom Pelops, and Atreus, and Menelaus, and Agamemnon, the king of men, had held their antique sway, and might still more have saddened the philosopher who believed, as Menander has nobly written, "that Nature knows no slaves."

Suddenly, in the midst of the confused and uproarious
9*

hubbub, the door opened, and Alcman the Mothon entered the chamber. At this sight the clamor ceased in an instant. The party rose, as by a general impulse, and crowded round the new-comer.

"My friends," said he, regarding them with the same calm and frigid indifference which usually characterized his demeanor, "you do well to make merry while you may, for something tells me it will not last long. We shall return to Lacedæmon. You look black. So, then, is there no delight in the thought of home?"

"*Home!*" muttered one of the Helots, and the word, sounding drearily on his lips, was echoed by many, so that it circled like a groan.

"Yet ye have your children as much as if ye were free," said Alcman.

"And for that reason it pains us to see them play, unaware of the future," said a Helot of better mien than his comrades.

"But do you know," returned the Mothon, gazing on the last speaker steadily, "that for your children there may not be a future fairer than that which your fathers knew?"

"Tush!" exclaimed one of the unhappy men, old before his time, and of an aspect singularly sullen and ferocious. "Such have been your half hints and mystic prophecies for years. What good comes of them? Was there ever an oracle for Helots?"

"There was no repute in the oracles even of Apollo," returned Alcman, "till the Apollo-serving Dorians became conquerors. Oracles are the children of victories."

"But there are no victories for us," said the first speaker, mournfully.

"Never, if ye despair," said the Mothon, loftily. "What!" he added, after a pause, looking round at the crowd, "what! do ye not see that hope dawned upon us from the hour when thirty-five thousand of us were admitted as soldiers, ay, and as conquerors, at Platæa? From that moment we knew our strength. Listen to me. At Samos once a thousand slaves—mark me, but a thousand—escaped the yoke, seized on arms, fled to the mountains (we have mountains even in Laconia), descended from time to time to devastate the fields and to harass their ancient lords. By habit they learned war, by desperation they grew indomitable. What became of these slaves? Were they cut off? Did they perish by hunger, by the sword, in the dungeon or field? No; those brave men were the founders of Ephesus."*

"But the Samians were not Spartans," mumbled the old Helot.

"As ye will, as ye will," said Alcman, relapsing into his usual coldness. "I wish you never to strike unless ye are prepared to die or conquer."

"Some of us are," said the younger Helot.

"Sacrifice a cock to the Fates, then."

"But why, think you," asked one of the Helots, "that we shall be so soon summoned back to Laconia?"

"Because while ye are drinking and idling here—drones that ye are—there is commotion in the Athenian bee-

---

* Malacus *ap.* Athen., 6.

hive yonder.   Know that Ariamanes the Persian, and Datis the Mede, have escaped.   The allies, especially the Athenians, are excited and angry; and many of them are already come in a body to Pausanias, whom they accuse of abetting the escape of the fugitives."

" Well ?"

" Well, and if Pausanias does not give honey in his words—and few flowers grow on his lips—the bees will sting, that is all.   A trireme will be dispatched to Sparta with complaints.   Pausanias will be recalled—perhaps his life endangered."

" Endangered !" echoed several voices.

" Yes.   What is that to you—what care you for his danger ?   He is a Spartan."

" Ay," cried one; " but he has been kind to the Helots."

" And we have fought by his side," said another.

" And he dressed my wound with his own hand," murmured a third.

" And we have got money under him," growled a fourth.

" And, more than all," said Alcman, in a loud voice, " if he lives, he will break down the Spartan government.   Ye will not let this man die ?"

" Never !" exclaimed the whole assembly.   Alcman gazed with a kind of calm and strange contempt on the flashing eyes, the fiery gestures, of the throng, and then said, coldly,

" So, then, ye would fight for one man ?"

" Ay, ay, that would we."

" But not for your own liberties, and those of your children unborn ?"

There was a dead silence; but the taunt was felt, and its logic was already at work in many of these rugged breasts.

At this moment, the door was suddenly thrown open; and a Helot, in the dress worn by the attendants of the Regent, entered, breathless and panting.

"Alcman! the gods be praised, you are here. Pausanias commands your presence. Lose not a moment. And you too, comrades, by Demeter! do you mean to spend whole days at your cups? Come to the citadel; ye may be wanted."

This was spoken to such of the Helots as belonged to the train of Pausanias.

"Wanted—what for?" said one. "Pausanias gives us a holiday while he employs the sleek Egyptians."

"Who that serves Pausanias ever asks that question, or can foresee from one hour to another what he may be required to do?" returned the self-important messenger, with great contempt. Meanwhile the Mothon, all whose movements were peculiarly silent and rapid, was already on his way to the citadel. The distance was not inconsiderable, but Alcman was swift of foot. Tightening the girdle round his waist, he swung himself, as it were, into a kind of run, which, though not seemingly rapid, cleared the ground with a speed almost rivaling that of the ostrich, from the length of the stride and the extreme regularity of the pace. Such was at that day the method by which messages were dispatched from state to state, especially in mountainous countries; and the length of way which was performed, without stopping, by the foot-couriers might startle the best-trained pedestrians in our times. So swiftly, indeed, did the Mothon pursue his course, that just by the citadel he came up with the Grecian captains who, before he joined the Helots, had set off for their audience with Pausanias. There were some fourteen or fifteen of them, and they so filled up the path, which, just there, was not broad, that Alcman was obliged to pause as he came upon their rear.

"And whither so fast, fellow?" said Uliades the Samian, turning round as he heard the strides of the Mothon.

"Please you, master, I am bound to the General."

"Oh, his slave! Is he going to free you?"

"I am already as free as a man who has no city can be."

"Pithy. The Spartan slaves have the dryness of their masters. How, sirrah! do you jostle me?"

"I crave pardon. I only seek to pass."

"Never! to take precedence of a Samian. Keep back."

"I dare not."

"Nay, nay, let him pass," said the young Chian, Antagoras; "he will get scourged if he is too late. Perhaps, like the Persians, Pausanias wears false hair, and wishes the slave to dress it in honor of us."

"Hush!" whispered an Athenian. "Are these taunts prudent?"

Here there suddenly broke forth a loud oath from Uliades, who, lingering a little behind the rest, had laid rough hands on the Mothon, as the latter once more attempted to pass him. With a dexterous and abrupt agility, Alcman had extricated himself from the Samian's grasp, but with a force that swung the captain on his knee. Taking advantage of the position of the foe, the Mothon darted onward, and, threading the rest of the party, disappeared through the neighboring gates of the citadel.

"You saw the insult?" said Uliades, between his ground teeth, as he recovered himself. "The master shall answer for the slave; and to me, too, who have forty slaves of my own at home!"

"Pooh! think no more of it," said Antagoras, gayly; "the poor fellow meant only to save his own hide."

"As if that were of any consequence! My slaves are brought up from the cradle not to know if they have hides or not. You may pinch them by the hour together, and they don't feel you. My little ones do it, in rainy weather, to strengthen their fingers. The gods keep them!"

"An excellent gymnastic invention. But we are now within the citadel. Courage! The Spartan greyhound has long teeth."

Pausanias was striding with hasty steps up and down a long and narrow peristyle or colonnade that surrounded the apartments appropriated to his private use, when Alcman joined him.

"Well, well," cried he, eagerly, as he saw the Mothon, "you have mingled with the common gangs of these worshipful seamen, these new men, these Ionians. Think you they have so far overcome their awe of the Spartan that they would obey the mutinous commands of their officers?"

"Pausanias, the truth must be spoken—Yes!"

"Ye gods! one would think each of these wranglers imagined he had a whole Persian army in his boat. Why, I have seen the day when, if in any assembly of Greeks a Spartan entered, the sight of his very hat and walking-staff cast a terror through the whole conclave."

"True, Pausanias; but they suspect that Sparta herself will disown her General."

"Ah! say they so?"

"With one voice."

Pausanias paused a moment in deep and perturbed thought.

"Have they dared yet, think you, to send to Sparta?"

"I hear not; but a trireme is in readiness to sail after your conference with the captains."

"So, Alcman, it were ruin to my schemes to be recalled —until—until—"

"The hour to join the Persians on the frontier—yes."

"One word more. Have you had occasion to sound the Helots?"

"But half an hour since. They will be true to you. Lift your right hand, and the ground where you stand will bristle with men who fear death even less than the Spartans."

"Their aid were useless here against the whole Grecian fleet; but in the defiles of Laconia, otherwise. I am prepared, then, for the worst, even recall."

Here a slave crossed from a kind of passage that led from the outer chambers into the peristyle.

"The Grecian Captains have arrived to demand audience."

"Bid them wait," cried Pausanias, passionately.

"Hist! Pausanias," whispered the Mothon. "Is it not best to soothe them—to play with them—to cover the lion with the fox's hide?"

The Regent turned with a frown to his foster-brother, as if surprised and irritated by his presumption in advising; and indeed of late, since Pausanias had admitted the son of the Helot into his guilty intrigues, Alcman had assumed a bearing and tone of equality which Pausanias, wrapped in his dark schemes, did not always notice, but at which from time to time he chafed angrily, yet again permitted it, and the custom gained ground; for in guilt conventional distinctions rapidly vanish, and mind speaks freely out to mind. The presence of the slave, however, restrained him, and after a momentary silence his natural acuteness, great when undisturbed by passion or pride, made him sensible of the wisdom of Alcman's counsel.

"Hold!" he said to the slave. "Announce to the Grecian Chiefs that Pausanias will await them forthwith. Begone! Now, Alcman, I will talk over these gentle monitors. Not in vain have I been educated in Sparta; yet if by chance I fail, hold thyself ready to haste to Sparta at a minute's warning. I must forestall the foe. I have gold, gold; and he who employs most of the yellow orators will prevail most with the Ephors. Give me my staff; and tarry in yon chamber to the left."

CHAPTER II.

In a large hall, with a marble fountain in the middle of it, the Greek Captains awaited the coming of Pausanias. A low and muttered conversation was carried on among them, in small knots and groups, amidst which the voice of Uliades was heard the loudest. Suddenly the hum was hushed, for footsteps were heard without. The thick curtains that at one extreme screened the door-way were drawn aside, and, attended by three of the Spartan knights, among whom was Lysander, and by two soothsayers, who were seldom absent, in war or warlike council, from the side of the Royal Heracleid, Pausanias slowly entered the hall. So majestic, grave, and self-collected were the bearing and aspect of the Spartan General, that the hereditary awe inspired by his race was once more awakened, and the angry crowd saluted him, silent and half abashed. Although the strong passions and the daring arrogance of Pausanias did not allow him the exercise of that enduring, systematic, unsleeping hypocrisy which, in relations with the foreigner, often characterized his countrymen, and which, from its outward dignity and profound craft, exalted the vice into genius; yet, trained from earliest childhood in the arts that hide design, that control the countenance, and convey in the fewest words the most ambiguous meanings, the Spar-

tan General could, for a brief period, or for a critical purpose, command all the wiles for which the Greek was na-
tionally famous, and in which Thucydides believed that, of
all Greeks, the Spartan was the most skillful adept. And
now, as, uniting the courtesy of the host with the dignity
of the chief, he returned the salute of the officers, and
smiled his gracious welcome, the unwonted affability of his
manner took the discontented by surprise, and half propiti-
ated the most indignant in his favor.

"I need not ask you, O Greeks," said he, why ye have
sought me. Ye have learned the escape of Ariamanes and
Datis—a strange and unaccountable mischance."

The captains looked round at each other in silence, till
at last every eye rested upon Cimon, whose illustrious birth,
as well as his known respect for Sparta, combined with
his equally well-known dislike of her chief, seemed to
mark him, despite his youth, as the fittest person to be
speaker for the rest. Cimon, who understood the mute appeal, and whose courage never failed his ambition, raised
his head, and, after a moment's hesitation, replied to the
Spartan:

"Pausanias, you guess rightly the cause which leads us
to your presence. These prisoners were our noblest; their
capture the reward of our common valor; they were generals, moreover, of high skill and repute. They had become
experienced in our Grecian warfare, even by their defeats.
Those two men, should Xerxes again invade Greece, are
worth more to his service than half the nations whose
myriads crossed the Hellespont. But this is not all. The

arms of the Barbarians we can encounter undismayed. It is treason at home which can alone appall us."

There was a low murmur among the Ionians at these words. Pausanias, with well-dissembled surprise on his countenance, turned his eyes from Cimon to the murmurers, and from them again to Cimon, and repeated,

"Treason! son of Miltiades; and from whom?"

"Such is the question that we would put to thee, Pausanias—to thee, whose eyes, as leader of our armies, are doubtless vigilant daily and nightly over the interests of Greece."

"I am not blind," returned Pausanias, appearing unconscious of the irony; "but I am not Argus. If thou hast discovered aught that is hidden from me, speak boldly."

"Thou hast made Gongylus the Eretrian governor of Byzantium; for what great services we know not. But he has lived much in Persia."

"For that reason, on this the frontier of her domains, he is better enabled to penetrate her designs and counteract her ambition."

"This Gongylus," continued Cimon, "is well known to have much frequented the Persian captives in their confinement."

"In order to learn from them what may yet be the strength of the king. In this he had my commands."

"I question it not. But, Pausanias," continued Cimon, raising his voice, and with energy, "had he also thy commands to leave thy galley last night, and to return to the citadel?"

"He had. What then?"

"And on his return the Persians disappear—a singular chance, truly. But that is not all. Last night, before he returned to the citadel, Gongylus was perceived, alone, in a retired spot on the outskirts of the city."

"Alone?" echoed Pausanias.

"Alone. If he had companions, they were not discerned. This spot was out of the path he should have taken. By this spot, on the soft soil, are the marks of hoofs, and in the thicket close by were found these witnesses;" and Cimon drew from his vest a handful of the pearls only worn by the Eastern captives.

"There is something in this," said Xanthippus, "which requires at least examination. May it please you, Pausanias, to summon Gongylus hither?"

A momentary shade passed over the brow of the conspirator, but the eyes of the Greeks were on him, and to refuse were as dangerous as to comply. He turned to one of his Spartans, and ordered him to summon the Eretrian.

"You have spoken well, Xanthippus. This matter must be sifted."

With that, motioning the captains to the seats that were ranged round the walls and before a long table, he cast himself into a large chair at the head of the table, and waited in silent anxiety the entrance of the Eretrian. His whole trust now was in the craft and penetration of his friend. If the courage or the cunning of Gongylus failed him—if but a word betrayed him—Pausanias was lost. He was girt by men who hated him; and he read in the dark, fierce eyes of the Ionians—whose pride he had so

10*   H

often galled, whose revenge he had so carelessly provoked
—the certainty of ruin. One hand hidden within the folds
of his robe convulsively clenched the flesh, in the stern agony of his suspense. His calm and composed face nevertheless exhibited to the captains no trace of fear.

The draperies were again drawn aside, and Gongylus
slowly entered.

Habituated to peril of every kind from his earliest youth,
the Eretrian was quick to detect its presence. The sight of
the silent Greeks, formally seated round the hall, and watching his steps and countenance with eyes whose jealous and
vindictive meaning it required no Œdipus to read; the
grave and half-averted brow of Pausanias; and the angry
excitement that had prevailed amidst the host at the news
of the escape of the Persians—all sufficed to apprise him of
the nature of the council to which he had been summoned.

Supporting himself on his staff, and dragging his limbs
tardily along, he had leisure to examine, though with apparent indifference, the whole group; and when, with a
calm salutation, he arrested his steps at the foot of the table
immediately facing Pausanias, he darted one glance at the
Spartan, so fearless, so bright, so cheering, that Pausanias
breathed hard, as if a load were thrown from his breast,
and, turning easily toward Cimon, said,

"Behold your witness. Which of us shall be questioner,
and which judge?"

"That matters but little," returned Cimon. "Before
this audience justice must force its way."

"It rests with you, Pausanias," said Xanthippus, "to acquaint the Governor of Byzantium with the suspicions he has excited."

"Gongylus," said Pausanias, "the captive Barbarians, Ariamanes and Datis, were placed by me especially under thy vigilance and guard. Thou knowest that, while (for humanity becomes the victor) I ordered thee to vex them by no undue restraints, I nevertheless commanded thee to consider thy life itself answerable for their durance. They have escaped. The Captains of Greece demand of thee, as I demanded—by what means—by what connivance? Speak the truth, and deem that in falsehood, as well as in treach. ery, detection is easy, and death certain."

The tone of Pausanias, and his severe look, pleased and re-assured all the Greeks, except the wiser Cimon, who, though his suspicions were a little shaken, continued to fix his eyes rather on Pausanias than on the Eretrian.

"Pausanias," replied Gongylus, drawing up his lean frame, as with the dignity of conscious innocence, "that suspicion could fall upon me, I find it difficult to suppose. Raised by thy favor to the command of Byzantium, what have I to gain by treason or neglect? These Persians—I knew them well. I had known them in Susa—known them when I served Darius, being then an exile from Eretria. Ye know, my countrymen, that when Darius invaded Greece I left his court and armies, and sought my native land, to fall or to conquer in its cause. Well, then, I knew these Barbarians. I sought them frequently; partly, it may be, to return to them in their adversity the courtesies shown me in mine. Ye are Greeks: ye will not condemn me for

humanity and gratitude. Partly with another motive. I
knew that Ariamanes had the greatest influence over Xerxes. I knew that the great king would at any cost seek to
regain the liberty of his friend. I urged upon Ariamanes
the wisdom of a peace with the Greeks even on their own
terms. I told him that when Xerxes sent to offer the ran-
som, conditions of peace would avail more than sacks of
gold. He listened and approved. Did I wrong in this,
Pausanias? No; for thou, whose deep sagacity has made
thee condescend even to appear half Persian, because thou
art all Greek—thou thyself didst sanction my efforts on behalf of Greece."

Pausanias looked with a silent triumph round the conclave, and Xanthippus nodded approval.

"In order to conciliate them, and with too great confidence in their faith, I relaxed by degrees the rigor of their
confinement; that was a fault, I own it. Their apartments
communicated with a court in which I suffered them to
walk at will. But I placed there two sentinels in whom I
deemed I could repose all trust—not my own countrymen
—not Eretrians—not thy Spartans or Laconians, Pausanias.
No; I deemed that if ever the jealousy (a laudable jealousy)
of the Greeks should demand an account of my faith and
vigilance, my witnesses should be the countrymen of those
who have ever the most suspected me. Those sentinels
were, the one a Samian, the other a Platæan. These men
have betrayed me and Greece. Last night, on returning
hither from the vessel, I visited the Persians. They were
about to retire to rest, and I quit them soon, suspecting

nothing. This morning they had fled, and with them their abettors, the sentinels. I hastened, first, to send soldiers in search of them; and, secondly, to inform Pausanias in his galley. If I have erred, I submit me to your punishment. Punish my error, but acquit my honesty."

"And what," said Cimon, abruptly, "led thee far from thy path, between the Heracleid's galley and the citadel, to the fields near the temple of Aphrodite, between the citadel and the bay? Thy color changes. Mark him, Greeks. Quick; thine answer."

The countenance of Gongylus had indeed lost its color and hardihood. The loud tone of Cimon—the effect his confusion produced on the Greeks, some of whom, the Ionians, less self-possessed and dignified than the rest, half rose, with fierce gestures and muttered exclamations—served still more to embarrass and intimidate him. He cast a hasty look on Pausanias, who averted his eyes. There was a pause. The Spartan gave himself up for lost; but how much more was his fear increased when Gongylus, casting an imploring gaze upon the Greeks, said, hesitatingly,

"Question me no further. I dare not speak;" and as he spoke he pointed to Pausanias.

"It was the dread of thy resentment, Pausanias," said Cimon, coldly, "that withheld his confession. Vouchsafe to re-assure him."

"Eretrian," said Pausanias, striking his clenched hand on the table, "I know not what tale trembles on thy lips; but, be it what it may, give it voice, I command thee."

"Thou thyself, thou wert the cause that led me toward the temple of Aphrodite," said Gongylus, in a low voice.

At these words there went forth a general deep-breathed murmur. With one accord every Greek rose to his feet. The Spartan attendants in the rear of Pausanias drew closer to his person; but there was nothing in their faces—yet more dark and vindictive than those of the other Greeks— that promised protection. Pausanias alone remained seated and unmoved. His imminent danger gave him back all his valor, all his pride, all his passionate and profound disdain. With unbleached cheek, with haughty eyes, he met the gaze of the assembly; and then waving his hand as if that gesture sufficed to restrain and awe them, he said,

"In the name of all Greece, whose chief I yet am, whose protector I have once been, I command ye to resume your seats, and listen to the Eretrian. Spartans, fall back. Governor of Byzantium, pursue your tale."

"Yes, Pausanias," resumed Gongylus, "you alone were the cause that drew me from my rest. I would fain be silent, but—"

"Say on!" cried Pausanias, fiercely, and measuring the space between himself and Gongylus, in doubt whether the Eretrian's head were within reach of his cimeter; so at least Gongylus interpreted that freezing look of despair and vengeance, and he drew back some paces. "I place myself, O Greeks, under your protection; it is dangerous to reveal the errors of the great. Know that, as Governor of Byzantium, many things ye wot not of reach my ears. Hence, I guard against dangers while ye sleep. Learn, then, that Pausanias is not without the weakness of his ancestor, Alcides; he loves a maiden—a Byzantine—Cleonice, the daughter of Diagoras."

This unexpected announcement, made in so grave a tone, provoked a smile among the gay Ionians; but an exclamation of jealous anger broke from Antagoras, and a blush, partly of wounded pride, partly of warlike shame, crimsoned the swarthy cheek of Pausanias. Cimon, who was by no means free from the joyous infirmities of youth, relaxed his severe brow, and said, after a short pause,

"Is it, then, among the grave duties of the Governor of Byzantium to watch over the fair Cleonice, or to aid the suit of her illustrious lover?"

"Not so," answered Gongylus; "but the life of the Grecian General is dear, at least, to the grateful Governor of Byzantium. Greeks, ye know that among you Pausanias has many foes. Returning last night from his presence, and passing through the thicket, I overheard voices at hand. I caught the name of Pausanias. 'The Spartan,' said one voice, 'nightly visits the house of Diagoras. He goes usually alone. From the height near the temple we can watch well, for the night is clear; if he goes alone, we can intercept his way on his return.' 'To the height!' cried the other. I thought to distinguish the voices, but the trees hid the speakers. I followed the footsteps toward the temple, for it behooved me to learn who thus menaced the chief of Greece. But ye know that the wood reaches even to the sacred building, and the steps gained the temple before I could recognize the men. I concealed myself, as I thought, to watch; but it seems that I was perceived, for he who saw me, and now accuses, was doubtless one of the assassins. Happy I, if the sight of a witness scared him from the crime. Either fearing detection, or aware that their intent that night was frustrated—for Pausanias, visiting Cleonice earlier than his wont, had already resought his galley—the men retreated as they came, unseen, not unheard. I caught their receding steps through the brush-wood. Greeks, I have said. Who is my accuser? in him behold the would-be murderer of Pausanias!"

"Liar!" cried an indignant and loud voice among the captains, and Antagoras stood forth from the circle.

"It is who saw thee. Darest thou accuse Antagoras of Chios?"

"What at that hour brought Antagoras of Chios to the Temple of Aphrodite?" retorted Gongylus.

The eyes of the Greeks turned toward the young captain, and there was confusion on his face. But, recovering himself quickly, the Chian answered, "Why should I blush to own it? Aphrodite is no dishonorable deity to the men of the Ionian Isles. I sought the temple at that hour, as is our wont, to make my offering and record my prayer."

"Certainly," said Cimon. "We must own that Aphrodite is powerful at Byzantium. Who can acquit Pausanias and blame Antagoras?"

"Pardon me—one question," said Gongylus. "Is not the female heart which Antagoras would beseech the goddess to soften toward him that of the Cleonice of whom we spoke? See, he denies it not. Greeks, the Chians are warm lovers, and warm lovers are revengeful rivals."

This artful speech had its instantaneous effect among the younger and more unthinking loiterers. Those who at once would have disbelieved the imputed guilt of Antagoras upon motives merely political, inclined to a suggestion that ascribed it to the jealousy of a lover. And his character, ardent and fiery, rendered the suspicion yet more plausible. Meanwhile the minds of the audience had been craftily drawn from the grave and main object of the meeting—the flight of the Persians—and a lighter and livelier curiosity had supplanted the eager and dark resentment which had hitherto animated the circle. Pausanias, with the subtle genius that belonged to him, hastened to seize advantage of the momentary diversion in his favor, and before the Chian could recover from his consternation, both at the charge and the evident effect it had produced upon a part of the assembly, the Spartan stretched his hand, and spake.

"Greeks, Pausanias listens to no tale of danger to himself. Willingly he believes that Gongylus either misinterpreted the intent of some jealous and heated threats, or that the words he overheard were not uttered by Antagoras. Possible is it, too, that others may have sought the temple with less gentle desires than our Chian ally. Let this pass. Unworthy such matters of the councils of bearded men; too much reference has been made to those follies which our idleness has given birth to. Let no fair Briseis renew strife among chiefs and soldiers. Excuse not thyself, An-

11   6

tagoras; we dismiss all charge against thee. On the other hand, Gongylus will doubtless seem to you to have accounted for his appearance near the precincts of the temple. And it is but a coincidence, natural enough, that the Persian prisoners should have chosen, later in the night, the same spot for the steeds to await them. The thickness of the wood round the temple, and the direction of the place toward the east, points out the neighborhood as the very one in which the fugitives would appoint the horses. Waste no further time, but provide at once for the pursuit. To you, Cimon, be this case confided. Already have I dispatched fifty light-armed men on fleet Thessalian steeds. You, Cimon, increase the number of the pursuers. The prisoners may be yet recaptured. Doth aught else remain worthy of our ears? If so, speak; if not, depart."

"Pausanias," said Antagoras, firmly, "let Gongylus retract, or not, his charge against me, I retain mine against Gongylus. Wholly false is it that in word or deed I plotted violence against thee, though of much—not as Cleonice's lover, but as Grecian captain—I have good reason to complain. Wholly false is it that I had a comrade. I was alone. And coming out from the temple, where I had hung my chaplet, I perceived Gongylus clearly under the starlit skies. He stood in listening attitude close by the sacred myrtle grove. I hastened toward him, but methinks he saw me not; he turned slowly, penetrated the wood, and vanished. I gained the spot on the soft sward which the dropping boughs make ever humid. I saw the print of hoofs. Within the thicket I found the pearls that

Cimon has displayed to you. Clear, then, is it that this man lies—clear that the Persians must have fled already—although Gongylus declares that on his return to the citadel he visited them in their prison. Explain this, Eretrian!"

"He who would speak false witness," answered Gongylus, with a firmness equal to the Chian's, "can find pearls at whatsoever hour he pleases. Greeks, this man presses me to renew the charge which Pausanias generously sought to stifle. I have said. And I, Governor of Byzantium, call on the council of the Grecian Leaders to maintain my authority, and protect their own Chief."

Then arose a vexed and perturbed murmur, most of the Ionians siding with Antagoras, such of the allies as yet clung to the Dorian ascendency grouping round Gongylus.

The persistence of Antagoras had made the dilemma of no slight embarrassment to Pausanias. Something lofty in his original nature urged him to shrink from supporting Gongylus in an accusation which he believed untrue. On the other hand, he could not abandon his accomplice in an effort, as dangerous as it was crafty, to conceal their common guilt.

"Son of Miltiades," he said, after a brief pause, in which his dexterous resolution was formed, "I invoke your aid to appease a contest in which I foresee no result but that of schism among ourselves. Antagoras has no witness to support his tale, Gongylus none to support his own. Who shall decide between conflicting testimonies which rest but on the lips of accuser and accused? Hereafter, if the matter be deemed sufficiently grave, let us refer the decision

to the oracle that never errs. Time and chance meanwhile
may favor us in clearing up the darkness we can not now
penetrate. For you, Governor of Byzantium, it behooves
me to say that the escape of prisoners intrusted to your
charge justifies vigilance, if not suspicion. We shall con-
sult at our leisure whether or not that course suffices to
remove you from the government of Byzantium. Heralds,
advance ; our council is dissolved."

With these words Pausanias rose, and the majesty of his
bearing, with the unwonted temper and conciliation of his
language, so came in aid of his high office, that no man
ventured a dissentient murmur.

The conclave broke up, and not till its members had gained the outer air did any signs of suspicion or dissatisfaction
evince themselves ; but then, gathering in groups, the Ionians with especial jealousy discussed what had passed, and
with their native shrewdness ascribed the moderation of
Pausanias to his desire to screen Gongylus and avoid further inquisition into the flight of the prisoners. The dis-
contented looked round for Cimon, but the young Athenian
had hastily retired from the throng, and, after issuing orders to pursue the fugitives, sought Aristides in the house
near the quay in which he lodged.

Cimon related to his friend what had passed at the meeting, and, terminating his recital, said,

" Thou shouldst have been with us. With thee we might
have ventured more."

"And if so," returned the wise Athenian, with a smile,
" ye would have prospered less. Precisely because I would

not commit our country to the suspicion of fomenting intrigues and mutiny to her own advantage, did I abstain from the assembly, well aware that Pausanias would bring his minion harmless from the unsupported accusation of Antagoras. Thou hast acted with cool judgment, Cimon. The Spartan is weaving the webs of the Parcæ for his own feet. Leave him to weave on, undisturbed. The hour in which Athens shall assume the sovereignty of the seas is drawing near. Let it come, like Jove's thunder, in a calm sky."

11*

CHAPTER III.

PAUSANIAS did not that night quit the city. After the meeting, he held a private conference with the Spartan Equals, whom custom and the government assigned, in appearance as his attendants, in reality as witnesses, if not spies, of his conduct. Though every pure Spartan, as compared with the subject Laconian population, was noble, the republic acknowledged two main distinctions in class— the higher, entitled Equals, a word which we might not inaptly and more intelligibly render Peers; the lower, Inferiors. These distinctions, though hereditary, were not immutable. The peer could be degraded, the inferior could become a peer. To the royal person in war three peers were allotted. Those assigned to Pausanias, of the tribe called the Hyllcans, were naturally of a rank and influence that constrained him to treat them with a certain deference, which perpetually chafed his pride and confirmed his discontent; for these three men were precisely of the mold which at heart he most despised. Polydorus, the first in rank—for, like Pausanias, he boasted his descent from Hercules—was the personification of the rudeness and bigotry of a Spartan who had never before stirred from his rocky home, and who disdained all that he could not

comprehend. Gelon, the second, passed for a very wise
man, for he seldom spoke but in monosyllables; yet, probably, his words were as numerous as his ideas. Cleomenes, the third, was as distasteful to the Regent from his
merits as the others from their deficiencies. He had risen
from the grade of the Inferiors by his valor: blunt, homely,
frank, sincere, he never disguised his displeasure at the
manner of Pausanias; though a true Spartan in discipline,
he never transgressed the respect which his chief commanded in time of war.

Pausanias knew that these officers were in correspondence
with Sparta, and he now exerted all his powers to remove
from their minds any suspicion which the disappearance of
the prisoners might have left in them.

In this interview he displayed all those great natural
powers which, rightly trained and guided, might have made
him not less great in council than in war. With masterly
precision he enlarged on the growing ambition of Athens,
on the disposition in her favor evinced by all the Ionian
confederates. "Hitherto," he said truly, "Sparta has uni-
formly held rank as the first state of Greece; the leader-
ship of the Greeks belongs to us by birth and renown. But
see you not that the war is now shifting from land to sea?
Sea is not our element; it is that of Athens, of all the Ionian race. If this continue, we lose our ascendency, and
Athens becomes the sovereign of Hellas. Beneath the calm
of Aristides I detect his deep design. In vain Cimon affects
the manner of the Spartan; at heart he is Athenian. This
charge against Gongylus is aimed at me. Grant that the

plot which it conceals succeed; grant that Sparta share the
affected suspicions of the Ionians, and recall me from Byzantium; deem you that there lives one Spartan who could
delay for a day the supremacy of Athens? Naught save
the respect the Dorian Greeks at least attach to the General
at Platæa could restrain the secret ambition of the city
of the demagogues. Deem not that I have been as rash
and vain as some hold me for the stern visage I have shown
to the Ionians. Trust me that it was necessary to awe
them, with a view to maintain our majesty. For Sparta to
preserve her ascendency two things are needful: first, to
continue the war by land; secondly, to disgust the Ionians
with their sojourn here, send them with their ships to their
own havens, and so leave Hellas under the sole guardianship of ourselves and our Peloponnesian allies. Therefore
I say, bear with me in this double design; chide me not
if my haughty manner disperse these subtle Ionians. If I
bore with them to-day, it was less from respect than, shall
I say it, my fear lest you should misinterpret me. Beware
how you detail to Sparta whatever might rouse the jealousy
of her government. Trust to me, and I will extend the dominion of Sparta till it grasp the whole of Greece. We
will depose everywhere the revolutionary Demos, and establish our own oligarchies in every Grecian state. We will
Laconize all Hellas."

Much of what Pausanias said was wise and profound.
Such statesmanship, narrow and congenial, but vigorous
and crafty, Sparta taught in later years to her alert politi-
cians. And we have already seen that, despite the dazzling

prospects of Oriental dominion, he as yet had separated himself rather from the laws than the interests of Sparta, and still incorporated his own ambition with the extension of the sovereignty of his country over the rest of Greece.

But the Peers heard him in dull and gloomy silence; and not till he had paused and thrice asked for a reply did Polydorus speak.

"You would increase the dominion of Sparta, Pausanias. Increase of dominion is waste of life and treasure. We have few men, little gold; Sparta is content to hold her own."

"Good," said Gelon, with impassive countenance. "What care we who leads the Greeks into blows? The fewer blows the better. Brave men fight if they must; wise men never fight if they can help it."

"And such is your counsel, Cleomenes?" asked Pausanias, with a quivering lip.

"Not from the same reasons," answered the nobler and more generous Spartan. "I presume not to question your motives, Pausanias. I leave you to explain them to the Ephors and the Gerusia. But since you press me, this I say. First, all the Greeks, Ionian as well as Dorian, fought equally against the Mede, and from the commander of the Greeks all should receive fellowship and courtesy. Secondly, I say if Athens is better fitted than Sparta for the maritime ascendency, let Athens rule, so that Hellas be saved from the Mede. Thirdly, O Pausanias, I pray that Sparta may rest satisfied with her own institutions, and not disturb the peace of Greece by forcing them upon other states, and thereby enslaving Hellas. What more could the Persian do? Finally, my advice is to suspend Gongylus from his office, to conciliate the Ionians, to remain as a Grecian armament firm and united, and so procure, on better terms, peace with Persia. And then let each state retire within itself, and none aspire to rule the other. A thousand free cities are better guard against the Barbarian than a single state made up of republics overthrown and resting its strength upon hearts enslaved."

"Do you too," said Pausanias, gnawing his nether lip, "do you too, Polydorus; you too, Gelon, agree with Cleomenes, that, if Athens is better fitted than Sparta for the sovereignty of the seas, we should yield to that restless rival so perilous a power?"

"Ships cost gold," said Polydorus; "Spartans have none to spare. Mariners require skillful captains; Spartans know nothing of the sea."

"Moreover," quoth Gelon, "the ocean is a terrible element. What can valor do against a storm? We may lose more men by adverse weather than a century can repair. Let who will have the seas. Sparta has her rocks and defiles."

"Men and Peers," said Pausanias, ill repressing his scorn, "ye little dream what arms ye place in the hands of the Athenians. I have done. Take only this prophecy: You are now the head of Greece. You surrender your sceptre to Athens, and become a second-rate power."

"Never second-rate when Greece shall demand armed men," said Cleomenes, proudly.

"Armed men, armed men!" cried the more profound Pausanias. "Do you suppose that commerce—that trade —that maritime energy—that fleets which ransack the shores of the world, will not obtain a power greater than mere brute-like valor? But as ye will, as ye will."

"As we speak, our forefathers thought," said Gelon.

"And, Pausanias," said Cleomenes, gravely, "as we speak, so think the Ephors."

Pausanias fixed his dark eye on Cleomenes, and, after a brief pause, saluted the Equals and withdrew. "Sparta," he muttered, as he regained his chamber, "Sparta, thou refusest to be great; but greatness is necessary to thy son. Ah, their iron laws would constrain my soul! but it shall wear them as a warrior wears his armor and adapts it to his body. Thou shalt be queen of all Hellas, despite thyself, thine Ephors, and thy laws. Then only will I forgive thee."

CHAPTER IV.

DIAGORAS was sitting outside his door and giving various instructions to the slaves employed on his farm, when, through an arcade thickly covered with the vine, the light form of Antagoras came slowly in sight.

"Hail to thee, Diagoras!" said the Chian; "thou art the only wise man I meet with. Thou art tranquil while all else are disturbed; and, worshiping the great Mother, thou carest naught, methinks, for the Persian who invades or the Spartan who professes to defend."

"Tut!" said Diagoras, in a whisper; "thou knowest the contrary: thou knowest that if the Persian comes, I am ruined; and, by the gods, I am on a bed of thorns as long as the Spartan stays."

"Dismiss thy slaves," exclaimed Antagoras, in the same undertone; "I would speak with thee on grave matters that concern us both."

After hastily finishing his instructions and dismissing his slaves, Diagoras turned to the impatient Chian, and said,

"Now, young warrior, I am all ears for thy speech."

"Truly," said Antagoras, "if thou wert aware of what I am about to utter, thou wouldst not have postponed consideration for thy daughter to thy care for a few jars of beggarly olives."

"Hem!" said Diagoras, peevishly. "Olives are not to be despised: oil to the limbs makes them supple; to the stomach it gives gladness. Oil, moreover, bringeth money, when sold. But a daughter is the plague of a man's life. First, one has to keep away lovers; and, next, to find a husband; and when all is done, one has to put one's hand in one's chest, and pay a tall fellow like thee for robbing one of one's own child. That custom of dowries is abominable. In the good old times a bridegroom, as was meet and proper, paid for his bride; now we poor fathers pay him for taking her. Well, well, never bite thy forefinger, and curl up thy brows. What thou hast to say, say."

"Diagoras, I know that thy heart is better than thy speech, and that, much as thou covetest money, thou lovest thy child more. Know, then, that Pausanias—a curse light on him!—brings shame upon Cleonice. Know that already her name hath grown the talk of the camp. Know that his visit to her the night before last was proclaimed in the Council of the Captains as a theme for jest and rude laughter. By the head of Zeus, how thinkest thou to profit by the stealthy wooings of this black-browed Spartan? Knowest thou not that his laws forbid him to marry Cleonice? Wouldst thou have him dishonor her? Speak out to him as thou speakest to men, and tell him that the maidens of Byzantium are not in the control of the General of the Greeks."

"Youth, youth," cried Diagoras, greatly agitated,

12

"wouldst thou bring my gray hairs to a bloody grave?
Wouldst thou see my daughter reft from me by force,
and—"

"How darest thou speak thus, old man?" interrupted
the indignant Chian. "If Pausanias wronged a virgin, all
Hellas would rise against him."

"Yes, but not till the ill were done, till my throat were
cut, and my child dishonored. Listen. At first, indeed,
when, as ill-luck would have it, Pausanias, lodging a few
days under my roof, saw and admired Cleonice, I did venture to remonstrate; and how think you he took it? 'Never,' quoth he, with his stern, quivering lip, 'never did conquest forego its best right to the smiles of beauty. The
legends of Hercules, my ancestor, tell thee that to him who
labors for men, the gods grant the love of women. Fear
not that I should wrong thy daughter; to woo her is not
to wrong. But close thy door on me; immure Cleonice
from my sight; and nor armed slaves, nor bolts, nor bars
shall keep love from the loved one.' Therewith he turned
on his heel and left me. But the next day came a Lydian
in his train, with a goodly pannier of rich stuffs and a
short Spartan sword. On the pannier was written '*Friendship;*' on the sword, '*Wrath;*' and Alcman gave me a scrap
of parchment, whereon, with the cursed brief wit of a Spartan, was inscribed '*Choose!*' Who could doubt which to
take? who, by the gods, would prefer three inches of Spar-
tan-iron in his stomach to a basketful of rich stuffs for his
shoulders? Wherefore, from that hour, Pausanias comes
as he lists. But Cleonice humors him not, let tongues wag

as they may. Easier to take three cities than that child's heart."

"Is it so, indeed?" exclaimed the Chian, joyfully. "Cleonice loves him not?"

"Laughs at him to his beard that is, would laugh if he wore one."

"O Diagoras!" cried Antagoras, "hear me, hear me. I need not remind thee that our families are united by the hospitable ties; that among thy treasures thou wilt find the gifts of my ancestors for five generations; that when, a year since, my affairs brought me to Byzantium, I came to thee with the symbols of my right to claim thy hospitable cares. On leaving thee, we broke the sacred die. I have one half, thou the other. In that visit I saw and loved Cleonice. Fain would I have told my love, but then my father lived, and I feared lest he should oppose my suit; therefore, as became me, I was silent. On my return home, my fears were confirmed; my father desired that I, a Chian, should wed a Chian. Since I have been with the fleet, news has reached me that the urn holds my father's ashes." Here the young Chian paused. "Alas! alas!" he murmured, smiting his breast, "and I was not at hand to fix over thy doors the sacred branch, to give thee the parting kiss, and receive into my lips thy latest breath! May Hermes, O father, have led thee to pleasant groves!"

Diagoras, who had listened attentively to the young Chian, was touched by his grief, and said, pityingly:

"I know thou art a good son, and thy father was a worthy man, though harsh. It is a comfort to think that all does not die with the dead. His money at least sur-vives him."

"But," resumed Antagoras, not heeding this consolation —"but now I am free; and ere this, so soon as my mourn-ing garment had been laid aside, I had asked thee to bless me with Cleonice, but that I feared her love was gone—gone to the haughty Spartan. Thou re-assurest me; and, in so doing, thou confirmest the fair omens with which Aphrodite has received my offerings. Therefore, I speak out. No dowry ask I with Cleonice, save such, more in name than amount, as may distinguish the wife from the concubine, and assure her an honored place among my kins-men. Thou knowest I am rich; thou knowest that my birth dates from the oldest citizens of Chios. Give me thy child, and deliver her thyself at once from the Spartan's power. Once mine, all the fleets of Hellas are her protec-tion, and our marriage-torches are the swords of a Grecian army. O Diagoras, I clasp thy knees; put thy right hand in mine. Give me thy child as wife!"

The Byzantine was strongly affected. The suitor was one who, in birth and possessions, was all that he could desire for his daughter; and at Byzantium there did not exist that feeling against intermarriages with the foreigner which prevailed in towns more purely Greek, though in many of them, too, that antique prejudice had worn away. On the other hand, by transferring to Antagoras his anxious charge, he felt that he should take the best course to pre-serve it untarnished from the fierce love of Pausanias, and there was truth in the Chian's suggestion. The daughter of a Byzantine might be unprotected; the wife of an Ionian captain was safe, even from the power of Pausanias. As these reflections occurred to him, he placed his right hand in the Chian's, and said:

"Be it as thou wilt; I consent to betroth thee to Cleonice. Follow me; thou art free to woo her."

So saying, he rose, and, as if in fear of his own second thoughts, he traversed the hall with hasty strides to the interior of the mansion. He ascended a flight of steps, and, drawing aside a curtain suspended between two columns, Antagoras, who followed timidly behind, beheld Cleonice.

As was the wont in the domestic life of all Grecian states, her handmaids were around the noble virgin. Two were engaged on embroidery, one in spinning, a fourth was reading aloud to Cleonice, and that at least was a rare diversion to women, for few had the education of the fair Byzantine. Cleonice herself was half reclined upon a bench inlaid with ivory and covered with cushions; before her stood a small tripod table on which she leaned the arm the hand of which supported her cheek, and she seemed listening to the lecture of the slave with earnest and absorbed attention, so earnest, so absorbed, that she did not for some moments perceive the entrance of Diagoras and the Chian.

"Child," said the former—and Cleonice started to her feet, and stood modestly before her father, her eyes downcast, her arms crossed upon her bosom—"child, I bid thee welcome my guest-friend, Antagoras of Chios. Slaves, ye may withdraw."

12*

Cleonice bowed her head; and an unquiet, anxious change came over her countenance.

As soon as the slaves were gone, Diagoras resumed:

"Daughter, I present to thee a suitor for thy hand. Receive him as I have done, and he shall have my leave to carve thy name on every tree in the garden, with the lover's epithet of 'Beautiful' attached to it. Antagoras, look up, then, and speak for thyself."

But Antagoras was silent; and a fear unknown to his frank, hardy nature came over him. With an arch smile, Diagoras, deeming his presence no longer necessary or expedient, lifted the curtain, and lover and maid were left alone.

Then, with an effort, and still with hesitating accents, the Chian spoke:

"Fair virgin, not in the groves of Byzantium will thy name be first written by the hand of Antagoras. In my native Chios the myrtle-trees are already eloquent of thee. Since I first saw thee, I loved. Maiden, wilt thou be my wife?"

Thrice moved the lips of Cleonice, and thrice her voice seemed to fail her. At length she said, "Chian, thou art a stranger, and the laws of the Grecian cities dishonor the stranger whom the free citizen stoops to marry."

"Nay," cried Antagoras, "such cruel laws are obsolete in Chios. Nature and custom, and love's almighty goddess, long since have set them aside. Fear not, the haughtiest matron of my native state will not be more honored than the Byzantium bride of Antagoras."

"Is it in Sparta only that such laws exist?" said Cleonice, half unconsciously, and to the sigh with which she spoke a deep blush succeeded.

"Sparta!" exclaimed Antagoras, with a fierce and jealous pang—"ah, are thy thoughts, then, upon the son of Sparta? Were Pausanias a Chian, wouldst thou turn from him scornfully as thou now dost from me?"

"Not scornfully, Antagoras," answered Cleonice (who had indeed averted her face at his reproachful question; but now turned it full upon him, with an expression of sad and pathetic sweetness), "not scornfully do I turn from thee, though with pain; for what worthier homage canst thou render to woman than honorable love? Gratefully do I hearken to the suit that comes from thee; but gratitude is not the return thou wouldst ask, Antagoras. My hand is my father's; my heart, alas! is mine. Thou mayst claim from him the one; the other, neither he can give, nor thou receive."

"Say not so, Cleonice," cried the Chian; "say not that thou canst not love me, if so I am to interpret thy words. Love brings love with the young. How canst thou yet know thine own heart? Tarry till thou hast listened to mine. As the fire on the altar spreads from offering to offering, so spreads love; its flame envelops all that are near to it. Thy heart will catch the heavenly spark from mine."

"Chian," said Cleonice, gently withdrawing the hand that he sought to clasp, "when as my father's guest-friend thou wert a sojourner within these walls, oft have I heard thee speak, and all thy words spoke the thoughts of a noble soul. Were it otherwise, not thus would I now address thee. Didst thou love gold, and wooed in me but the child of the rich Diagoras, or wert thou one of those who would treat for a wife, as a trader for a slave, invoking Herè, but disdaining Aphrodite, I should bow my head to my doom. But thou, Antagoras, askest love for love; this I can not give thee. Spare me, O generous Chian. Let not my father enforce his right to my obedience."

"Answer me but one question," interrupted Antagoras in a low voice, though with compressed lips, "dost thou, then, love another?"

The blood mounted to the virgin's cheeks; it suffused her brow, her neck, with burning blushes, and then, receding, left her face colorless as a statue. Then with tones low and constrained as his own, she pressed her hand on her heart, and replied, "Thou sayest it; I love another."

"And that other is Pausanias? Alas! thy silence, thy trembling, answer me."

Antagoras groaned aloud, and covered his face with his hands; but after a short pause he exclaimed, with great emotion, "No, no—say not that thou lovest Pausanias; say not that Aphrodite hath so accursed thee: for to love Pausanias is to love dishonor."

"Hold, Chian! Not so; for my love has no hope. Our hearts are not our own, but our actions are."

Antagoras gazed on her with suspense and awe; for as she spoke her slight form dilated, her lip curled, her cheek glowed again, but with the blush less of love than of pride. In her countenance, her attitude, there was something divine and holy, such as would have beseemed a priestess of Diana.

"Yes," she resumed, raising her eyes, and with a still and mournful sweetness in her upraised features. "What I love is not Pausanias, it is the glory of which he is the symbol, it is the Greece of which he has been the savior. Let him depart, as soon he must—let these eyes behold him no more; still there exists for me all that exists now—a name, a renown, a dream. Never for me may the nuptial hymn resound, or the marriage-torch be illumined. O goddess of the silver bow, O chaste and venerable Artemis, receive, protect thy servant! and ye, O funereal gods, lead me soon, lead the virgin unreluctant to the shades!"

A superstitious fear, a dread as if his earthly love would violate something sacred, chilled the ardor of the young Chian; and for several moments both were silent.

At length, Antagoras, kissing the hem of her robe, said:

"Maiden of Byzantium, like thee, then, I will love, though without hope. I will not, I dare not, profane thy presence by prayers which pain thee, and seem to me, having heard thee, almost guilty, as if proffered to some nymph circling in choral dance the moonlit mountain-tops of Delos. But ere I depart, and tell thy father that my suit is over, oh, place at least thy right hand in mine, and swear to me, not the bride's vow of faith and troth, but that vow which a virgin sister may pledge to a brother, mindful to protect and to avenge her. Swear to me, that if this haughty Spartan, contemning alike men, laws, and the household gods, should seek to constrain thy purity to his will; if thou shouldst have cause to tremble at power and force; and fierce desire should demand what gentle love would but reverently implore—then, Cleonice, seeing how little thy father can defend thee, wilt thou remember Antagoras, and through him summon around thee all the majesty of Hellas? Grant me but this prayer, and I leave thee, if in sorrow, yet not with terror."

"Generous and noble Chian," returned Cleonice, as her tears fell upon the hand he extended to her, " why, why do I so ill repay thee? Thy love is indeed that which ennobles the heart that yields it, and her who shall one day recompense thee for the loss of me. Fear not the power of Pausanias: dream not that I shall need a defender, while above us reign the gods, and below us lies the grave. Yet, to appease thee, take my right hand, and hear my oath: If the hour comes when I have need of man's honor against man's wrong, I will call on Antagoras as a brother."

Their hands closed in each other; and, not trusting himself to speech, Antagoras turned away his face and left the room.

CHAPTER V.

For some days, an appearance, at least, of harmony was restored to the contending factions in the Byzantine camp.

Pausanias did not dismiss Gongylus from the government of the city; but he sent, one by one, for the more important of the Ionian complainants, listened to their grievances, and promised redress. He adopted a more popular and gracious demeanor, and seemed, with a noble grace, to submit to the policy of conciliating the allies.

But discontent arose from causes beyond his power, had he genuinely exerted it, to remove. For it was a discontent that lay in the hostility of race to race. Though the Spartan Equals had preached courtesy to the Ionians, the ordinary manner of the Spartan warriors was invariably offensive to the vain and susceptible confederates of a more polished race. A Spartan, wherever he might be placed, unconsciously assumed superiority. The levity of an Ionian was ever displeasing to him. Out of the actual battle-field, they could have no topics in common, none which did not provoke irritation and dispute. On the other hand, most of the Ionians could ill conceal their disaffection, mingled with something of just contempt at the notorious and confessed incapacity of the Spartans for maritime affairs, while a Spartan was yet the commander of the fleet. And many

of them, wearied with inaction and anxious to return home,
were willing to seize any reasonable pretext for desertion.
In this last motive lay the real strength and safety of Pausanias.   And to this end his previous policy of arrogance
was not so idle as it had seemed to the Greeks, and appears
still in the page of history.   For a Spartan really anxious
to preserve the pre-eminence of his country, and to prevent
the sceptre of the seas passing to Athens, could have devised
no plan of action more sagacious and profound than one
which would disperse the Ionians, and the Athenians themselves, and reduce the operations of the Grecian force to that
land warfare in which the Spartan pre-eminence was equally indisputable and undisputed.   And still Pausanias, even
in his change of manner, plotted and intrigued and hoped
for this end.   Could he once sever from the encampment
the Athenians and the Ionian allies, and yet remain with his
own force at Byzantium until the Persian army could collect on the Phrygian frontier, the way seemed clear to his
ambition.   Under ordinary circumstances, in this object he
might easily have succeeded.   But it chanced that all his
schemes were met with invincible mistrust by those in
whose interest they were conceived, and on whose co-operation they depended for success.   The means adopted by
Pausanias in pursuit of his policy were too distasteful to
the national prejudices of the Spartan government, to en-
able him to elicit from the national ambition of that government sufficient sympathy with the object of it.   The more
he felt himself uncomprehended and mistrusted by his
countrymen, the more personal became the character, and

the more unscrupulous the course, of his ambition. Unhappily for Pausanias, moreover, the circumstances which
chafed his pride also thwarted the satisfaction of his affections; and his criminal ambition was stimulated by that
less guilty passion which shared with it the mastery of a
singularly turbulent and impetuous soul. Not his the love
of sleek, gallant, and wanton youth; it was the love of man
in his mature years, but of man to whom love till then had
been unknown. In that large and dark and stormy nature,
all passions, once admitted, took the growth of Titans.
He loved as those long lonely at heart alone can love; he
loved as love the unhappy when the unfamiliar bliss of the
sweet human emotion descends like dew upon the desert.
To him Cleonice was a creature wholly out of the range of
experience. Differing in every shade of her versatile humor
from the only women he had known—the simple, sturdy,
uneducated maids and matrons of Sparta—her softness en-
thralled him, her anger awed. In his dreams of future
power, of an absolute throne and unlimited dominion, Pausanias beheld the fair Byzantine crowned by his side.
Fiercely as he loved, and little as the *sentiment* of love mingled with his *passion*, he yet thought not to dishonor a victim, but to elevate a bride. What though the laws of
Sparta were against such nuptials, was not the hour approaching when these laws should be trampled under his
armed heel? Since the contract with the Persians, which
Gongylus assured him Xerxes would joyously and promptly
fulfill, Pausanias already felt, in a soul whose arrogance
arose from the consciousness of powers that had not yet

found their field, as if he were not the subject of Sparta, but her lord and king. In his interviews with Cleonice, his language took a tone of promise and of hope that at times lulled her fears, and communicated its sanguine colorings of the future to her own dreams. With the elasticity of youth her spirits rose from the solemn despondency with which she had replied to the reproaches of Antagoras. For though Pausanias spoke not openly of his schemes, though his words were mysterious, and his replies to her questions ambiguous and equivocal, still it seemed to her, seeing in him the hero of all Hellas, so natural that he could make the laws of Sparta yield to the weight of his authority, or relax in homage to his renown, that she indulged the belief that his influence would set aside the iron customs of his country. Was it too extravagant a reward to the conqueror of the Mede to suffer him to select at least the partner of his hearth? No, Hope was not dead in that young breast. Still might she be the bride of him whose glory had dazzled her noble and sensitive nature, till the faults that darkened it were lost in the blaze. Thus, insensibly to herself, her tones became softer to her stern lover, and her heart betrayed itself more in her gentle looks. Yet again were there times when doubt and alarm returned with more than their earlier force—times when, wrapped in his lurid and absorbing ambition, Pausanias escaped from his usual suppressed reserve—times when she recalled that night in which she had witnessed his interview with the strangers of the East, and had trembled lest the altar should be kindled upon the ruins of his fame. For Cleonice was wholly, ardently, sublimely Greek, filled in each crevice of her soul with its lovely poetry, its beautiful superstition, its heroic freedom. As Greek, she had loved Pausanias, seeing in him the lofty incarnation of Greece itself. The descendant of the demi-god, the champion of Platæa, the savior of Hellas—theme for song till song should be no more—these attributes were what she beheld and loved; and not to have reigned by his side over a world would she have welcomed one object of that evil ambition which renounced the loyalty of a Greek for the supremacy of a king.

Meanwhile, though Antagoras had, with no mean degree of generosity, relinquished his suit to Cleonice, he detected with a jealous vigilance the continued visits of Pausanias, and burned with increasing hatred against his favored and powerful rival. Though, in common with all the Greeks out of the Peloponnesus, he was very imperfectly acquainted with the Spartan constitution, he could not be blinded, like Cleonice, into the belief that a law so fundamental in Sparta, and so general in all the primitive states of Greece, as that which forbade intermarriage with a foreigner, could be canceled for the Regent of Sparta, and in favor of an obscure maiden of Byzantium. Every visit Pausanias paid to Cleonice but served, in his eyes, as a prelude to her ultimate dishonor. He lent himself, therefore, with all the zeal of his vivacious and ardent character, to the design of removing Pausanias himself from Byzantium. He plotted with the implacable Uliades and the other Ionian captains to send to Sparta a formal mission, stating their grievances

against the Regent and urging his recall.   But the altered
manner of Pausanias deprived them of their just pretext;
and the Ionians, more and more under the influence of the
Athenian chief, were disinclined to so extreme a measure
without the consent of Aristides and Cimon.   These two
chiefs were not passive spectators of affairs so critical to
their ambition for Athens—they penetrated into the motives of Pausanias in the novel courtesy of demeanor that
he adopted, and they foresaw that if he could succeed in
wearing away the patience of the allies and dispersing the
fleet, yet without giving occasion for his own recall, the
golden opportunity of securing to Athens the maritime ascendency would be lost.   They resolved, therefore, to make
the occasion which the wiles of the Regent had delayed;
and toward this object Antagoras, moved by his own jealous hate against Pausanias, worked incessantly.   Fearless
and vigilant, he was ever on the watch for some new charge
against the Spartan chief, ever relentless in stimulating suspicion, aggravating discontent, inflaming the fierce, and arguing with the timid.   His less exalted station allowed him
to mix more familiarly with the various Ionian officers than
would have become the high-born Cimon, and the dignified
repute of Aristides.   Seeking to distract his mind from the
haunting thought of Cleonice, he flung himself with the
ardor of his Greek temperament into the social pleasures,
which took a zest from the design that he carried into them
all.   In the banquets, in the sports, he was ever seeking to
increase the enemies of his rival; and where he charmed a
gay companion, there he often enlisted a bold conspirator.

Pausanias, the unconscious or the careless object of the Ionian's jealous hate, could not resist the fatal charm of Cleonice's presence; and if it sometimes exasperated the more evil elements of his nature, at other times it so lulled them to rest, that had the Fates given him the rightful claim to that single treasure, not one guilty thought might have disturbed the majesty of a soul which, though undisciplined and uncultured, owed half its turbulence and half its rebellious pride to its baffled yearnings for human affection and natural joy. And Cleonice, unable to shun the visits which her weak and covetous father, despite his promised favor to the suit of Antagoras, still encouraged; and feeling her honor, at least, if not her peace, was secured by that ascendency which, with each successive interview between them, her character more and more asserted over the Spartan's higher nature, relinquished the tormenting levity of tone whereby she had once sought to elude his earnestness, or conceal her own sentiments. An interest in a fate so solemn, an interest far deeper than mere human love, stole into her heart and elevated its instincts. She recognized the immense compassion which was due to the man so desolate at the head of armaments, so dark in the midst of glory. Centuries roll, customs change, but, ever since the time of the earliest mother, woman yearns to be the soother.

13*

CHAPTER VI.

IT was the hour of the day when between the two principal meals of the Greeks men surrendered themselves to idleness or pleasure; when groups formed in the market-place,
or crowded the barbers' shops, to gossip and talk of news;
when the tale-teller or ballad-singer collected round him
on the quays his credulous audience; when on playgrounds
that stretched behind the taverns or without the walls the
more active youths assembled, and the quoit was hurled, or
mimic battles waged with weapons of wood; or the Dorians weaved their simple, the Ionians their more intricate or
less decorous, dances. At that hour Lysander, wandering
from the circles of his countrymen, walked musingly by
the sea-shore.

"And why," said the voice of a person who had approached him unperceived, "and why, O Lysander, art thou
absent from thy comrades, thou model and theme of the
youths of Sparta, foremost in their manly sports, as in their
martial labors?"

Lysander turned and bowed low his graceful head, for he
who accosted him was scarcely more honored by the Athenians, whom his birth, his wealth, and his popular demeanor
dazzled, than by the plain sons of Sparta, who, in his simple garb, his blunt and hasty manner, his professed admira-

tion for all things Spartan, beheld one Athenian at least congenial to their tastes.

"The child that misses its mother," answered Lysander, "has small joy with its playmates. And I, a Spartan, pine for Sparta."

"Truly," returned Cimon, "there must be charms in thy noble country of which we other Greeks know but little, if amidst all the luxuries and delights of Byzantium thou canst pine for her rugged hills. And although, as thou knowest well, I was once a sojourner in thy city as embassador from my own, yet to foreigners so little of the inner Spartan life is revealed, that I pray thee to satisfy my curiosity and explain to me the charm that reconciles thee and thine to institutions which seem to the Ionians at war with the pleasures and the graces of social life."*

* Alexander, King of Macedon, had visited the Athenians with overtures of peace and alliance from Xerxes and Mardonius. These overtures were confined to the Athenians alone, and the Spartans were fearful lest they should be accepted. The Athenians, however, generously refused them. Gold, said they, hath no amount, earth no territory how beautiful soever that could tempt the Athenians to accept conditions from the Mede for the servitude of Greece. On this the Persians invaded Attica, and the Athenians, after waiting in vain for promised aid from Sparta, took refuge at Salamis. Meanwhile, they had sent messengers or embassadors to Sparta, to remonstrate on the violation of their agreement in delaying succor. This chanced at the very time when, by the death of his father, Cleombrotus, Pausanias became Regent. Slowly, and after much hesitation, the Spartans sent them aid under Pausanias. Two of the embassadors were Aristides and Cimon.

"Ill can the native of one land explain to the son of another why he loves it," returned Lysander. "That which the Ionian calls pleasure is to me but tedious vanity; that which he calls grace is to me but enervate levity. Me it pleases to find the day, from sunrise to night, full of occupations that leave no languor, that employ, but not excite. For the morning, our gymnasia, our military games, the chase—diversions that brace the limbs and leave us in peace fit for war—diversions which, unlike the brawls of the wordy Agora, bless us with the calm mind and clear spirit resulting from vigorous habits, and insuring jocund health. Noon brings our simple feast, shared in public, enlivened by jest; late at eve we collect in our Leschæ, and the winter nights seem short, listening to the old men's talk of our sires and heroes. To us life is one serene yet active holiday. No Spartan condescends to labor, yet no Spartan can womanize himself by ease. For us, too, differing from you Ionian Greeks, for us women are companions, not slaves. Man's youth is passed under the eyes and in the presence of those from whom he may select, as his heart inclines, the future mother of his children. Not for us your feverish and miserable ambitions, the intrigues of demagogues, the drudgery of the mart, the babble of the populace; we alone know the quiet repose of heart. That which I see everywhere else, the gnawing strife of passion, visits not the stately calm of the Spartan life. We have the leisure, not of the body alone, but of the soul. Equality with us is the all in all, and we know not that jealous anguish—the desire to rise one above the other. We busy

ourselves not in making wealth, in ruling mobs, in osten-
tatious rivalries of state, and gaud, and power—struggles
without an object. When we struggle, it is for an end.
Nothing moves us from our calm but danger to Sparta, or
woe to Hellas. Harmony, peace, and order—these are the
graces of our social life. Pity us, O Athenian!"

Cimon had listened with profound attention to a speech
unusually prolix and descriptive for a Spartan; and he
sighed deeply as it closed. For that young Athenian, destined to so renowned a place in the history of his country,
was, despite his popular manners, no favorer of the popular passions. Lofty and calm, and essentially an aristocrat
by nature and opinion, this picture of a life unruffled by
the restless changes of democracy, safe and aloof from the
shifting humors of the multitude, charmed and allured him.
He forgot for the moment those counter-propensities which
made him still Athenian—the taste for magnificence, the
love of women, and the desire of rule. His busy schemes
slept within him, and he answered:

"Happy is the Spartan who thinks with you. Yet," he
added, after a pause, "yet own that there are among you
many to whom the life you describe has ceased to proffer
the charms that inthrall you, and who envy the more diversified and exciting existence of surrounding states. Lysander's eulogiums shame his chief, Pausanias."

"It is not for me, nor for thee, whose years scarce exceed my own, to judge of our elders in renown," said Lysander, with a slight shade over his calm brow. "Pausanias will surely be found still a Spartan, when Sparta needs

7*

him; and the heart of the Heracleid beats under the robe of the Mede."

"Be frank with me, Lysander; thou knowest that my own countrymen often jealously accuse me of loving Sparta too well. I imitate, say they, the manners and dress of the Spartan, as Pausanias those of the Mede. Trust me, then, and bear with me, when I say that Pausanias ruins the cause of Sparta. If he tarry here longer in the command, he will render all the allies enemies to thy country. Already he has impaired his fame and dimmed his laurels; already, despite his pretexts and excuses, we perceive that his whole nature is corrupted. Recall him to Sparta while it is yet time—time to reconcile the Greeks with Sparta, time to save the hero of Platæa from the contaminations of the East. Preserve his own glory, dearer to thee as his special friend than to all men, yet dear to me, though an Athenian, from the memory of the deeds which delivered Hellas."

Cimon spoke with the blunt and candid eloquence natural to him, and to which his manly countenance and earnest tone and character for truth gave singular effect.

Lysander remained long silent. At length he said: "I neither deny nor assent to thine arguments, son of Miltiades. The Ephors alone can judge of their wisdom."

"But if we address them, by message, to the Ephors, thou and the nobler Spartans will not resent our remonstrances?"

"All that injures Pausanias, Lysander will resent. Little know I of the fables of poets, but Homer is at least as familiar to the Dorian as to the Ionian, and I think with him that between friends there is but one love and one anger."

"Then are the frailties of Pausanias dearer to thee than his fame, or Pausanias himself dearer to thee than Sparta —the erring brother than the venerable mother."

Lysander's voice died on his lips; the reproof struck home to him. He turned away his face, and, with a slow wave of his hand, seemed to implore forbearance. Cimon was touched by the action and the generous embarrassment of the Spartan; he saw, too, that he had left in the mind he had addressed thoughts that might work as he had designed; and he judged by the effect produced on Lysander what influence the same arguments might effect addressed to others less under the control of personal friendship. Therefore, with a few gentle words, he turned aside, continued his way, and left Lysander alone.

Entering the town, the Athenian threaded his path through some of the narrow lanes and alleys that wound from the quays toward the citadel, avoiding the broader and more frequented streets. The course he took was such as rendered it little probable that he should encounter any of the higher classes, and especially the Spartans, who from their constitutional pride shunned the resorts of the populace. But as he came nearer the citadel, stray Helots were seen at times emerging from the inns and drinking-houses, and these stopped short and inclined low if they caught sight of him at a distance; for his hat and staff, his majestic stature and composed step, made them take him for a Spartan.

One of these slaves, however, emerging suddenly from a house close by which Cimon passed, recognized him, and, retreating within abruptly, entered a room in which a man sat alone, and seemingly in profound thought; his cheek rested on one hand, with the other he leaned upon a small lyre; his eyes were bent on the ground, and he started, as a man does dream-like from a reverie, when the Helot touched him, and said abruptly, and in a tone of surprise and inquiry,

"Cimon the Athenian is ascending the hill toward the Spartan quarter."

"The Spartan quarter! Cimon!" exclaimed Alcman, for it was he. "Give me thy cap and hide."

Hastily enduing himself in these rough garments, and drawing the cap over his face, the Mothon hurried to the threshold, and, seeing the Athenian at the distance, followed his footsteps, though, with the skill of a man used to ambush, he kept himself unseen — now under the projecting roofs of the houses, now skirting the wall, which, heavy with buttresses, led toward the outworks of the citadel. And with such success did he pursue his track, that when Cimon paused at last at the place of his destination, and gave one vigilant and searching glance around him, he detected no living form.

He had then reached a small space of table-land on which stood a few trees of great age—all that time and the encroachments of the citadel and the town had spared of the sacred grove which formerly surrounded a rude and primitive temple, the gray columns of which gleamed through the heavy foliage. Passing, with a slow and cautious step,

under the thick shadow of these trees, Cimon now arrived
before the open door of the temple, placed at the east so as
to admit the first beams of the rising sun. Through the
threshold, in the middle of the fane, the eye rested on the
statue of Apollo, raised upon a lofty pedestal and surrounded by a rail—a statue not such as the later genius of the
Athenian represented the god of light, and youth, and
beauty; not wrought from Parian marble, or smoothest
ivory, and in the divinest proportions of the human form,
but rude, formal, and roughly hewn from the wood of the
yew-tree—some early effigy of the god, made by the simple
piety of the first Dorian colonizers of Byzantium. Three
forms stood mute by an altar equally homely and ancient,
and adorned with horns, placed a little apart, and consider-
ably below the statue.

As the shadow of the Athenian, who halted at the
threshold, fell long and dark along the floor, the figures
turned slowly, and advanced toward him. With an inclina-
tion of his head, Cimon retreated from the temple, and,
looking round, saw abutting from the rear of the building a
small cell or chamber, which doubtless in former times had
served some priestly purpose, but now, doorless, empty,
desolate, showed the utter neglect into which the ancient
shrine of the Dorian god had fallen amidst the gay and dis-
solute Byzantians. To this cell Cimon directed his steps;
the men he had seen in the temple followed him; and all
four, with brief and formal greeting, seated themselves,
Cimon on a fragment of some broken column, the others
on a bench that stretched along the wall.

14

"Peers of Sparta," said the Athenian, "ye have doubtless ere this revolved sufficiently the grave matter which I opened to you in a former conference, and in which, to hear your decision, I seek at your appointment these sacred precincts."

"Son of Miltiades," answered the blunt Polydorus, "you inform us that it is the intention of the Athenians to dispatch a messenger to Sparta demanding the instant recall of Pausanias. You ask us to second that request. But without our aid the Athenians are masters to do as they will. Why should we abet your quarrel against the Regent ?"

"Friend," replied Cimon, " we, the Athenians, confess to no quarrel with Pausanias; what we demand is to avoid all quarrel with him or yourselves. You seem to have overlooked my main arguments. Permit me to re-urge them briefly. If Pausanias remains, the allies have resolved openly to revolt; if you, the Spartans, assist your chief, as methinks you needs must do, you are at once-at war with the rest of the Greeks. If you desert him, you leave Hellas without a chief, and we will choose one of our own. Meanwhile, in the midst of our dissensions, the towns and states well affected to Persia will return to her sway; and Persia herself falls upon us as no longer a united enemy, but an easy prey. For the sake, therefore, of Sparta and of Greece, we entreat you to co-operate with us; or, rather, to let the recall of Pausanias be effected more by the wise precaution of the Spartans than by the fierce resolve of the other Greeks. So you save best the dignity of your state, and so, in reality, you best serve your chief. For less shameful to him is it to be recalled by you than to be deposed by us."

"I know not," said Gelon, surlily, "what Sparta hath to do at all with this foreign expedition. We are safe in our own defiles."

"Pardon me, if I remind you that you were scarcely safe at Thermopylæ, and that had the advice Demaratus proffered to Xerxes been taken, and that island of Cythera, which commands Sparta itself, been occupied by Persian troops, as in a future time, if Sparta desert Greece, it may be, you were undone. And, wisely or not, Sparta is now in command at Byzantium, and it behooves her to maintain, with the dignity she assumes, the interests she represents. Grant that Pausanias be recalled, another Spartan can succeed him. Whom of your countrymen would you prefer to that high post, if you, O Peers, aid us in the dismissal of Pausanias?"[*]

     *   *   *   *   *   *   *

---

[*] This chapter was left unfinished by the author; probably with the intention of recasting it. Such an intention, at least, is indicated by the marginal marks upon the MS.—L.

BOOK III.

CHAPTER I.

THE fountain sparkled to the noonday, the sward around it was sheltered from the sun by vines formed into shadowy arcades, with interlaced leaves for roof. Afar through the vistas thus formed gleamed the blue of a sleeping sea.

Under the hills, or close by the margin of the fountain, Cleonice was seated upon a grassy knoll, covered with wild flowers. Behind her, at a little distance, grouped her handmaids, engaged in their womanly work, and occasionally conversing in whispers. At her feet reposed the grand form of Pausanias. Alcman stood not far behind him, his hand resting on his lyre, his gaze fixed upon the upward jet of the fountain.

"Behold," said Cleonice, "how the water soars up to the level of its source!"

"As my soul would soar to thy love," said the Spartan, amorously.

"As thy soul should soar to the stars. O son of Hercules, when I hear thee burst into thy wild flights of ambition, I see not thy way to the stars."

"Why dost thou ever thus chide the ambition which may give me thee?"

"No, for thou mightest then be as much below me as thou art now above. Too humble to mate with the Heracleid, I am too proud to stoop to the Tributary of the Mede."

"Tributary for a sprinkling of water and a handful of earth. Well, my pride may revolt, too, from that tribute. But, alas! what is the tribute Sparta exacts from me now? —personal liberty—freedom of soul itself. The Mede's Tributary may be a king over millions; the Spartan Regent is a slave to the few."

"Cease—cease—cease. I will not hear thee," cried Cleonice, placing her hands on her ears.

Pausanias gently drew them away; and holding them both captive in the large clasp of his own right hand, gazed eagerly into her pure, unshrinking eyes.

"Tell me," he said, "for in much thou art wiser than I am, unjust though thou art. Tell me this. Look onward to the future with a gaze as steadfast as now meets mine, and say if thou canst discover any path, except that which it pleases thee to condemn, which may lead thee and me to the marriage altar!"

Down sunk those candid eyes, and the virgin's cheek grew first rosy red, and then pale, as if every drop of blood had receded to the heart.

"Speak!" insisted Pausanias, softening his haughty voice to its meekest tone.

"I can not see the path to the altar," murmured Cleonice, and the tears rolled down her cheeks.

"And if thou seest it not," returned Pausanias, "art thou brave enough to say, 'Be we lost to each other for life?' I, though man and Spartan, am not brave enough to say that."

He released her hands as he spoke, and clasped his own over his face. Both were long silent.

Alcman had for some moments watched the lovers with deep interest, and had caught into his listening ears the purport of their words. He now raised his lyre, and swept his hand over the chords. The touch was that of a master, and the musical sounds produced their effect on all. The handmaids paused from their work. Cleonice turned her eyes wistfully toward the Mothon. Pausanias drew his hands from his face, and cried joyously: "I accept the omen. Foster-brother, I have heard that measure to a hymeneal song. Sing us the words that go with the melody."

"Nay," said Alcman, gently, "the words are not those which are sung before youth and maiden when they walk over perishing flowers to bridal altars. They are the words which embody a legend of the land in which the heroes of old dwell, removed from earth, yet preserved from Hades."

"Ah," said Cleonice — and a strange expression, calmly mournful, settled on her features — "then the words may haply utter my own thoughts. Sing them to us, I pray thee."

The Mothon bowed his head, and thus began:

THE ISLE OF SPIRITS.

Many wonders on the ocean
  By the moonlight may be seen;
Under moonlight on the Euxine
  Rose the blessed silver isle,

As Leostratus of Croton,
  At the Pythian god's behest,
Steer'd along the troubled waters
  To the tranquil spirit-land.

In the earthquake of the battle,
  When the Locrians reel'd before
Croton's shock of marching iron,
  Strode a Phantom to their van:

Strode the shade of Locrian Ajax,
  Guarding still the native soil,
And Leostratus, confronting,
  Wounded fell before the spear.

Leech and herb the wound could heal not;
  Said the Pythian god, "Depart,
Voyage o'er the troubled Euxine
  To the tranquil spirit-land.

"There abides the Locrian Ajax,
  He who gave the wound shall heal;
Godlike souls are in their mercy
  Stronger yet than in their wrath."

While at ease on lulled waters
  Rose the blessed silver isle,
Purple vines in lengthening vistas
  Knit the hill-top to the beach.

And the beach had sparry caverns,
  And a floor of golden sands,
And wherever soar'd the cypress,
  Underneath it bloom'd the rose.

Glimmer'd there amid the vine-trees,
  Thoro' cavern, over beach,

Life-like shadows of a beauty
  Which the living know no more;

 Towering statures of great heroes,
  They who fought at Thebes and Troy;
And with looks that poets dream of
  Beam'd the women heroes loved.

Kingly, forth before their comrades,
  As the vessel touch'd the shore,
Came the stateliest Two by Hymen
  Ever hallow'd into One.

As He strode, the forests trembled
  To the awe that crown'd his brow:
As She stepp'd, the ocean dimpled
  To the ray that left her smile.

"Welcome hither, fearless warrior!"
  Said a voice in which there slept
Thunder-sounds to scatter armies,
  As a north wind scatters leaves.

"Welcome hither, wounded sufferer,"
  Said a voice of music low
As the coo of doves that nestle
  Under summer boughs at noon.

"Who are ye, O shapes of glory?"
  Ask'd the wondering living man:
Quoth the Man-ghost, "This is Helen,
  And the Fair is for the Brave.

"Fairest prize to bravest victor;
  Whom doth Greece her bravest deem?"
Said Leostratus, "Achilles:"
  "Bride and bridegroom then are we."

"Low I kneel to thee, Pelides,
 But, O marvel, she thy bride,
 She whose guilt unpeopled Hellas,
  She whose marriage lights fired Troy !"

 Frown'd the large front of Achilles,
  Overshadowing sea and sky,
 Even as when between Olympus
  And Oceanus hangs storm.

"Know, thou dullard," said Pelides,
 "That on the funereal pyre
 Earthly sins are purged from glory,
  And the Soul is as the Name.

"If to her in life—a Paris,
 If to me in life—a slave,
 Helen's mate is *here* Achilles,
  Mine—the sister of the stars.

"Naught of her survives but beauty,
 Naught of me survives but fame ;
 Here the Beautiful and Famous
  Intermingle evermore."

 Then throughout the Blessed Island
  Sung aloud the Race of Light,
"Know, the Beautiful and Famous
 Marry here for evermore !"

"Thy song bears a meaning deeper than its words," said Pausanias ; "but if that meaning be consolation, I comprehend it not."

"I do," said Cleonice. "Singer, I pray thee draw near. Let us talk of what my lost mother said was the favorite theme of the grander sages of Miletus. Let us talk of what lies afar and undiscovered amidst waters more troubled than the Euxine. Let us speak of the Land of Souls."

"Who ever returned from that land to tell us of it?" said Pausanias. "Voyagers that never voyaged thither save in song."

"Son of Cleombrotus," said Alcman, "hast thou not heard that in one of the cities founded by thine ancestor, Hercules, and named after his own name, there yet dwells a Priesthood that can summon to living eyes the Phantoms of the Dead?"

"No," answered Pausanias, with the credulous wonder common to eager natures which philosophy has not withdrawn from the realm of superstition.

"But," asked Cleonice, "does it need the Necromancer to convince us that the soul does not perish when the breath leaves the lips? If I judge the burden of thy song aright, thou art not, O singer, uninitiated in the divine and consoling doctrines which, emanating, it is said, from the schools of Miletus, establish the immortality of the soul, not for demi-gods and heroes only, but for us all; which imply the soul's purification from earthly sins, in some regions less chilling and stationary than the sunless and melancholy Hades."

Alcman looked at the girl surprised.

"Art thou not, maiden," said he, "one of the many female disciples whom the successors of Pythagoras the Samian have enrolled?"

"Nay," said Cleonice, modestly; "but my mother had

listened to great teachers of wisdom, and I speak imperfectly the thoughts I have heard her utter when she told me
she had no terror of the grave."

" Fair Byzantine," returned the Mothon, while Pausanias,
leaning his upraised face on his hand, listened mutely to
themes new to his mind and foreign to his Spartan culture
—" fair Byzantine, we in Lacedæmon, whether free or enslaved, are not educated to the subtle learning which dis-
tinguishes the intellect of Ionian Sages. But I, born and
licensed to be a poet, converse eagerly with all who swell
the stores which enrich the treasure-house of song. And
thus, since we have left the land of Sparta, and more especially in yon city, the centre of many tribes and of many
minds, I have picked up, as it were, desultory and scattered notions, which, for want of a fitting teacher, I bind and
arrange for myself as well as I may. And since the ideas
that now float through the atmosphere of Hellas are not
confined to the great, nay, perhaps are less visible to them
than to those whose eyes are not riveted on the absorbing
substances of ambition and power, so I have learned something, I know not how, save that I have listened and re-
flected. And here, where I have heard what sages conjecture of a world which seems so far off, but to which we are
so near that we may reach it in a moment, my interest
might indeed be intense. For what is this world to him
who came into it a slave?"

"Alcman," exclaimed Pausanias, "the foster-brother of
the Heracleid is no more a slave."

The Mothon bowed his head gratefully, but the expression on his face retained the same calm and sombre resignation.

"Alas!" said Cleonice, with the delicacy of female consolation, "who in this life is really free? Have citizens no thralldom in custom and law? Are we not all slaves?"

"True. All slaves!" murmured the royal victor. "Envy none, O Alcman. Yet," he continued, gloomily, "what is the life beyond the grave which sacred tradition and ancient song holds out to us? Not thy silver island, vain singer, unless it be only for an early race more immediately akin to the gods. Shadows in the shade are the dead, at the best reviving only their habits when on earth, in phantom-like delusions; aiming spectral darts, like Orion, at spectral lions; things bloodless and pulseless; existences followed to no purpose through eternity, as dreams are through a night. Who cares so to live again? Not I."

"The sages that now rise around, and speak oracles different from those heard at Delphi," said Alcman, "treat not thus the soul's immortality. They begin by inquiring how creation rose; they seek to find the primitive element; what that may be they dispute; some say the fiery, some the airy, some the ethereal element. Their language here is obscure. But it is a something which forms, harmonizes, works, and lives on forever. And of that something is the soul; creative, harmonious, active, an element in itself. Out of its development here, that soul comes on to a new development elsewhere. If here the beginning lead to that new development in what we call virtue, it moves to light and joy; if it can only roll on through the grooves

it has here made for itself, in what we call vice and crime,
its path is darkness and wretchedness."

"In what we call virtue—what we call vice and crime?
Ah," said Pausanias, with a stern sneer, "Spartan virtue, O
Alcman, is what a Helot may call crime. And if ever the
Helot rose and shouted freedom, would he not say, This is
virtue? Would the Spartan call it virtue, too, my foster-
brother?"

"Son of Cleombrotus," answered Alcman, "it is not for
me to vindicate the acts of the master; nor to blame the
slave who is of my race. Yet the sage definers of virtue
distinguish between the Conscience of a Polity and that of
the Individual Man. Self-preservation is the instinct of every community, and all the ordinances ascribed to Lycurgus
are designed to preserve the Spartan existence. For what
are the pure Spartan race? a handful of men established as
lords in the midst of a hostile population. Close by the
eyrie thine eagle fathers built in the rocks, hung the silent
Amyclæ, a city of foes that cost the Spartans many generations to subdue. Hence thy state was a camp, its citizens sentinels; its children were brought up from the cradle
to support the stern life to which necessity devoted the
men. Hardship and privation were second nature. Not
enough to be brave; vigilance was equally essential. Every
Spartan life was precious; therefore came the cunning
which characterizes the Spartan; therefore the boy is permitted to steal, but punished if detected; therefore the
whole Commonwealth strives to keep aloof from the wars
of Greece unless itself be threatened. A single battle in a

common cause might suffice to depopulate the Spartan race, and leave it at the mercy of the thousands that so reluctantly own its dominion. Hence the ruthless determination to crush the spirit, to degrade the class of the enslaved Helots; hence its dread lest the slumbering brute force of the Servile find in its own masses a head to teach the consciousness, and a hand to guide the movements, of its power. These are the necessities of the Polity; its vices are the outgrowth of its necessities; and the life that so galls thee, and which has sometimes rendered mad those who return to it from having known another, and the danger that evermore surrounds the lords of a sullen multitude, are the punishments of these vices. Comprehendest thou?"

"I comprehend."

"But individuals have a conscience apart from that of the Community. Every community has its errors in its laws. No human laws, how skillfully soever framed, but give to a national character defects as well as merits, merits as well as defects. Craft, selfishness, cruelty to the subdued, inhospitable frigidity to neighbors, make the defects of the Spartan character. But," added Alcman, with a kind of reluctant anguish in his voice, "the character has its grand virtues, too, or would the Helots not be the masters? Valor indomitable; grand scorn of death; passionate ardor for the State, which is so severe a mother to them; antique faith in the sacred altars; sublime devotion to what is held to be duty. Are these not found in the Spartan beyond all the Greeks, as thou seest them in thy friend Lysander—in that soul, stately, pure, compact in its own firm

15*

substance as a statue within a temple is in its Parian stone?
But what the gods ask from man is virtue in himself, according as he comprehends it.   And, therefore, here all so-
cieties are equal ; for the gods pardon in the man the faults
he shares with his Community, and ask from him but the
good and the beautiful, such as the nature of his Community will permit him to conceive and to accomplish.   Thou
knowest that there are many kinds of music—for instance,
the Doric, the Æolian, the Ionian—in Hellas.   The Lydians
have their music, the Phrygians theirs, too.   The Scyth and
the Mede doubtless have their own.   Each race prefers the
music it cultivates, and finds fault with the music of other
races.   And yet a man who has learned melody and measure
will recognize a music in them all.   So it is with virtue,
the music of the human soul.   It differs in differing races.
But he who has learned to know what virtue is can recognize its harmonies, wherever they be heard.   And thus
the soul that fulfills its own notions of music, and carries
them up to its idea of excellence, is the master soul ; and
in the regions to which it goes, when the breath leaves the
lips, it pursues the same art set free from the trammels that
confined and the false judgments that marred it here.   For
then the soul is no longer Spartan, or Ionian, Lydian, Median, or Scythian.   Escaped into the upper air, it is the citizen of universal freedom and universal light.   And hence
it does not live as a ghost in gloomy shades, being merely
a pale memory of things that have passed away ; but in its
primitive being as an emanation from the one divine principle which penetrates everywhere, vivifies all things, and

enjoys in all. This is what I weave together from the doctrines of varying schools; schools that collect from the fields of thought flowers of different kinds which conceal, by adorning it, the ligament that unites them all: this, I say, O Pausanias, is my conception of the soul."

Cleonice rose softly, and, taking from her bosom a rose, kissed it fervently, and laid it at the feet of the singer.

"Were this my soul," cried she, "I would ask thee to bind it in the wreath."

Vague and troubled thoughts passed meanwhile through the mind of the Heracleid: old ideas being disturbed and dislodged, the new ones did not find easy settlement in a brain occupied with ambitious schemes and a heart agitated by stormy passions. In much superstitious, in much skeptical, as education had made him the one, and experience but of worldly things was calculated to make him the other, he followed not the wing of the philosophy which passed through heights not occupied by Olympus, and dived into depths where no Tartarus echoed to the wail of Cocytus.

After a pause he said, in his perplexity,

"Well mayst thou own that no Delphian oracle tells thee all this. And when thou speakest of the Divine Principle as one, dost thou not, O presumptuous man, depopulate the Halls of Ida? Nay, is it not Zeus himself whom thou dethronest? is not thy Divine Principle the Fate which Zeus himself must obey?"

"There is a young man of Clazomenæ," answered the singer, "named Anaxagoras, who, avoiding all active life, though of birth the noblest, gives himself up to contemplation, and whom I have listened to in the city as he passed through it, on his way into Egypt. And I heard him say, 'Fate is an empty name.'* Fate is blind, the Divine is All-seeing."

"How!" cried Cleonice. "An empty name—she! Necessity, the All-compelling."

The musician drew from the harp one of the most artful of Sappho's exquisite melodies.

"What drew forth that music?" he asked, smiling. "My hand and my will, from a genius not present, not visible. Was that genius a blind fate? No, it was a grand intelligence. Nature is to the Deity what my hand and will are to the unseen genius of the musician. They obey an intelligence and they form a music. If creation proceed from an intelligence, what we call fate is but the consequence of its laws. And Nature operates not in the external world alone, but in the core of all life; therefore in the mind of man obeying only what some supreme intelligence has placed there; therefore in man's mind producing music or discord, according as he has learned the principles of harmony, that is, of good. And there be sages who declare that Intelligence and Love are the same. Yet," added the Mothon, with an aspect solemnly compassionate, "not the love thou mockest by the name of Aphrodite. No mortal eye hath ever seen that love within the known sphere, yet all insensibly feel its reign. What keeps the world togeth-

---

* Anaxagoras was then between twenty and thirty years of age.—See Ritter, vol. ii., for the sentiment here ascribed to him, and a general view of his tenets.

er but affection? What makes the earth bring forth its fruits but the kindness which beams in the sunlight and descends in the dews? What makes the lioness watch over her cubs, and the bird, with all air for its wanderings, come back to the fledglings in its nest? Strike love, the conjoiner, from creation, and creation returns to a void. Destroy love, the parental, and life is born but to perish. Where stop the influence of love, or how limit its multiform degrees? Love guards the fatherland; crowns with turrets the walls of the freeman. What but love binds the citizens of states together, and frames and heeds the laws that submit individual liberty to the rule of the common good? Love creates, love cements, love enters and harmonizes all things. And as like attracts like, so love attracts in the hereafter the loving souls that conceived it here. From the region where it summons them, its opposites are excluded. There ceases war; there ceases pain. There, indeed, intermingle the beautiful and glorious, but beauty purified from earthly sin, the glorious resting from earthly toil. Ask ye how to know on earth where love is really presiding? Not in Paphos, not in Amathus. Wherever thou seest beauty and good; wherever thou seest life, and that life pervaded with faculties of joy, there thou seest love; there thou shouldst recognize the Divinity."

"And where I see misery and hate," said the Spartan, "what should I recognize there?"

"Master," returned the singer, "can the good come without a struggle? Is the beautiful accomplished without strife? Recall the tales of primeval chaos, when, as

8*   M

sung the Ascræan singer, love first darted into the midst;
imagine the heave and throe of joining elements; conjure
up the first living shapes, born of the fluctuating slime
and vapor.   Surely they were things incomplete, deformed
ghastly fragments of being, as are the dreams of a maniac.
Had creative Love stopped there, and then, standing on the
height of some fair completed world, had viewed the war-
ring portents, wouldst thou not have said, But these are
the works of Evil and Hate?   Love did not stop there, it
worked on; and out of the chaos once ensouled, this glorious world swung itself into ether, the completed sister of
the stars.   Again, O my listeners, contemplate the sculptor,
when the block from the granite shaft first stands, rude
and shapeless, before him.   See him in his earlier strife
with the obstinate matter—how uncouth the first outline
of limb and feature; unlovelier often in the rugged com-
mencements of shape than when the dumb mass stood
shapeless.   If the sculptor had stopped there, the thing
might serve as an image for the savage of an abominable
creed, engaged in the sacrifice of human flesh.   But he
pauses not, he works on.   Stroke by stroke comes from
the stone a shape of more beauty than man himself is
endowed with, and in a human temple stands a celestial
image.

"Thus is it with the soul in the mundane sphere; it
works its way on through the adverse matter.   We see its
work half completed; we cry, 'Lo! this is misery, this is
hate,' because the chaos is not yet a perfected world, and
the stone block is not yet a statue of Apollo.   But for that

reason must we pause? No; we must work on, till the victory brings the repose.

"All things come into order from the war of contraries; the elements fight and wrestle to produce the wild flower at our feet; from a wild flower man hath striven and toiled to perfect the marvelous rose of the hundred leaves. Hate is necessary for the energies of love, evil for the activity of good; until, I say, the victory is won, until Hate and Evil are subdued, as the sculptor subdues the stone; and then rises the divine image serene forever, and rests on its pedestal in the Uranian Temple. Lift thine eyes; that temple is yonder. O Pausanias, the sculptor's work-room is the earth."

Alcman paused, and, sweeping his hand once more over his lyre, chanted as follows:

"Dew-drop that weepest on the sharp-barbed thorn,
   Why didst thou fall from Day's golden chalices?
      'My tears bathe the thorn,' said the Dew-drop,
      'To nourish the bloom of the rose.'

"Soul of the Infant, why to calamity
   Comest thou wailing from the calm spirit-source?
      'Ask of the Dew,' said the Infant,
      'Why it descends on the thorn!'

"Dew-drop from storm, and soul from calamity.
   Vanish soon—whither? let the Dew answer thee;
      'Have not my tears been my glory?
      Tears drew me up to the sun.'

"What were thine uses, that thou art glorified?
   What did thy tears give, profiting earth or sky?
      'There, to the thorn-stem a blossom;
      Here, to the Iris a tint.'"

Alcman had modulated the tones of his voice into a sweetness so plaintive and touching, that, when he paused, the handmaidens had involuntarily risen and gathered round, hushed and noiseless. Cleonice had lowered her veil over her face and bosom; but the heaving of its tissue betrayed her half-suppressed, gentle sob; and the proud mournfulness on the Spartan's swarthy countenance had given way to a soft composure, melancholy still—but melancholy as a lulled though dark water, over which starlight steals through disparted cloud.

Cleonice was the first to break the spell which bound them all. "I would go within," she murmured, faintly. "The sun, now slanting, strikes through the vine-leaves, and blinds me with its glare."

Pausanias approached timidly, and, taking her by the hand, drew her aside, along one of the grassy alleys that stretched onward to the sea.

The handmaidens tarried behind, to cluster nearer round the singer. They forgot he was a slave.

CHAPTER II.

"Thou art weeping still, Cleonice!" said the Spartan, "and I have not the privilege to kiss away thy tears."

"Nay, I weep not," answered the girl, throwing up her veil; and her face was calm, if still sad—the tear yet on the eyelids, but the smile upon the lip—δακρυόεν γελάοισα. "Thy singer has learned his art from a teacher heavenlier than the Pierides, and its name is Hope."

"But if I understand him aright," said Pausanias, "the Hope that inspires him is a goddess who blesses us little on the earth."

As if the Mothon had overheard the Spartan, his voice here suddenly rose behind them, singing:

> "*There* the Beautiful and Glorious
> Intermingle evermore."

Involuntarily both turned. The Mothon seemed as if explaining to the handmaids the allegory of his marriage-song upon Helen and Achilles, for his hand was raised on high, and again, with an emphasis, he chanted:

> "There, throughout the Blessed Islands,
>   And amid the Race of Light,
> Do the Beautiful and Glorious
>   Intermingle evermore."

16

"Canst thou not wait, if thou so lovest me?" said Cleonice, with more tenderness in her voice than it had ever yet betrayed to him; "life is very short. Hush!" she continued, checking the passionate interruption that burst from his lips; "I have something I would confide to thee: listen. Know that in my childhood I had a dear friend, a maiden a few years older than myself, and she had the divine gift of trance which comes from Apollo. Often, gazing into space, her eyes became fixed, and her frame still as a statue's; then a shiver seized her limbs, and prophecy broke from her lips. And she told me in one of these hours, when, as she said, 'all space and all time seemed spread before her like a sunlit ocean,' she told me of my future, so far as its leaves have yet unfolded from the stem of my life. Spartan, she prophesied that I should see thee—and—" Cleonice paused, blushing, and then hurried on, "and she told me that suddenly her eye could follow my fate on the earth no more, that it vanished out of the time and the space on which it gazed, and, saying it, she wept, and broke into funeral song. And therefore, Pausanias, I say life is very short for me at least—"

"Hold," cried Pausanias; "torture not me, nor delude thyself with the dreams of a raving girl. Lives she near? Let me visit her with thee, and I will prove thy prophetess an impostor."

"They whom the Priesthood of Delphi employ throughout Hellas to find the fit natures for a Pythoness heard of her, and heard herself. She whom thou callest impostor gives the answer to perplexed nations from the Pythian shrine. But wherefore doubt her?—where the sorrow? I feel none. If love does rule the worlds beyond, and does unite souls who love nobly here, yonder we shall meet, O descendant of Hercules, and human laws will not part us there!"

"Thou die! die before me! thou, scarcely half my years! And I be left here, with no comfort but a singer's dreamy verse, not even mine ambition! Thrones would vanish out of earth, and turn to cinders in thine urn."

"Speak not of thrones," said Cleonice, with imploring softness, "for the prophetess, too, spake of steps that went toward a throne, and vanished at the threshold of darkness, beside which sat the Furies. Speak not of thrones, dream but of glory and Hellas—of what thy soul tells thee is that virtue which makes life a Uranian music, and thus unites it to the eternal symphony, as the breath of the single flute melts when it parts from the instrument into the great concord of the choir. Knowest thou not that in the creed of the Persians each mortal is watched on earth by a good spirit and an evil one? And they who loved us below, or to whom we have done beneficent and gentle deeds, if they go before us into death, pass to the side of the good spirit, and strengthen him to save and to bless thee against the malice of the bad, and the bad is strengthened in his turn by those whom we have injured. Wouldst thou have all the Greeks whose birthright thou wouldst barter, whose blood thou wouldst shed for barbaric aid to thy solitary and lawless power, stand by the side of the evil Fiend? And what could I do against so many? what could my soul do," added Cleonice, with simple pathos, "by the side of the kinder spirit?"

Pausanias was wholly subdued. He knelt to the girl, he kissed the hem of her robe, and for the moment ambition, luxury, pomp, pride fled from his soul, and left there only the grateful tenderness of the man, and the lofty instincts of the hero. But just then—was it the evil spirit that sent him?—the boughs of the vine were put aside, and Gongylus the Eretrian stood before them. His black eyes glittered keen upon Pausanias, who rose from his knee, startled and displeased.

"What brings thee hither, man?" said the Regent, haughtily.

"Danger," answered Gongylus, in a hissing whisper. "Lose not a moment—come."

"Danger!" exclaimed Cleonice, tremblingly, and clasping her hands, and all the human love at her heart was visible in her aspect. "Danger, and to *him!*"

"Danger is but as the breeze of my native air," said the Spartan, smiling; "thus I draw it in and thus breathe it away. I follow thee, Gongylus. Take my greeting, Cleonice—the Good to the Beautiful. Well, then, keep Alcman yet a while to sing thy kind face to repose, and this time let him tune his lyre to songs of a more Dorian strain—songs that show what a Heracleid thinks of danger."

He waved his hand, and the two men, striding hastily, passed along the vine alley, darkened its vista for a few minutes, then vanishing down the descent to the beach, the wide blue sea again lay lone and still before the eyes of the Byzantine maid.

CHAPTER III.

PAUSANIAS and the Eretrian halted on the shore.

"Now speak," said the Spartan Regent. "Where is the danger?"

"Before thee," answered Gongylus, and his hand pointed to the ocean.

"I see the fleet of the Greeks in the harbor — I see the flag of my galley above the forest of their masts. I see detached vessels skimming along the waves hither and thither as in holiday and sport; but discipline slackens where no foe dares to show himself. Eretrian, I see no danger."

"Yet danger is there, and where danger is thou shouldst be. I have learned from my spies, not an hour since, that there is a conspiracy formed — a mutiny on the eve of an outburst. Thy place now should be in thy galley."

"My boat waits yonder in that creek, overspread by the wild shrubs," answered Pausanias; "a few strokes of the oar, and I am where thou seest. And in truth, without thy summons, I should have been on board ere sunset, seeing that on the morrow I have ordered a general review of the vessels of the fleet. Was that to be the occasion for the mutiny?"

"So it is supposed."

"I shall see the faces of the mutineers," said Pausanias,

16*

with a calm visage, and an eye which seemed to brighten the very atmosphere. "Thou shakest thy head; is this all?"

"Thou art not a bird—this moment in one place, that moment in another. There, with yon armament, is the danger thou canst meet. But yonder sails a danger which thou canst not, I fear me, overtake."

"Yonder!" said Pausanias, his eye following the hand of the Eretrian. "I see naught save the white wing of a sea-gull—perchance, by its dip into the water, it foretells a storm."

"Farther off than the sea-gull, and seeming smaller than the white spot of its wing, seest thou nothing?"

"A dim speck on the farthest horizon, if mine eyes mistake not."

"The speck of a sail that is bound to Sparta. It carries with it a request for thy recall."

This time the cheek of Pausanias paled, and his voice slightly faltered as he said,

"Art thou sure of this?"

"So I hear that the Samian captain, Uliades, has boasted at noon in the public baths."

"A Samian!—is it only a Samian who hath ventured to address to Sparta a complaint of her General?"

"From what I could gather," replied Gongylus, "the complaint is more powerfully backed. But I have not, as yet, heard more, though I conjecture that Athens has not been silent, and before the vessel sailed Ionian captains were seen to come with joyous faces from the lodgings of Cimon."

The Regent's brow grew yet more troubled. "Cimon, of all the Greeks out of Laconia, is the one whose word would weigh most in Sparta. But my Spartans themselves are not suspected of privity and connivance in this mission?"

"It is not said that they are."

Pausanias shaded his face with his hand for a moment in deep thought. Gongylus continued,

"If the Ephors recall thee before the Asian army is on the frontier, farewell to the sovereignty of Hellas!"

"Ha!" cried Pausanias, "tempt me not. Thinkest thou I need other tempter than I have here?"—smiting his breast.

Gongylus recoiled in surprise. "Pardon me, Pausanias, but temptation is another word for hesitation. I dreamed that I could not tempt; I did not know that thou didst hesitate."

The Spartan remained silent.

"Are not thy messengers on the road to the great king? —nay, perhaps already they have reached him. Didst thou not say how intolerable to thee would be life henceforth in the iron thralldom of Sparta—and now?"

"And now—I forbid thee to question me more. Thou hast performed thy task; leave me to mine."

He sprung with the spring of the mountain goat from the crag on which he stood—over a precipitous chasm, lighted on a narrow ledge, from which a slip of the foot would have been sure death, another bound yet more fearful, and his whole weight hung suspended by the bough of the ilex which he grasped with a single hand; then from bough to bough, from crag to crag, the Eretrian saw him descending till he vanished amidst the trees that darkened over the fissures at the foot of the cliff.

And before Gongylus had recovered his amaze at the almost preterhuman agility and vigor of the Spartan, and his dizzy sense at the contemplation of such peril braved by another, a boat shot into the sea from the green creek, and he saw Pausanias seated beside Lysander on one of the benches, and conversing with him, as if in calm earnestness, while the ten rowers sent the boat toward the fleet with the swiftness of an arrow to its goal.

"Lysander," said Pausanias, "hast thou heard that the Ionians have offered to me the insult of a mission to the Ephors demanding my recall?"

"No.   Who would tell me of insult to thee?"

"But hast thou any conjecture that other Spartans around me, and who love me less than thou, would approve, nay, have approved, this embassy of spies and malcontents?"

"I think none have so approved.   I fear some would so approve.   The Spartans round thee would rejoice did they know that the pride of their armies, the Victor of Platæa, were once more within their walls."

"Even to the danger of Hellas from the Mede?"

"They would rather all Hellas were Medized than Pausanias the Heracleid."

"Boy, boy," said Pausanias, between his ground teeth, "dost thou not see that what is sought is the disgrace of Pausanias the Heracleid?   Grant that I am recalled from the head of this armament, and on the charge of Ionians, and I am dishonored in the eyes of all Greece. Dost thou remember in the last Olympiad that when Themistocles, the only rival now to me in glory, appeared on the Altis, assembled Greece rose to greet and do him honor? And if I, deposed, dismissed, appeared at the next Olympiad, how would assembled Greece receive me? Couldst thou not see the pointed finger and hear the muttered taunt, 'That is Pausanias, whom the Ionians banished from Byzantium.' No, I must abide here; I must prosecute the vast plans which shall dwarf into shadow the petty genius of Themistocles. I must counteract this mischievous embassy to the Ephors. I must send to them an embassador of my own. Lysander, wilt thou go, and, burying in thy bosom thine own Spartan prejudices, deem that thou canst only serve me by proving the reasons why I should remain here; pleading for me, arguing for me, and winning my suit?"

"It is for thee to command, and for me to obey thee," answered Lysander, simply. "Is not that the duty of soldier to chief? When we converse as friends I may contend with thee in speech. When thou sayest, 'Do this,' I execute thine action. To reason with thee would be revolt."

Pausanias placed his clasped hands on the young man's shoulder, and, leaving them there, impressively said:

"I select thee for this mission because thee alone can I trust. And of me hast thou a doubt? Tell me."

"If I saw thee taking the Persian gold, I should say that the Demon had mocked mine eyes with a delusion. Never could I doubt, unless—unless—"

"Unless what?"

"Thou wert standing under Jove's sky, against the arms of Hellas."

"And then, if some other chief bid thee raise thy sword against me, thou art Spartan, and wouldst obey?"

"I am Spartan, and can not believe that I should ever have a cause, or listen to a command, to raise my sword against the chief I now serve and love," replied Lysander.

Pausanias withdrew his hands from the young man's broad shoulder. He felt humbled beside the quiet truth of that sublime soul. His own deceit became more black to his conscience. "Methinks," he said, tremulously, "I will not send thee, after all—and perhaps the news may be false."

The boat had now gained the fleet, and, steering amidst the crowded triremes, made its way toward the floating banner of the Spartan Serpent. More immediately round the General's galley were the vessels of the Peloponnesian allies, by whom he was still honored. A welcoming shout rose from the seamen lounging on their decks as they caught sight of the renowned Heracleid. Cimon, who was on his own galley, at some distance, heard the shout.

"So Pausanias," he said, turning to the officers round him, "has deigned to come on board, to direct, I suppose, the manœuvres for to-morrow."

"I believe it is but the form of a review for manœuvres," said an Athenian officer, "in which Pausanias will inspect the various divisions of the fleet, and, if more be intended, will give the requisite orders for a subsequent day. No ar-

rangements demanding much preparation can be anticipated, for Antagoras, the rich Chian, gives a great banquet
this day—a supper to the principal captains of the Isles."

"A frank and hospitable reveler is Antagoras," answered Cimon. "He would have extended his invitation to the
Athenians—me included—but in their name I declined."

"May I ask wherefore?" said the officer who had before
spoken. "Cimon is not held averse to wine-cup and myrtle bough."

"But things are said over some wine-cups and under
some myrtle boughs," answered Cimon, with a quiet laugh,
"which it is imprudence to hear, and would be treason to
repeat. Sup with me here on deck, friends—a supper for
sober companions—sober as the Laconian Syssitia, and let
not Spartans say that *our* manners are spoiled by the luxuries of Byzantium."

CHAPTER IV.

In an immense peristyle of a house which a Byzantine noble, ruined by lavish extravagance, had been glad to cede to the accommodation of Antagoras and other officers of Chios, the young rival of Pausanias feasted the chiefs of the Ægean. However modern civilization may in some things surpass the ancient, it is certainly not in luxury and splendor. And although the Hellenic States had not, at that period, aimed at the pomp of show and the refinements of voluptuous pleasure which preceded their decline, and although they never did carry luxury to the wondrous extent which it reached in Asia, or even in Sicily, yet even at that time a wealthy sojourner in such a city as Byzantium could command an entertainment that no monarch in our age would venture to parade before royal guests, and submit to the criticism of taxpaying subjects.

The columns of the peristyle were of dazzling alabaster, with their capitals richly gilt. The space above was roofless; but an immense awning of purple, richly embroidered in Persian looms—a spoil of some gorgeous Mede—shaded the feasters from the summer sky. The couches on which the banqueters reclined were of citron-wood, inlaid with ivory, and covered with the tapestries of Asiatic looms. At the four corners of the vast hall played four fountains,

and their spray sparkled to a blaze of light from colossal
candelabra, in which burned perfumed oil. The guests
were not assembled at a single table, but in small groups;
to each group its tripod of exquisite workmanship. To that
feast of fifty revelers no less than seventy cooks had contributed the inventions of their art, but under one great master, to whose care the banquet had been consigned by the
liberal host, and who ransacked earth, sky, and sea for dainties more various than this degenerate age ever sees ac-
cumulated at a single board. And the epicure who has but
glanced over the elaborate page of Athenæus must own with
melancholy self-humiliation that the ancients must have carried the art of flattering the palate to a perfection as absolute as the art which built the Parthenon and sculptured out
of gold and ivory the Olympian Jove. But the first course,
with its profusion of birds, flesh, and fishes, its marvelous
combinations of forced meats, and inventive poetry of
sauces, was now over. And in the interval preceding that
second course, in which gastronomy put forth its most exquisite masterpieces, the slaves began to remove the tables,
soon to be replaced. Vessels of fragrant waters, in which
the banqueters dipped their fingers, were handed round;
perfumes, which the Byzantine marts collected from every
clime, escaped from their precious receptacles.

Then were distributed the garlands. With these each
guest crowned locks that steamed with odors; and in them
were combined the flowers that most charm the eye, with
bud or herb that most guards from the head the fumes of
wine: with hyacinth and flax, with golden asphodel and

silver lily, the green of ivy and parsley leaf were thus en-twined; and above all, the rose, said to convey a delicious coolness to the temples on which it bloomed. And now for the first time wine came to heighten the spirits and test the charm of the garlands. Each, as the large goblet passed to him, poured from the brim, before it touched his lips, his libation to the good spirit. And as Antagoras, rising first, set this pious example, out from the farther ends of the hall, behind the fountains, burst a concert of flutes, and the great Hellenic Hymn of the Pæan.

As this ceased, the fresh tables appeared before the ban-queters, covered with all the fruits in season, and with those triumphs in confectionery, of which honey was the main ingredient, that well justified the favor in which the Greeks held the bee.

Then, instead of the pure juice of the grape, from which the libation had been poured, came the wines, mixed at least three parts with water, and deliciously cooled.

Up again rose Antagoras, and every eye turned to him.

"Companions," said the young Chian, "it is not held in free states well for a man to seize by himself upon supreme authority. We deem that a magistracy should only be ob-tained by the votes of others. Nevertheless, I venture to think that the latter plan does not always insure to us a good master. I believe it was by election that we Greeks have given to ourselves a generalissimo, not contented, it is said, to prove the invariable wisdom of that mode of gov-ernment; wherefore this seems an occasion to revive the good custom of tyranny. And I propose to do so in my person by proclaiming myself Symposiarch and absolute Promander in the Commonwealth here assembled. But if ye prefer the chance of the die—"

"No, no," cried the guests almost universally; "Antagoras, the Symposiarch, we submit. Issue thy laws."

"Hearken, then, and obey. First, then, as to the strength of the wine. Behold the crater in which there are three Naiades to one Dionysos. He is a match for them; not for more. No man shall put into his wine more water than the slaves have mixed. Yet if any man is so diffident of the god that he thinks three Naiades too much for him, he may omit one or two, and let the wine and the water fight it out upon equal terms. So much for the quality of the drink. As to quantity, it is a question to be deliberated hereafter. And now this cup to Zeus the Preserver."

The toast went round.

"Music, and the music of Lydia!" then shouted Antagoras, and resumed his place on the couch beside Uliades.

The music proceeded, the wines circled.

"Friend," whispered Uliades to the host, "thy father left thee wines, I know. But if thou givest many banquets like this, I doubt if thou wilt leave wines to thy son."

"I shall die childless, perhaps," answered the Chian; "and any friend will give me enough to pay Charon's fee across the Styx."

"That is a melancholy reflection," said Uliades, "and there is no subject of talk that pleases me less than that same Styx. Why dost thou bite thy lip, and choke the sigh? By the gods! art thou not happy?"

"Happy!" repeated Antagoras, with a bitter smile. "Oh yes!"

"Good. Cleonice torments thee no more. I myself have gone through thy trials; ay, and oftentimes. Seven times at Samos, five at Rhodes, once at Miletus, and forty-three times at Corinth, have I been an impassioned and unsuccessful lover. Courage; I love still."

Antagoras turned away. By this time the hall was yet more crowded, for many not invited to the supper came, as was the custom with the Greeks, to the Symposium; but these were all of the Ionian race.

"The music is dull without the dancers," cried the host. "Ho, there! the dancing-girls. Now would I give all the rest of my wealth to see among these girls one face that yet but for a moment could make me forget—"

"Forget what, or whom?" said Uliades; "not Cleonice?"

"Man, man, wilt thou provoke me to strangle thee?" muttered Antagoras.

Uliades edged himself away.

"Ungrateful!" he cried. "What are a hundred Byzantine girls to one tried male friend?"

"I will not be ungrateful, Uliades, if thou stand by my side against the Spartan."

"Thou art, then, bent upon this perilous hazard?"

"Bent on driving Pausanias from Byzantium, or into Hades—yes."

"Touch!" said Uliades, holding out his right hand. "By Cypris, but these girls dance like the daughters of Oceanus; every step undulates as a wave."

Antagoras motioned to his cup-bearer. "Tell the leader of that dancing choir to come hither." The cup-bearer obeyed.

A man with a solemn air came to the foot of the Chian's couch, bowing low. He was an Egyptian—one of the meanest castes.

"Swarthy friend," said Antagoras, "didst thou ever hear of the Pyrrhic dance of the Spartans?"

"Surely, of all dances am I teacher and preceptor."

"Your girls know it, then?"

"Somewhat, from having seen it; but not from practice. 'Tis a male dance and a warlike dance, O magnanimous, but, in this instance, untutored, Chian!"

"Hist, and listen." Antagoras whispered. The Egyptian nodded his head, returned to the dancing-girls, and when their measure had ceased, gathered them round him.

Antagoras again rose.

"Companions, we are bound now to do homage to our masters—the pleasant, affable, and familiar warriors of Sparta."

At this the guests gave way to their applauding laughter.

"And, therefore, these delicate maidens will present to us that flowing and Amathusian dance which the Graces taught to Spartan sinews. Ho, there—begin!"

The Egyptian had by this time told the dancers what they were expected to do; and they came forward with an affectation of stern dignity, the burlesque humor of which delighted all those lively revelers. And when, with adroit mimicry, their slight arms and mincing steps mocked that

17*

grand and masculine measure so associated with images of
Spartan austerity and decorum, the exhibition became so
humorously ludicrous that perhaps a Spartan himself would
have been compelled to laugh at it. But the merriment
rose to its height, when the Egyptian, who had withdrawn
for a few minutes, re-appeared with a Median robe and
mitred cap, and, calling out in his barbarous African accent,
" Way for the conqueror !" threw into his mien and gestures all the likeness to Pausanias himself which a practiced
mime and posture-master could attain. The laughter of
Antagoras alone was not loud—it was low and sullen, as if
sobs of rage were stifling it ; but his eye watched the effect
produced, and it answered the end he had in view.

As the dancers now, while the laughter was at its loudest
roar, vanished behind the draperies, the host rose, and his
countenance was severe and grave.

" Companions, one cup more, and let it be to Harmodius
and Aristogiton. Let the song in their honor come only
from the lips of free citizens, of our Ionian comrades.
Uliades, begin ! I pass to thee a myrtle bough ; and under
it I pass a sword."

Then he began the famous hymn ascribed to Callistratus,
commencing with a clear and sonorous voice, and the guests
repeating each stanza after him with the enthusiasm which
the words usually produced among the Hellenic republicans :

> I in a myrtle bough the sword will carry,
> As did Harmodius and Aristogiton ;
> When they the tyrant slew,
> And back to Athens gave her equal laws.

Thou art in nowise dead, best-loved Harmodius;
Isles of the Blessed are, they say, thy dwelling;
There swift Achilles dwells,
And there, they say, with thee dwells Diomed.

I in a myrtle bough the sword will carry,
As did Harmodius and Aristogiton,
When to Atheue's shrine
They gave their sacrifice—a tyrant man.

Ever on earth for both of you lives glory,
O loved Harmodius, loved Aristogiton,
For ye the tyrant slew,
And back to Athens ye gave equal laws.

When the song had ceased, the dancers, the musicians, the attendant slaves, had withdrawn from the hall, dismissed by a whispered order from Antagoras.

He, now standing up, took from his brows the floral crown, and, first sprinkling them with wine, replaced the flowers by a wreath of poplar. The assembly, a little while before so noisy, was hushed into attentive and earnest silence. The action of Antagoras, the expression of his countenance, the exclusion of the slaves, prepared all present for something more than the convivial address of a Symposiarch.

"Men and Greeks," said the Chian, "on the evening before Teucer led his comrades in exile over the wide waters to found a second Salamis, he sprinkled his forehead with Lyæan dews, being crowned with the poplar leaves—emblems of hardihood and contest; and, this done, he invited his companions to dispel their cares for the night, that their hearts might with more cheerful hope and bolder courage meet what the morrow might bring to them on the ocean. I imitate the ancient hero, in honor less of him than of the name of Salamis. We, too, have a Salamis to remember, and a second Salamis to found. Can ye forget that, had the advice of the Spartan leader Eurybiades been adopted, the victory of Salamis would never have been achieved? He was for retreat to the Isthmus; he was for defending the Peloponnese, because in the Peloponnesus was the unsocial, selfish Sparta, and leaving the rest of Hellas to the armament of Xerxes. Themistocles spoke against the ignoble counsel; the Spartan raised his staff to strike him. Ye know the Spartan manners. 'Strike if you will, but hear me,' cried Themistocles. He was heard, Xerxes was defeated, and Hellas saved. I am not Themistocles; nor is there a Spartan staff to silence free lips. But I too say, Hear me! for a new Salamis is to be won. What was the former Salamis?—the victory that secured independence to the Greeks, and delivered them from the Mede and the Medizing traitors. Again we must fight a Salamis. Where, ye say, is the Mede?—not at Byzantium, it is true, in person; but the Medizing traitor is here."

A profound sensation thrilled through the assembly.

"Enough of humility do the maritime Ionians practice when they accept the hegemony of a Spartan landsman; enough of submission do the free citizens of Hellas show when they suffer the imperious Dorian to sentence them to punishments only fit for slaves. But when the Spartan appears in the robes of the Mede, when the imperious Dorian places in the government of a city, which our joint arms now occupy, a recreant who has changed an Eretrian birthright for a Persian satrapy; when prisoners, made by the valor of all Hellas, mysteriously escape the care of the Lacedæmonian, who wears their garb, and imitates their manners — say, O ye Greeks, O ye warriors, if there is no second Salamis to conquer!"

The animated words, and the wine already drunk, produced on the banqueters an effect sudden, electrical, universal. They had come to the hall gay revelers; they were prepared to leave the hall stern conspirators.

Their hoarse murmur was as the voice of the sea before a storm.

Antagoras surveyed them with a fierce joy, and, with a change of tone, thus continued: "Ye understand me, ye know already that a delivery is to be achieved. I pass on: I submit to your wisdom the mode of achieving it. While I speak, a swift-sailing vessel bears to Sparta the complaints of myself, of Uliades, and of many Ionian captains here present, against the Spartan General. And although the Athenian chiefs decline to proffer complaints of their own, lest their State, which has risked so much for the common cause, be suspected of using the admiration it excites for the purpose of subserving its ambition, yet Cimon, the young son of the great Miltiades, who has ties of friendship and hospitality with families of high mark in Sparta, has been persuaded to add to our public statement a private letter to the effect that, speaking for himself, not in the name of Athens, he deems our complaints justly founded,

and the recall of Pausanias expedient for the discipline of
the armament. But can we say what effect this embassy
may have upon a sullen and haughty goverñment; against,
too, a royal descendant of Hercules; against the General
who at Platæa flattered Sparta with a renown to which her
absence from Marathon, and her meditated flight from
Salamis, gave but disputable pretensions?"

"And," interrupted Uliades, rising, "and—if, O Antagoras, I may crave pardon for standing a moment between
thee and thy guests—and this is not all, for even if they recall Pausanias, they may send us another general as bad, and
without the fame which somewhat reconciles our Ionian
pride to the hegemony of a Dorian. Now, whatever my
quarrel with Pausanias, I am less against a man than a
principle. I am a seaman, and against the principle of having for the commander of the Greek fleet a Spartan who
does not know how to handle a sail. I am an Ionian, and
against the principle of placing the Ionian race under the
imperious domination of a Dorian. Therefore I say, now
is the moment to emancipate our blood and our ocean—the
one from an alien, the other from a landsman. And the
hegemony of the Spartan should pass away."

Uliades sat down with an applause more clamorous than
had greeted the eloquence of Antagoras, for the pride of
race and of special calling is ever more strong in its im-
pulses than hatred to a single man. And, despite of all that
could be said against Pausanias, still these warriors felt awe
for his greatness, and remembered that at Platæa, where
all were brave, he had been proclaimed the bravest.

Antagoras, with the quickness of a republican Greek, trained from earliest youth to sympathy with popular assemblies, saw that Uliades had touched the right key, and swallowed down with a passionate gulp his personal wrath against his rival, which might otherwise have been carried too far, and have lost him the advantage he had gained.

"Rightly and wisely speaks Uliades," said he. "Our cause is that of our whole race; and clear has that true Samian made it to you all, O Ionians and captains of the seas, that we must not wait for the lordly answer Sparta may return to our embassage. Ye know that while night lasts we must return to our several vessels; an hour more, and we shall be on deck. To-morrow Pausanias reviews the fleet, and we may be some days before we return to land, and can meet in concert. Whether to-morrow or later the occasion for action may present itself, is a question I would pray you to leave to those whom you intrust with the discretionary power to act."

"How act?" cried a Lesbian officer.

"Thus would I suggest," said Antagoras, with well-dissembled humility: "let the captains of one or more Ionian vessels perform such a deed of open defiance against Pausanias as leaves to them no option between death and success; having so done, hoist a signal, and, sailing at once to the Athenian ships, place themselves under the Athenian leader; all the rest of the Ionian captains will then follow their example. And then, too numerous and too powerful to be punished for a revolt, we shall proclaim a revolution, and declare that we will all sail back to our native havens unless we have the liberty of choosing our own hegemon."

"But," said the Lesbian who had before spoken, "the Athenians as yet have held back and declined our overtures, and without them we are not strong enough to cope with the Peloponnesian allies."

"The Athenians will be compelled to protect the Ionians, if the Ionians in sufficient force demand it," said Uliades. "For as we are naught without them, they are naught without us. Take the course suggested by Antagoras: I advise it. Ye know me, a plain man, but I speak not without warrant. And before the Spartans can either contemptuously dismiss our embassy or send us out another general, the Ionian will be the mistress of the Hellenic seas, and Sparta, the land of oligarchies, will no more have the power to oligarchize democracy. Otherwise, believe me, that power she has now from her hegemony, and that power, whenever it suit her, she will use."

Uliades was chiefly popular in the fleet as a rough, good seaman, as a blunt and somewhat vulgar humorist. But whenever he gave advice, the advice carried with it a weight not always bestowed upon superior genius, because, from the very commonness of his nature, he reached at the common sense and the common feelings of those whom he addressed. He spoke, in short, what an ordinary man thought and felt. He was a practical man, brave, but not overaudacious, not likely to run himself or others into idle dangers; and when he said he had a warrant for his advice, he was believed to speak from his knowledge of the course which the Athenian chiefs, Aristides and Cimon, would pursue if the plan recommended were actively executed.

"I am convinced," said the Lesbian. "And since all are grateful to Athens for that final stand against the Mede, to which all Greece owes her liberties, and since the chief of her armaments here is a man of so modest a virtue, and so clement a justice, as we all acknowledge in Aristides, fitting is it for us Ionians to constitute Athens the maritime sovereign of our race."

"Are ye all of that mind?" cried Antagoras, and was answered by the universal shout, "We are—all!" or if the shout was not universal, none heeded the few whom fear or prudence might keep silent. "All that remains, then, is to appoint the captain who shall hazard the first danger and make the first signal. For my part, as one of the electors, I give my vote for Uliades, and this is my ballot." He took from his temples the poplar wreath, and cast it into a silver vase on the tripod placed before him.

"Uliades by acclamation!" cried several voices.

"I accept," said the Ionian; "and as Ulysses, a prudent man, asked for a colleague in enterprises of danger, so I ask for a companion in the hazard I undertake, and I select Antagoras."

This choice received the same applauding acquiescence as that which had greeted the nomination of the Ionian.

And in the midst of the applause was heard without the sharp, shrill sound of the Phrygian pipe.

"Comrades," said Antagoras, "ye hear the summons to our ships? Our boats are waiting at the steps of the quay,

18

by the Temple of Neptune.   Two sentences more, and then
to sea.   First, silence and fidelity; the finger to the lip, the
right hand raised to Zeus Horkios.   For a pledge, here is
an oath.   Secondly, be this the signal: whenever ye shall
see Uliades and myself steer our triremes out of the line in
which they may be marshaled, look forth and watch, breathless; and the instant you perceive that beside our flags of
Samos and Chios we hoist the ensign of Athens, draw off
from your stations, and follow the wake of our keels, to the
Athenian navy.   Then, as the gods direct us.   Hark! a second time shrills the fife."

CHAPTER V.

AT the very hour when the Ionian captains were hurrying toward their boats Pausanias was pacing his decks alone, with irregular strides, and through the cordage and the masts the starshine came fitfully on his troubled features. Long undecided he paused, as the waves sparkled to the stroke of oars, and beheld the boats of the feasters making toward the division of the fleet in which lay the navy of the isles. Farther on, remote and still, anchored the ships of Athens. He clenched his hand, and turned from the sight.

"To lose an empire," he muttered, "and without a struggle; an empire over yon mutinous rivals, over yon happy and envied Athens: an empire—where its limits?—if Asia puts her armies to my lead, why should not Asia be Hellenized, rather than Hellas be within the tribute of the Mede? Dull, dull, stolid Sparta! methinks I could pardon the slavery thou inflictest on my life, didst thou but leave unshackled my intelligence. But each vast scheme to be thwarted, every thought for thine own aggrandizement beyond thy barren rocks, met and inexorably baffled by a selfish aphorism, a cramping saw — 'Sparta is wide eno' for Spartans.'—'Ocean is the element of the fickle.'—'What matters the ascendency of Athens?—it does not cross the

Isthmus.'—'Venture nothing where I want nothing.' Why, this is the soul's prison! Ah, had I been born Athenian, I had never uttered a thought against my country. She and I would have expanded and aspired together."

Thus arguing with himself, he at length confirmed his resolve, and with a steadfast step entered his pavilion. There, not on broidered cushions, but by preference on the hard floor, without coverlet, lay Lysander calmly sleeping, his crimson warlike cloak, weather-stained, partially wrapped around him; no pillow to his head but his own right arm.

By the light of the high lamp that stood within the pavilion, Pausanias contemplated the slumberer.

"He says he loves me, and yet can sleep," he murmured, bitterly. Then, seating himself before a table, he began to write, with slowness and precision, whether as one not accustomed to the task or weighing every word.

When he had concluded, he again turned his eyes to the sleeper. "How tranquil! Was my sleep ever as serene? I will not disturb him to the last."

The fold of the curtain was drawn aside, and Alcman entered noiselessly.

"Thou hast obeyed?" whispered Pausanias.

"Yes; the ship is ready, the wind favors. Hast thou decided?"

"I have," said Pausanias, with compressed lips.

He rose, and touched Lysander lightly, but the touch sufficed; the sleeper woke on the instant, casting aside slumber easily as a garment.

"My Pausanias," said the young Spartan, "I am at

thine orders—shall I go? Alas! I read thine eye, and I shall leave thee in peril."

"Greater peril in the council of the Ephors and in the babbling lips of the hoary Gerontes than amidst the meeting of armaments. Thou wilt take this letter to the Ephors. I have said in it but little; I have said that I confide my cause to thee. Remember that thou insist on the disgrace to me—the Heracleid, and through me to Sparta, that my recall would occasion; remember that thou prove that my alleged harshness is but necessary to the discipline that preserves armies, and to the ascendency of Spartan rule. And as to the idle tale of Persian prisoners escaped, why thou knowest how even the Ionians could make nothing of that charge. Crowd all sail, strain every oar; no ship in the fleet so swift as that which bears thee. I care not for the few hours' start the tale-bearers have. Our Spartan forms are slow; they can scarce have an audience ere thou reach. The gods speed and guard thee, beloved friend. With thee goes all the future of Pausanias."

Lysander grasped his hand in a silence more eloquent than words, and a tear fell on that hand which he clasped. "Be not ashamed of it," he said then, as he turned away, and, wrapping his cloak round his face, left the pavilion. Alcman followed, lowered a boat from the side, and in a few moments the Spartan and the Mothon were on the sea. The boat made to a vessel close at hand—a vessel built in Cyprus, manned by Bithynians; its sails were all up, but it bore no flag. Scarcely had Lysander climbed the deck when it heaved to and fro, swaying as the anchor was drawn up,

then, righting itself, sprung forward, like a hound unleash-
ed for the chase. Pausanias, with folded arms, stood on the
deck of his own vessel, gazing after it, gazing long, till,
shooting far beyond the fleet, far toward the melting line
between sea and sky, it grew less and lesser; and as the
twilight dawned, it had faded into space.

The Heracleid turned to Alcman, who, after he had con-
veyed Lysander to the ship, had regained his master's side.

"What thinkest thou, Alcman, will be the result of all
this?"

"The emancipation of the Helots," said the Mothon,
quietly. "The Athenians are too near thee; the Persians
are too far. Wouldst thou have armies Sparta can neither
give nor take away from thee, bind to thee a race by the
strongest of human ties—make them see in thy power the
necessary condition of their freedom."

Pausanias made no answer. He turned within his pavilion, and, flinging himself down on the same spot from
which he had disturbed Lysander, said, "Sleep here was so
kind to him that it may linger where he left it. I have
two hours yet for oblivion before the sun rise."

CHAPTER VI.

If we were enabled minutely to examine the mental organization of men who have risked great dangers, whether by the impulse of virtue or in the perpetration of crime, we should probably find therein a large preponderance of hope. By that preponderance we should account for those heroic designs which would annihilate prudence as a calculator, did not a sanguine confidence in the results produce special energies to achieve them, and thus create a prudence of its own, being, as it were, the self-conscious admeasurement of the diviner strength which justified the preterhuman spring. Nor less should we account by the same cause for that audacity which startles us in criminals on a colossal scale, which blinds them to the risks of detection, and often at the bar of justice, while the evidences that insure condemnation are thickening round them, with the persuasion of acquittal or escape. Hope is thus alike the sublime inspirer or the arch corrupter; it is the foe of terror, the defier of consequences, the buoyant gamester which at every loss doubles the stakes, with a firm hand rattles the dice, and, invoking ruin, cries within itself, "How shall I expend the gain?"

In the character, therefore, of a man like Pausanias, risking so much glory, daring so much peril, strong indeed

must have been this sanguine motive power of human action. Nor is a large and active development of hope incompatible with a temperament habitually grave and often
profoundly melancholy. For hope itself is often engendered by discontent. A vigorous nature keenly susceptible
to joy, and deprived of the possession of the joy it yearns
for by circumstances that surround it in the present, is
goaded on by its impatience and dissatisfaction; it hopes
for the something it has not got, indifferent to the things
it possesses, and saddened by the want which it experiences. And therefore it has been well said by philosophers
that real happiness would exclude desire; in other words,
not only at the gates of hell, but at the porch of heaven,
he who entered would leave hope behind him. For perfect
bliss is but supreme content. And if content could say to
itself, "But I hope for something more," it would destroy
its own existence.

From his brief slumber the Spartan rose refreshed.
The trumpets were sounding near him, and the very sound
brightened his aspect, and animated his spirits.

Agreeably to orders he had given the night before, the
anchor was raised, the rowers were on their benches, the
libation to the Carnean Apollo, under whose special protection the ship was placed, had been poured forth, and
with the rising sea and to the blare of trumpets the gorgeous trireme moved forth from the bay.

It moved, as the trumpets ceased, to the note of a sweeter, but not less exciting, music. For, according to Hellenic
custom, to the rowers was allotted a musician, with whose

harmony their oars, when first putting forth to sea, kept
time.   And on this occasion Alcman superseded the wonted performer by his own more popular song and the melody
of his richer voice.   Standing by the mainmast, and holding
the large harp, which was stricken by the quill, its strings
being deepened by a sounding-board, he chanted an Io
Pæan to the Dorian god of light and poesy.   The harp at
stated intervals was supported by a burst of flutes, and the
burden of the verse was caught up by the rowers as in
chorus.   Thus, far and wide over the shining waves, went
forth the hymn.

Io, Io Pæan! slowly.   Song and oar must chime together:
Io, Io Pæau! by what title call Apollo?
   Clarian? Xauthian? Boëdromian?
   Countless are thy names, Apollo.
        Io Carnëe, Io Carnëe!
        By the margent of Eurotas,
        'Neath the shadows of Taygetus,
        Thee the sons of Lacedæmon
        Name Carneus.   Io, Io!
           Io Carnëe!   Io Carnëe!

Io, Io Pæan! quicker.   Song and voice must chime together:
Io Pæau! Io Pæan!   King Apollo, Io, Io!
Io Carnëe!
   For thine altars do the seasons
   Paint the tributary flowers,
   Spring thy hyacinth restores,
   Summer greets thee with the rose,
   Autumn the blue Cyane mingles
   With the coronals of corn,
   And in every wreath thy laurel
   Weaves its everlasting green.

Io Carnëe! Io Carnëe!
For the brows Apollo favors
Spring and winter does the laurel
Weave its everlasting green.

Io, Io Pæan! louder.   Voice and oar must chime together :
For the brows Apollo favors
Even Ocean bears the laurel.
Io Carnëe! Io Carnëe!

Io, Io Pæan! stronger.   Strong are those who win the laurel.

As the ship of the Spartan commander thus bore out to sea, the other vessels of the armament had been gradually forming themselves into a crescent, preserving still the order in which the allies maintained their several contributions to the fleet, the Athenian ships at the extreme end occupying the right wing, the Peloponnesians massed together at the left.

The Chian galleys adjoined the Samian ; for Uliades and Antagoras had contrived that their ships should be close to each other, so that they might take counsel at any moment and act in concert.

And now when the fleet had thus opened its arms, as it were, to receive the commander, the great trireme of Pausanias began to veer round, and to approach the half moon of the expanded armament.   On it came, with its beaked prow, like a falcon swooping down on some array of the lesser birds.

From the stern hung a gilded shield and a crimson pennon.   The heavy - armed soldiers in their Spartan mail occupied the centre of the vessel, and the sun shone full upon their armor.

"By Pallas the guardian," said Cimon, "it is the Athenian vessels that the strategus honors with his first visit."

And indeed the Spartan galley now came along-side that of Aristides, the admiral of the Athenian navy.

The soldiers on board the former gave way on either side. And a murmur of admiration circled through the Athenian ship, as Pausanias suddenly appeared. For, as if bent that day on either awing mutiny or conciliating the discontented, the Spartan chief had wisely laid aside the wondrous Median robes. He stood on her stern in the armor he had worn at Platæa, resting one hand upon his shield, which itself rested on the deck. His head alone was uncovered, his long sable locks gathered up into a knot, in the Spartan fashion, a crest, as it were, in itself to that lofty head. And so imposing were his whole air and carriage, that Cimon, gazing at him, muttered, "What profane hand will dare to rob that demi-god of command?"

CHAPTER VII.

PAUSANIAS came on board the vessel of the Athenian admiral, attended by the five Spartan chiefs who have been mentioned before as the warlike companions assigned to him. He relaxed the haughty demeanor which had given so much displeasure, adopting a tone of marked courtesy. He spoke with high and merited praise of the seaman-like appearance of the Athenian crews, and the admirable build and equipment of their vessels.

"Pity only," said he, smiling, "that we have no Persians on the ocean now, and that instead of their visiting us we must go in search of them."

"Would that be wise on our part?" said Aristides. "Is not Greece large enough for Greeks?"

"Greece has not done growing," answered the Spartan; "and the gods forbid that she should do so. When man ceases to grow in height he expands in bulk; when he stops there too, the frame begins to stoop, the muscles to shrink, the skin to shrivel, and decrepit old age steals on. I have heard it said of the Athenians that they think nothing done while aught remains to do. Is it not truly said, worthy son of Miltiades?"

Cimon bowed his head. "General, I can not disavow the sentiment. But if Greece entered Asia, would it not be as a river that runs into a sea? it expands, and is merged."

"The river, Cimon, may lose the sweetness of its wave, and take the brine of the sea. But the Greek can never lose the flavor of the Greek genius; and could he penetrate the universe, the universe would be Hellenized. But if, O Athenian chiefs, ye judge that we have now done all that is needful to protect Athens, and awe the Barbarian, ye must be longing to retire from the armament and return to your homes."

"When it is fit that we should return, we shall be recalled," said Aristides, quietly.

"What, is your state so unerring in its judgment? Experience does not permit me to think so, for it ostracized Aristides."

"An honor," replied the Athenian, "that I did not deserve, but an action that, had I been the adviser of those who sent me forth, I should have opposed as too lenient. Instead of ostracizing me, they should have cast both myself and Themistocles into the Barathrum."

"You speak with true Attic honor, and I comprehend that where, in commonwealths constituted like yours, party runs high, and the state itself is shaken, ostracism may be a necessary tribute to the very virtues that attract the zeal of a party and imperil the equality ye so prize. But what can compensate to a state for the evil of depriving itself of its greatest citizens?"

"Peace and freedom," said Aristides. "If you would have the young trees thrive, you must not let one tree be so large as to overshadow them. Ah, General, at Platæa," added the Athenian, in a benignant whisper, for the grand

19   10   ·

image before him moved his heart with a mingled feeling of generous admiration and prophetic pity — "ah, pardon me if I remind thee of the ring of Polycrates, and say that Fortune is a queen that requires tribute, Man should tremble most when most seemingly fortune-favored, and guard most against a fall when his rise is at the highest."

"But it is only at its highest flight that the eagle is safe from the arrow," answered Pausanias.

"And the nest the eagle has forgotten in her soaring is the more exposed to the spoiler."

"Well, my nest is in rocky Sparta; hardy the spoiler who ventures thither. Yet, to descend from these speculative comparisons, it seems that thou hast a friendly and meaning purpose in thy warnings. Thou knowest that there are in this armament men who grudge to me whatever I now owe to Fortune; who would topple me from the height to which I did not climb, but was led by the congregated Greeks; and who, while, perhaps, they are forging arrow-heads for the eagle, have sent to place poison and a snare in its distant nest. So the *Nausicaa* is on its voyage to Sparta, conveying to the Ephors complaints against me —complaints from men who fought by my side against the Mede!"

"I have heard that a Cyprian vessel left the fleet yesterday, bound to Laconia. ·I have heard that it does bear men charged by some of the Ionians with representations unfavorable to the continuance of thy command. It bears none from me as the Nauarchus of the Athenians. But—"

"But—what ?"

"But I have complained to thyself, Pausanias, in vain."

"Hast thou complained of late, and in vain?"

"Nay."

"Honest men may err. If they amend, do just men continue to accuse?"

"I do not accuse, Pausanias; I but imply that those who do may have a cause; but it will be heard before a tribunal of thine own countrymen, and doubtless thou hast sent to the tribunal those who may meet the charge on thy behalf."

"Well," said Pausanias, still preserving his studied urbanity and lofty smile, "even Agamemnon and Achilles quarreled; but Greece took Troy not the less. And, at least, since Aristides does not denounce me, if I have committed even worse faults than Agamemnon, I have not made an enemy of Achilles. And if," he added, after a pause, "if some of these Ionians, not waiting for the return of their envoys, openly mutiny, they must be treated as Thersites was." Then he hurried on quickly, for, observing that Cimon's brow lowered and his lips quivered, he desired to cut off all words that might lead to altercation.

"But I have a request to ask of the Athenian Nauarchus. Will you gratify myself and the fleet by putting your Athenian triremes into play? Your seamen are so famous for their manœuvres that they might furnish us with sports of more grace and agility than do the Lydian dancers. Landsman though I be, no sight more glads mine eye than these sea-lions of pine and brass, bounding under the yoke of their tamers. I presume not to give thee instructions what to perform. Who can dictate to the seamen of Salamis? But when your ships have played out their martial sport, let them exchange stations with the Peloponnesian vessels, and occupy for the present the left of the armament. Ye object not?"

"Place us where thou wilt, as was said to thee at Platæa," answered Aristides.

"I now leave ye to prepare, Athenians, and greet ye, saying, The Good to the Beautiful."

"A wondrous presence for a Greek commander!" said Cimon, as Pausanias again stood on the stern of his own vessel, which moved off toward the ships of the Islands.

"And no mean capacity," returned Aristides. "See you not his object in transplacing us?"

"Ha, truly; in case of mutiny on board the Ionian ships, he separates them from Athens. But woe to him if he thinks in his heart that an Ionian is a Thersites, to be silenced by the blow of a sceptre. Meanwhile let the Greeks see what manner of seamen are the Athenians. Methinks this game ordained to us is a contest before Neptune, and for a crown."

Pausanias bore right on toward the vessels from the Ægean Isles. Their masts and prows were heavy with garlands, but no music sounded from their decks, no welcoming shout from their crews.

"Son of Cleombrotus," said the prudent Erasinidas, "sullen dogs bite. Unwise the stranger who trusts himself to their kennel. Pass not to those triremes; let the captains, if thou wantest them, come to thee."

Pausanias replied, "Dogs fear the steady eye and spring at the recreant back. Helmsman, steer to yonder ship with the olive-tree on the parasemon, and the image of Bacchus on the guardian standard. It is the ship of Antagoras, the Chian captain."

Pausanias turned to his warlike Five. "This time, forgive me, I go alone." And before their natural Spartan slowness enabled them to combat this resolution, their leader was by the side of his rival, alone in the Chian vessel, and surrounded by his sworn foes.

"Antagoras," said the Spartan, "a Chian seaman's ship is his dearest home. I stand on thy deck as at thy hearth, and ask thy hospitality; a crust of thy honeyed bread, and a cup of thy Chian wine. For from thy ship I would see the Athenian vessels go through their nautical gymnastics."

The Chian turned pale and trembled; his vengeance was braved and foiled. He was powerless against the man who trusted to his honor, and asked to break of his bread and eat of his cup. Pausanias did not appear to heed the embarrassment of his unwilling host, but, turning round, addressed some careless words to the soldiers on the raised central platform, and then quietly seated himself, directing his eyes toward the Athenian ships. Upon these all the sails were now lowered. In nice manœuvres the seamen preferred trusting to their oars. Presently one vessel started forth, and with a swiftness that seemed to increase at every stroke.

A table was brought upon deck and placed before Pausanias, and the slaves began to serve to him such light food

19*

as sufficed to furnish the customary meal of the Greeks in the earlier forenoon.

"But where is mine host?" asked the Spartan. "Does Antagoras himself not deign to share a meal with his guest?"

On receiving the message, Antagoras had no option but to come forward. The Spartan eyed him deliberately, and the young Chian felt with secret rage the magic of that commanding eye.

Pausanias motioned to him to be seated, making room beside himself. The Chian silently obeyed.

"Antagoras," said the Spartan, in a low voice, "thou art doubtless one of those who have already infringed the laws of military discipline and obedience. Interrupt me not yet. A vessel, without waiting my permission, has left the fleet with accusations against me, thy commander; of what nature I am not even advised. Thou wilt scarcely deny that thou art one of those who sent forth the ship and shared in the accusations. Yet I had thought that if I had ever merited thine ill-will, there had been reconciliation between us in the council-hall. What has chanced since? Why shouldst thou hate me? Speak frankly; frankly have I spoken to thee."

"General," replied Antagoras, "there is no hegemony over men's hearts; thou sayest truly, as man to man, I hate thee. Wherefore? Because, as man to man, thou standest between me and happiness. Because thou wooest, and canst only woo to dishonor, the virgin in whom I would seek the sacred wife."

Pausanias slightly recoiled, and the courtesy he had sim-

ulated, and which was essentially foreign to his vehement
and haughty character, fell from him like a mask. For
with the words of Antagoras, jealousy passed within him,
and for the moment its agony was such that the Chian was
avenged. But he was too habituated to the stateliness of
self-control to give vent to the rage that seized him. He
only said, with a whitened and writhing lip, "Thou art
right; all animosities may yield, save those which a woman's eye can kindle. Thou hatest me—be it so—that is as
man to man. But as officer to chieftain, I bid thee henceforth beware how thou givest me cause to set this foot on
the head that lifts itself to the height of mine."

With that he rose, turned on his heel, and walked toward
the stern, where he stood apart, gazing on the Athenian
triremes, which by this time were in the broad sea. And
all the eyes in the fleet were turned toward that exhibition.
For marvelous were the ease and beauty with which these
ships went through their nautical movements: now as in
chase of each other; now approaching as in conflict, veering
off, darting aside, threading, as it were, a harmonious maze,
gliding in and out, here, there, with the undulous celerity
of the serpent. The admirable build of the ships; the perfect skill of the seamen; the noiseless docility and instinc-
tive comprehension by which they seemed to seize and to
obey the unforeseen signals of their Admiral—all struck the
lively Greeks that beheld the display, and universal was the
thought, if not the murmur, There was the power that
should command the Grecian seas.

Pausanias was too much accustomed to the sway of

masses not to have acquired that electric knowledge of what circles among them from breast to breast, to which habit gives the quickness of an instinct. He saw that he had committed an imprudence, and that in seeking to divert a mutiny he had incurred a yet greater peril.

He returned to his own ship without exchanging another word with Antagoras, who had retired to the centre of the vessel, fearing to trust himself to a premature utterance of that defiance which the last warning of his chief provoked, and who was therefore arousing the soldiers to louder shouts of admiration at the Athenian skill.

Rowing back toward the wing occupied by the Peloponnesian allies, of whose loyalty he was assured, Pausanias then summoned on board their principal officer, and communicated to him his policy of placing the Ionians not only apart from the Athenians, but under the vigilance and control of Peloponnesian vessels in the immediate neighborhood. "Therefore," said he, "while the Athenians will occupy this wing, I wish you to divide yourselves; the Lacedæmonian ships will take the way the Athenians abandon, but the Corinthian triremes will place themselves between the ships of the Islands and the Athenians. I shall give further orders toward distributing the Ionian navy. And thus I trust either all chance of a mutiny is cut off, or it will be put down at the first outbreak. Now, give orders to your men to take the places thus assigned to you. And having gratified the vanity of our friends, the Athenians, by their holiday evolutions, I shall send to thank and release them from the fatigue so gracefully borne."

All those with whom he here conferred, and who had no love for Athens or Ionia, readily fell into the plan suggested. Pausanias then dispatched a Laconian vessel to the Athenian Admiral, with complimentary messages and orders to cease the manœuvres, and then, heading the rest of the Laconian contingent, made slow and stately way toward the station deserted by the Athenians. But, pausing once more before the vessels of the Isles, he dispatched orders to their several commanders, which had the effect of dividing their array, and placing between them the powerful Corinthian service. In the orders of the vessels he forwarded for this change, he took especial care to dislocate the dangerous contiguity of the Samian and Chian triremes.

The sun was declining toward the west when Pausanias had marshaled the vessels he headed, at their new stations, and the Athenian ships were already anchored close and secured. But there was an evident commotion in that part of the fleet to which the Corinthian galleys had sailed. The Ionians had received with indignant murmurs the command which divided their strength. Under various pretexts each vessel delayed to move; and when the Corinthian ships came to take a vacant space, they found a formidable array —the soldiers on the platforms armed to the teeth. The confusion was visible to the Spartan chief; the loud hubbub almost reached to his ears. He hastened toward the place; but anxious to continue the gracious part he had so unwontedly played that day, he cleared his decks of their formidable hoplites, lest he might seem to meet menace by menace, and, drafting them into other vessels, and accom-

10*   P

panied only by his personal serving-men and rowers, he put forth alone, the gilded shield and the red banner still displayed at his stern.

But as he was thus conspicuous and solitary, and midway in the space left between the Laconian and Ionian galleys, suddenly two ships from the latter darted forth, passed through the centre of the Corinthian contingent, and steered, with the force of all their rowers, right toward the Spartan's ship.

"Surely," said Pausanias, "that is the Chian's vessel. I recognize the vine-tree and the image of the Bromian god; and surely that other one is the *Chimera* under Uliades, the Samian. They come hither, the Ionian with them, to harangue against obedience to my orders."

"They come hither to assault us," exclaimed Erasinidas; "their beaks are right upon us."

He had scarcely spoken, when the Chian's brass prow smote the gilded shield, and rent the red banner from its staff. At the same time the *Chimera*, under Uliades, struck the right side of the Spartan ship, and with both strokes the stout vessel reeled and dived. "Know, Spartan," cried Antagoras, from the platform in the midst of his soldiers, "that we Ionians hold together. He who would separate means to conquer us. We disown thy hegemony. If ye would seek us, we are with the Athenians."

With that the two vessels, having performed their insolent and daring feat, veered and shot off with the same rapidity with which they had come to the assault; and, as they did so, hoisted the Athenian ensign over their own national standards. The instant that signal was given, from the other Ionian vessels, which had been evidently awaiting it, there came a simultaneous shout; and all, vacating their place and either gliding through or wheeling round the Corinthian galleys, steered toward the Athenian fleet.

The trireme of Pausanias, meanwhile, sorely damaged, part of its side rent away, and the water rushing in, swayed and struggled alone in great peril of sinking.

Instead of pursuing the Ionians, the Corinthian galleys made at once to the aid of the insulted commander.

"Oh," cried Pausanias, in powerless wrath, "oh, the accursed element! Oh that mine enemies had attacked me on the land!"

"How are we to act?" said Aristides.

"We are citizens of a Republic in which the majority govern," answered Cimon. "And the majority here tell us how we are to act. Hark to the shouts of our men, as they are opening way for their kinsmen of the Isles."

The sun sunk, and with it sunk the Spartan maritime ascendency over Hellas. And from that hour in which the Samian and the Chian insulted the galley of Pausanias, if we accord weight to the authority on which Plutarch must have based his tale, commenced the brief and glorious sovereignty of Athens. Commence when and how it might, it was an epoch most signal in the records of the ancient world for its results upon a civilization to which as yet human foresight can predict no end.

BOOK IV.

CHAPTER I.

WE pass from Byzantium; we are in Sparta. In the Archeion, or office of the Ephoralty, sat five men, all somewhat advanced in years. These constituted that stern and
terrible authority which had gradually, and from unknown
beginnings,* assumed a kind of tyranny over the descendants of Hercules themselves. They were the representatives
of the Spartan people, elected without reference to rank
or wealth,† and possessing jurisdiction not only over the
Helots and Laconians, but over most of the magistrates.
They could suspend or terminate any office; they could
accuse the kings, and bring them before a court in which
they themselves were judges upon trial of life and death.
They exercised control over the armies and the embassies
sent abroad; and the king, at the head of his forces, was
still bound to receive his instructions from this Council of

---

* K. O. Müller ("Dorians"), book 3, ch. 7, § 2. According to
Aristotle, Cicero, and others, the Ephoralty was founded by
Theopompus subsequently to the mythical time of Lycurgus.
To Lycurgus himself it is referred by Xenophon and Herod-
otus. Müller considers rightly that, though an ancient Doric
institution, it was incompatible with the primitive constitution
of Lycurgus, and had gradually acquired its peculiar character
by causes operating on the Spartan State alone.

† Aristot., Pol. ii.

Five. Their duty, in fact, was to act as a check upon the kings, and they were the representatives of that nobility which embraced the whole Spartan people, in contradistinction to the Laconians and Helots.

The conference in which they engaged seemed to rivet their most earnest attention. And as the presiding Ephor continued the observations he addressed to them, the rest listened with profound and almost breathless silence.

The speaker, named Periclides, was older than the others. His frame, still upright and sinewy, was yet lean almost to emaciation, his face sharp, and his dark eyes gleamed with a cunning and sinister light under his gray brows.

" If," said he, " we are to believe these Ionians, Pausanias meditates some deadly injury to Greece. As for the complaints of his arrogance, they are to be received with due caution. Our Spartans, accustomed to the peculiar discipline of the Laws of Ægimius, rarely suit the humors of Ionians and innovators. The question to consider is not whether he has been too imperious toward Ionians who were but the other day subjected to the Mede, but whether he can make the command he received from Sparta menacing to Sparta herself. We lend him iron, he hath holpen himself to gold."

" Besides the booty at Platæa, they say that he has amassed much plunder at Byzantium," said Zeuxidamus, one of the Ephors, after a pause.

Periclides looked hard at the speaker, and the two men exchanged a significant glance.

" For my part," said a third, a man of a severe but noble

countenance, the father of Lysander, and, what was not usual with the Ephors, belonging to one of the highest families of Sparta, "I have always held that Sparta should limit its policy to self-defense; that, since the Persian invasion is over, we have no business with Byzantium. Let the busy Athenians obtain, if they will, the empire of the sea. The sea is no province of ours. All intercourse with foreigners, Asiatics and Ionians, enervates our men and corrupts our generals. Recall Pausanias — recall our Spartans. I have said."

"Recall Pausanias first," said Periclides, "and we shall then hear the truth, and decide what is best to be done."

"If he has Medized, if he has conspired against Greece, let us accuse him to the death," said Agesilaus, Lysander's father.

"We may accuse, but it rests not with us to sentence," said Periclides, disapprovingly.

"And," said a fourth Ephor, with a visible shudder, "what Spartan dare counsel sentence of death to the descendant of the gods?"

"I dare," replied Agesilaus, "but provided only that the descendant of the gods had counseled death to Greece. And for that reason, I say that I would not, without evidence the clearest, even harbor the thought that a Heracleid could meditate treason to his country."

Periclides felt the reproof, and bit his lips.

"Besides," observed Zeuxidamus, "fines enrich the state."

Periclides nodded approvingly.

An expression of lofty contempt passed over the brow
20*

and lip of Agesilaus. But with national self-command, he replied gravely, and with equal laconic brevity, "If Pausanias hath committed a trivial error that a fine can expiate, so be it. But talk not of fines till ye acquit him of all treasonable connivance with the Mede."

At that moment an officer entered on the conclave, and, approaching the presiding Ephor, whispered in his ear.

"This is well," exclaimed Periclides, aloud. "A messenger from Pausanias himself. Your son Lysander has just arrived from Byzantium."

"My son!" exclaimed Agesilaus, eagerly, and then, checking himself, added calmly, "That is a sign no danger to Sparta threatened Byzantium when he left."

"Let him be admitted," said Periclides.

Lysander entered; and, pausing at a little distance from the council-board, inclined his head submissively to the Ephors: save a rapid interchange of glances, no separate greeting took place between son and father.

"Thou art welcome," said Periclides. "Thou hast done thy duty since thou hast left the city. Virgins will praise thee as the brave man; age, more sober, is contented to say thou hast upheld the Spartan name. And thy father without shame may take thy hand."

A warm flush spread over the young man's face. He stepped forward with a quick step, his eyes beaming with joy. Calm and stately, his father rose, clasped the extended hand, then, releasing his own, placed it an instant on his son's bended head, and reseated himself in silence.

"Thou camest straight from Pausanias?" said Periclides.

Lysander drew from his vest the dispatch intrusted to him, and gave it to the presiding Ephor. Periclides half rose, as if to take with more respect what had come from the hand of the son of Hercules.

"Withdraw, Lysander," he said, "and wait without while we deliberate on the contents herein."

Lysander obeyed, and returned to the outer chamber.

Here he was instantly surrounded by eager, though not noisy, groups. Some in that chamber were waiting on business connected with the civil jurisdiction of the Ephors. Some had gained admittance for the purpose of greeting their brave countryman, and hearing news of the distant camp from one who had so lately quit the great Pausanias. For men could talk without restraint of their General, though it was but with reserve and indirectly that they slid in some furtive question as to the health and safety of a brother or a son.

"My heart warms to be among ye again," said the simple Spartan youth. "As I came through the defiles from the sea-coast, and saw on the height the gleam from the old Temple of Pallas Chalcioecus, I said to myself, ' Blessed be the gods that ordained me to live with Spartans or die with Sparta !' "

"Thou wilt see how much we shall make of thee, Lysander," cried a Spartan youth a little younger than himself, one of the superior tribe of the Hylleans. "We have heard of thee at Platæa. It is said that had Pausanias not been there thou wouldst have been called the bravest Greek in the armament."

"Hush!" said Lysander, "thy few years excuse thee, young friend. Save our General, we were all equals in the day of battle."

"So thinks not my sister Percalus," whispered the youth, archly; "scold her as thou dost me, if thou dare."

Lysander colored, and replied in a voice that slightly trembled, "I can not hope that thy sister interests herself in me. Nay, when I left Sparta, I thought—" He checked himself.

"Thought what?"

"That among those who remained behind Percalus might find her betrothed long before I returned."

"Among those who remained *behind!* Percalus! How meanly thou must think of her!"

Before Lysander could utter the eager assurance that he was very far from thinking meanly of Percalus, the other by-standers, impatient at this whispered colloquy, seized his attention with a volley of questions, to which he gave but curt and not very relevant answers, so much had the lad's few sentences disturbed the calm tenor of his existing self-possession. Nor did he quite regain his presence of mind until he was once more summoned into the presence of the Ephors.

CHAPTER II.

THE communication of Pausanias had caused an animated discussion in the Council, and led to a strong division of opinion. But the faces of the Ephors, rigid and composed, revealed nothing to guide the sagacity of Lysander as he re-entered the chamber. He himself, by a strong effort, had recovered from the disturbance into which the words of the boy had thrown his mind, and he stood before the Ephors intent upon the object of defending the name and fulfilling the commands of his chief. So reverent and grateful was the love that he bore to Pausanias that he scarcely permitted himself even to blame the deviations from Spartan austerity which he secretly mourned in his mind; and as to the grave guilt of treason to the Hellenic cause, he had never suffered the suspicion of it to rest upon an intellect that only failed to be penetrating where its sight was limited by discipline and affection. He felt that Pausanias had intrusted to him his defense; and though he would fain, in his secret heart, have beheld the Regent once more in Sparta, yet he well knew that it was the duty of obedience and friendship to plead against the sentence of recall which was so dreaded by his chief.

With all his thoughts collected toward that end, he stood before the Ephors, modest in demeanor, vigilant in purpose.

"Lysander," said Periclides, after a short pause, "we know thy affection to the Regent, thy chosen friend; but we know, also, thy affection for thy native Sparta: where the two may come into conflict, it is, and it must be, thy country which will claim the preference. We charge thee, by virtue of our high powers and authority, to speak the truth on the questions we shall address to thee, without fear or favor."

Lysander bowed his head. "I am in presence of Sparta my mother, and Agesilaus my father. They know that I was not reared to lie to either."

"Thou say'st well. Now answer. Is it true that Pausanias wears the robes of the Mede?"

"It is true."

"And has he stated to thee his reasons?"

"Not only to me, but to others."

"What are they?"

"That, in the mixed and half-Medized population of Byzantium, splendor of attire has become so associated with the notion of sovereign power that the Eastern dress and attributes of pomp are essential to authority; and that men bow before his tiara who might rebel against the helm and the horse-hair. Outward signs have a value, O Ephors, according to the notions men are brought up to attach to them."

"Good," said one of the Ephors. "There is in this departure from our habits, be it right or wrong, no sign, then, of connivance with the Barbarian."

"Connivance is a thing secret and concealed, and shuns all outward signs."

"But," said Periclides, "what say the other Spartan captains to this vain fashion, which savors not of the laws of Ægimius?"

"The first law of Ægimius commands us to fight and to die for the king or the chief who has kingly sway. The Ephors may blame, but the soldier must not question."

"Thou speakest boldly for so young a man," said Periclides, harshly.

"I was commanded to speak the truth."

"Has Pausanias intrusted the command of Byzantium to Gongylus the Eretrian, who already holds four provinces under Xerxes?"

"He has done so."

"Know you the reason for that selection?"

"Pausanias says that the Eretrian could not more show his faith to Hellas than by resigning Eastern satrapies so vast."

"Has he resigned them?"

"I know not; but I presume that when the Persian king knows that the Eretrian is leagued against him with the other captains of Hellas, he will assign the satrapies to another."

"And is it true that the Persian prisoners, Ariamanes and Datis, have escaped from the custody of Gongylus?"

"It is true. The charge against Gongylus for that error was heard in a council of confederate captains, and no proof against him was brought forward. Cimon was intrusted with the pursuit of the prisoners. Pausanias himself sent forth fifty scouts on Thessalian horses. The prisoners were not discovered."

"Is it true," said Zeuxidamus, "that Pausanias has amassed much plunder at Byzantium ?"

"What he has won as a conqueror was assigned to him by common voice; but he has spent largely ont of his own resources in securing the Greek sway at Byzantium."

There was a silence. None liked to question the young soldier further; none liked to put the direct question, whether or not the Ionian embassador could have cause for suspecting the descendant of Hercules of harm against the Greeks. At length Agesilaus said:

"I demand the word, and I claim the right to speak plainly. My son is young, but he is of the blood of Hyllus.

"Son, Pausanias is dear to thee. Man soon dies: man's name lives forever. Dear to thee if Pausanias is, dearer must be his name. In brief, the Ionian embassadors complain of his arrogance toward the confederates; they demand his recall. Cimon has addressed a private letter to the Spartan host, with whom he lodged here, intimating that it may be the best for the honor of Pausanias, and for our weight with the allies, to hearken to the Ionian embassy. It is a grave question, therefore, whether we should recall the Regent or refuse to hear these charges. Thou art fresh from Byzantium; thou must know more of this matter than we. Loose thy tongue, put aside equivocation. Say thy mind; it is for us to decide afterward what is our duty to the state."

"I thank thee, my father," said Lysander, coloring deeply

at a compliment paid rarely to one so young, "and thus I answer thee:

"Pausanias, in seeking to enforce discipline and preserve the Spartan supremacy, was at first somewhat harsh and severe to these Ionians, who had indeed but lately emancipated themselves from the Persian yoke, and who were little accustomed to steady rule. But of late he has been affable and courteous, and no complaint was urged against him for austerity at the time when this embassy was sent to you. Wherefore was it then sent? Partly, it may be, from motives of private hate, not public zeal, but partly because the Ionian race sees with reluctance and jealousy the hegemony of Sparta. I would speak plainly. It is not for me to say whether ye will or not that Sparta should retain the maritime supremacy of Hellas; but if ye do will it, ye will not recall Pausanias. No other than the Conqueror of Platæa has a chance of maintaining that authority. Eager would the Ionians be upon any pretext, false or frivolous, to rid themselves of Pausanias. Artfully willing would be the Athenians in especial that ye listened to such pretexts; for Pausanias gone, Athens remains and rules. On what belongs to the policy of the state it becomes not me to proffer a word, O Ephors. In what I have said I speak what the whole armament thinks and murmurs. But this I may say as soldier to whom the honor of his chief is dear: The recall of Pausanias may or may not be wise as a public act, but it will be regarded throughout all Hellas as a personal affront to your General; it will lower the royalty of Sparta, it will be an insult to the blood of Hercules. Forgive me,

O venerable magistrates. I have fought by the side of Pausanias, and I can not dare to think that the great Conqueror of Platæa, the man who saved Hellas from the Mede, the man who raised Sparta on that day to a renown which penetrated the farthest corners of the East, will receive from you other return than fame and glory. And fame and glory will surely make that proud spirit doubly Spartan."

Lysander paused, breathing hard and coloring deeply—annoyed with himself for a speech of which both the length and the audacity were much more Ionian than Spartan.

The Ephors looked at each other, and there was again silence.

"Son of Agesilaus," said Periclides, "thou hast proved thy Lacedæmonian virtues too well, and too high and general is thy repute among our army, as it is borne to our ears, for us to doubt thy purity and patriotism; otherwise, we might fear that while thou speakest in some contempt of Ionian wolves, thou hadst learned the arts of Ionian Agoras. But enough : thou art dismissed. Go to thy home; glad the eyes of thy mother ; enjoy the honors thou wilt find awaiting thee among thy coevals. Thou wilt learn later whether thou return to Byzantium, or whether a better field for thy valor may not be found in the nearer war with which Arcadia threatens us."

As soon as Lysander left the chamber, Agesilaus spoke :

"Ye will pardon me, Ephors, if I bid my son speak thus boldly. I need not say I am no vain, foolish father, desiring to raise the youth above his years. But, making allowance for his partiality to the Regent, ye will grant that he is a fair specimen of our young soldiery. Probably, as he speaks, so will our young men think. To recall Pausanias is to disgrace our General. Ye have my mind. If the Regent be guilty of the darker charges insinuated—correspondence with the Persian against Greece—I know but one sentence for him—Death. And it is because I would have ye consider well how dread is such a charge, and how awful such a sentence, that I entreat ye not lightly to entertain the one unless ye are prepared to meditate the other. As for the maritime supremacy of Sparta, I hold, as I have held before, that it is not within our councils to strive for it: it must pass from us. We may surrender it later with dignity. If we recall our General on such complaints, we lose it with humiliation."

"I agree with Agesilaus," said another. "Pausanias is a Heracleid; my vote shall not insult him."

"I agree, too, with Agesilaus," said a third Ephor; "not because Pausanias is the Heracleid, but because he is the victorious General who demands gratitude and respect from every true Spartan."

"Be it so," said Periclides, who, seeing himself thus outvoted in the council, covered his disappointment with the self-control habitual to his race. "But be we in no hurry to give these Ionian legates their answer to-day. We must deliberate well how to send such a reply as may be most conciliating and prudent. And for the next few days we have an excuse for delay in the religious ceremonials due to the venerable Divinity of Fear, which commence to-morrow.

Pass we to the other business before us; there are many whom we have kept waiting. Agesilaus, thou art excused from the public table to-day, if thou wouldst sup with thy brave son at home."

"Nay," said Agesilaus, "my son will go to his pheidition and I to mine—as I did on the day when I lost my first-born."

CHAPTER III.

On quitting the Hall of the Ephors, Lysander found himself at once on the Spartan Agora, wherein that hall was placed. This was situated on the highest of the five hills, over which the unwalled city spread its scattered population, and was popularly called the Tower. Before the eyes of the young Spartan rose the statues, rude and antique, of Latona, the Pythian Apollo, and his sister Artemis —venerable images to Lysander's early associations. The place which they consecrated was called Chorus; for there, in honor of Apollo, and in the most pompous of all the Spartan festivals, the young men were accustomed to lead the sacred dance. The Temple of Apollo himself stood a little in the background, and near to it that of Hera. But more vast than any image of a god was a colossal statue which represented the Spartan people; while on a still loftier pinnacle of the hill than that table-land which inclosed the Agora—dominating, as it were, the whole city—soared into the bright-blue sky the sacred Chalciœcus, or Temple of the Brazen Pallas, darkening with its shadow another fane toward the left dedicated to the Lacedæmonian Muses, and receiving a gleam on the right from the brazen statue of Zeus, which was said by tradition to have been made by a disciple of Dædalus himself.

But short time had Lysander to note undisturbed the old
21*

familiar scenes. A crowd of his early friends had already
collected round the doors of the Archeion, and rushed forward to greet and welcome him. The Spartan coldness
and austerity of social intercourse vanished always before
the enthusiasm created by the return to his native city of
a man renowned for valor; and Lysander's fame had come
back to Sparta before himself. Joyously, and in triumph,
the young men bore away their comrade. As they passed
through the centre of the Agora, where assembled the various merchants and farmers, who, under the name of Periœci, carried on the main business of the Laconian mart, and
were often much wealthier than the Spartan citizens, trade
ceased its hubbub; all drew near to gaze on the young warrior; and now, as they turned from the Agora, a group of
eager women met them on the road, and shrill voices exclaimed, "Go, Lysander, thou hast fought well — go and
choose for thyself the maiden that seems to thee the fairest. Go, marry, and get sons for Sparta."

Lysander's step seemed to tread on air, and tears of rapture stood in his downcast eyes. But suddenly all the voices
hushed; the crowds drew back; his friends halted. Close
by the great Temple of Fear, and coming from some place
within its sanctuary, there approached toward the Spartan
and his comrades a majestic woman—a woman of so grand
a step and port, that, though her veil as yet hid her face,
her form alone sufficed to inspire awe. All knew her by
her gait; all made way for Alithea, the widow of a king,
the mother of Pausanias the Regent. Lysander, lifting his
eyes from the ground, impressed by the hush around him,

recognized the form as it advanced slowly toward him, and, leaving his comrades behind, stepped forward to salute the mother of his chief. She, thus seeing him, turned slightly aside, and paused by a rude building of immemorial antiquity which stood near the temple. That building was the tomb of the mythical Orestes, whose bones were said to have been interred there by the command of the Delphian Oracle. On a stone at the foot of the tomb sat calmly down the veiled woman, and waited the approach of Lysander. When he came near, and alone—all the rest remaining aloof and silent—Alithea removed her veil, and a countenance grand and terrible as that of a Fate lifted its rigid looks to the young Spartan's eyes. Despite her age—for she had passed into middle life before she had borne Pausanias—Alithea retained all the traces of a marvelous and almost preterhuman beauty. But it was not the beauty of woman. No softness sat on those lips; no love beamed from those eyes. Stern, inexorable—not a fault in her grand proportions—the stoutest heart might have felt a throb of terror as the eye rested upon that pitiless and imposing front. And the deep voice of the Spartan warrior had a slight tremor in its tone as it uttered its respectful salutation.

"Draw near, Lysander. What sayest thou of my son?"

"I left him well, and—"

"Does a Spartan mother first ask of the bodily health of an absent man-child? By the tomb of Orestes and near the Temple of Fear, a king's widow asks a Spartan soldier what he says of a Spartan chief."

"All Hellas," replied Lysander, recovering his spirit, "might answer thee best, Alithea. For all Hellas proclaimed that the bravest man at Platæa was thy son, my chief."

"And where did my son, thy chief, learn to boast of bravery? They tell me he inscribed the offerings to the gods with his name as the Victor of Platæa — the battle won, not by one man, but assembled Greece. The inscription that dishonors him by its vainglory will be erased. To be brave is naught. Barbarians may be brave. But to dedicate bravery to his native land becomes a Spartan. He who is every thing against a foe should count himself as nothing in the service of his country."

Lysander remained silent under the gaze of those fixed and imperious eyes.

"Youth," said Alithea, after a short pause, "if thou returnest to Byzantium, say this from Alithea to thy chief: 'From thy childhood, Pausanias, has thy mother feared for thee; and at the Temple of Fear did she sacrifice when she heard that thou wert victorious at Platæa; for in thy heart are the seeds of arrogance and pride; and victory to thine arms may end in ruin to thy name. And ever since that day does Alithea haunt the precincts of that temple. Come back and be Spartan, as thine ancestors were before thee, and Alithea will rejoice, and think the gods have heard her. But if thou seest within thyself one cause why thy mother should sacrifice to Fear, lest her son should break the laws of Sparta, or sully his Spartan name, humble thyself, and mourn that thou didst not perish at Platæa.

By a temple and from a tomb I send thee warning.' Say this. I have done; join thy friends."

Again the veil fell over the face, and the figure of the woman remained seated at the tomb long after the procession had passed on, and the mirth of young voices was again released.

11*

CHAPTER IV.

THE group that attended Lysander continued to swell as he mounted the acclivity on which his parental home was placed. The houses of the Spartan proprietors were at that day not closely packed together as in the dense population of commercial towns. More like the villas of a suburb, they lay a little apart, on the unequal surface of the rugged ground, perfectly plain and unadorned, covering a large space with ample court - yards, closed in, in front of the narrow streets. And still was in force the primitive law which ordained that door-ways should be shaped only by the saw, and the ceilings by the axe ; but in contrast to the rudeness of the private houses, at every opening in the street were seen the Doric pillars or graceful stairs of a temple; and high over all dominated the Tower - hill, or Acropolis, with the antique fane of Pallas Chalciœcus.

And so, loud and joyous, the procession bore the young warrior to the threshold of his home. It was an act of public honor to his fair repute and his proven valor. And the Spartan felt as proud of that unceremonious attendance as ever did Roman chief sweeping under arches of triumph in the curule car.

At the threshold of the door stood his mother—for the tidings of his coming had preceded him — and his little brothers and sisters. His step quickened at the sight of these beloved faces.

"Bound forward, Lysander," said one of the train; "thou hast won the right to thy mother's kiss."

"But fail us not at the pheidition before sunset," cried another. "Every one of the obe will send his best contribution to the feast to welcome thee back. We shall have a rare banquet of it."

And so, as his mother drew him within the doors, his arm round her waist, and the children clung to his cloak, to his knees, or sprung up to claim his kiss, the procession set up a kind of chanted shout, and left the warrior in his home.

"Oh, this is joy, joy!" said Lysander, with sweet tears in his eyes, as he sat in the women's apartment, his mother by his side, and the little ones round him. "Where, save in Sparta, does a man love a home?"

And this exclamation, which might have astonished an Ionian—seeing how much the Spartan civilians merged the individual in the state—was yet true, where the Spartan was wholly Spartan, where, by habit and association, he had learned to love the severities of the existence that surrounded him, and where the routine of duties which took him from his home, whether for exercises or the public tables, made yet more precious the hours of rest and intimate intercourse with his family. For the gay pleasures and lewd resorts of other Greek cities were not known to the Spartan. Not for him were the cook-shops and baths and revels of Ionian idlers. When the state ceased to claim him, he had nothing but his home.

As Lysander thus exclaimed, the door of the room had opened noiselessly, and Agesilaus stood unperceived at the entrance, and overheard his son. His face brightened singularly at Lysander's words. He came forward and opened his arms.

"Embrace me now, my boy! my brave boy! embrace me now! The Ephors are not here."

Lysander turned, sprung up, and was in his father's arms.

"So thou art not changed. Byzantium has not spoiled thee. Thy name is uttered with praise unmixed with fear. All Persia's gold, all the great king's satrapies, could not Medize my Lysander. Ah," continued the father, turning to his wife, "who could have predicted the happiness of this hour? Poor child! he was born sickly. Hera had already given us more sons than we could provide for, ere our lands were increased by the death of thy childless relatives. Wife, wife! when the family council ordained him to be exposed on Taygetus, when thou didst hide thyself lest thy tears should be seen, and my voice trembled as I said, 'Be the laws obeyed,' who could have guessed that the gods would yet preserve him to be the pride of our house? Blessed be Zeus the savior, and Hercules the warrior!"

"And," said the mother, "blessed be Pausanias, the descendant of Hercules, who took the forlorn infant to his father's home, and who has reared him now to be the example of Spartan youths."

"Ah," said Lysander, looking up into his father's eyes, "if I can ever be worthy of your love, O my father, forget not, I pray thee, that it is to Pausanias I owe life, home, and a Spartan's glorious destiny."

"I forget it not," answered Agesilaus, with a mournful and serious expression of countenance. "And on this I would speak to thee. Thy mother must spare thee a while to me. Come. I lean on thy shoulder instead of my staff."

Agesilaus led his son into the large hall, which was the main chamber of the house; and pacing up and down the wide and solitary floor, questioned him closely as to the truth of the stories respecting the Regent which had reach-ed the Ephors.

"Thou must speak with naked heart to me," said Agesilaus; "for I tell thee that, if I am Spartan, I am also man and father; and I would serve him, who saved thy life and taught thee how to fight for thy country, in every way that may be lawful to a Spartan and a Greek."

Thus addressed, and convinced of his father's sincerity, Lysander replied with ingenuous and brief simplicity. He granted that Pausanias had exposed himself with a haughty imprudence, which it was difficult to account for, to the charges of the Ionians. "But," he added, with that shrewd observation which his affection for Pausanias rather than his experience of human nature had taught him—"but we must remember that in Pausanias we are dealing with no ordinary man. If he has faults of judgment which a Spartan rarely commits, he has, O my father, a force of intellect and passion which a Spartan as rarely knows. Shall I tell you the truth? Our state is too small for him. But would it not have been too small for Hercules? Would the laws

22

of Ægimius have permitted Hercules to perform his labors and achieve his conquests? This vast and fiery nature sud-denly released from the cramps of our customs, which Pausanias never in his youth regarded save as galling, expands itself, as an eagle long caged would outspread its wings."

"I comprehend," said Agesilaus, thoughtfully, and some-what sadly. "There have been moments in my own life when I regarded Sparta as a prison. In my early manhood I was sent on a mission to Corinth. Its pleasures, its wild tumult of gay license, dazzled and inebriated me. I said, 'This it is to live.' I came back to Sparta sullen and dis-contented. But then, happily, I saw thy mother at the fes-tival of Diana. We loved each other, we married; and when I was permitted to take her to my home, I became sobered and was a Spartan again. I comprehend. Poor Pausanias! But luxury and pleasure, though they charm a while, do not fill up the whole of a soul like that of our Heracleid. From these he may recover; but ambition— that is the true liver of Tantalus, and grows larger under the beak that feeds on it. What is his ambition, if Sparta be too small for him?"

"I think his ambition would be to make Sparta as big as himself."

Agesilaus stroked his chin musingly.

"And how?"

"I can not tell, I can only guess. But the Persian war, if I may judge by what I hear and see, can not roll away and leave the boundaries of each Greek state the same. Two states now stand forth prominent, Athens and Sparta.

Themistocles and Cimon aim at making Athens the head of
Hellas. Perhaps Pausanias aims to effect for Sparta what
they would effect for Athens."

"And what thinkest thou of such a scheme?"

"Ask me not. I am too young, too inexperienced, and
perhaps too Spartan to answer rightly."

"Too Spartan, because thou art too covetous of power
for Sparta."

"Too Spartan, because I may be too anxious to keep
Sparta what she is."

Agesilaus smiled. "We are of the same mind, my son.
Think not that the rocky defiles which inclose us shut out
from our minds all the ideas that new circumstance strikes
from time. I have meditated on what thou sayest. Pausanias may scheme. It is true that the invasion of the
Mede must tend to raise up one state in Greece to which
the others will look for a head. I have asked myself, can
Sparta be that state? and my reason tells me, No; Sparta
is lost if she attempt it. She may become something else,
but she can not be Sparta. Such a state must become maritime, and depend on fleets. Our inland situation forbids
this. True, we have ports in which the Periœci flourish;
but did we use them for a permanent policy, the Periœci
must become our masters. These five villages would be
abandoned for a mart on the sea-shore. This mother of
men would be no more. A state that so aspires must have
ample wealth at its command. We have none. We might
raise tribute from other Greek cities, but for that purpose
we must have fleets again, to overawe and compel, for no

tribute will be long voluntary. A state that would be the active governor of Hellas must have lives to spare in abundance. We have none, unless we always do hereafter as we did at Platæa, raise an army of Helots—seven Helots to one Spartan. How long, if we did so, would the Helots obey us, and meanwhile how would our lands be cultivated? A state that would be the centre of Greece must cultivate all that can charm and allure strangers. We banish strangers, and what charms and allures them would womanize us. More than all, a state that would obtain the sympathies of the turbulent Hellenic populations must have the most popular institutions. It must be governed by a Demus. We are an Oligarchic Aristocracy—a disciplined camp of warriors, not a licentious Agora. Therefore, Sparta can not assume the head of a Greek Confederacy except in the rare seasons of actual war; and the attempt to make her the head of such a confederacy would cause changes so repugnant to our manners and habits, that it would be fraught with destruction to him who made the attempt, or to us if he succeeded. Wherefore, to sum up, the ambition of Pausanias is in this impracticable, and must be opposed."

"And Athens," cried Lysander, with a slight pang of natural and national jealousy, "Athens, then, must wrest from Pausanias the hegemony he now holds for Sparta, and Athens must be what the Athenian ambition covets."

"We can not help it—she must; but can it last? Impossible. And woe to her if she ever comes in contact with the bronze of Laconian shields. But, in the mean while, what is to be done with this great and awful Hera-

cleid? They accuse him of Medizing, of secret conspiracy
with Persia itself. Can that be possible?"

"If so, it is but to use Persia on behalf of Sparta. If he
would subdue Greece, it is not for the king—it is for the
race of Hercules."

"Ay, ay, ay," cried Agesilaus, shading his face with his
hand. "All becomes clear to me now. Listen. Did I
openly defend Pausanias before the Ephors, I should in-
jure his cause. But when they talk of his betraying Hellas
and Sparta, I place before them, nakedly and broadly, their
duty if that charge be true. For if true, O my son, Pausanias must die as criminals die."

"Die—criminal—a Heracleid—king's blood—the Victor of Platæa—my friend Pausanias!"

"Rather he than Sparta. What sayest thou?"

"Neither, neither," exclaimed Lysander, wringing his
hands—"impossible both."

"Impossible both, be it so. I place before the Ephors
the terrors of accrediting that charge, in order that they
may repudiate it. For the lesser ones it matters not; he is
in no danger there, save that of fine. And his gold," added Agesilaus, with a curved lip of disdain, "will both condemn and save him. For the rest, I would spare him the
dishonor of being publicly recalled, and, to say truth, I
would save Sparta the peril she might incur from his wrath,
if she inflicted on him that slight. But mark me, he himself must resign his command, voluntarily, and return to
Sparta. Better so for him and his pride, for he can not
keep the hegemony against the will of the Ionians, whose

fleet is so much larger than ours, and it is to his gain if
his successor lose it, not he.   But better, not only for his
pride, but for his glory and his name, that he should come
from these scenes of fierce temptation, and, since birth
made him a Spartan, learn here again to conform to what he
can not change.   I have spoken thus plainly to thee.   Use
the words I have uttered as thou best may, after thy return
to Pausanias, which I will strive to make speedy.   But
while we talk there goes on danger — danger still of his
abrupt recall—for there are those who will seize every excuse for it.   Enough of these grave matters : the sun is
sinking toward the west, and thy companions await thee at
thy feast ; mine will be eager to greet me on thy return,
and thy little brothers, who go with me to my pheidition,
will hear thee so praised that they will long for the crypteia
—long to be men, and find some future Platæa for themselves.   May the gods forbid it !   War is a terrible unset-
tler.   Time saps states, as a tide the cliff.   War is an inun-
dation ; and when it ebbs, a landmark has vanished."

CHAPTER V.

NOTHING so largely contributed to the peculiar character
of Spartan society as the uniform custom of taking the principal meal at a public table.   It conduced to four objects:
the precise status of aristocracy, since each table was formed
according to title and rank; equality among aristocrats,
since each at the same table was held the equal of the other; military union, for as they feasted so they fought, being
formed into divisions in the field according as they messed
together at home; and, lastly, that sort of fellowship in public opinion which intimate association among those of the
same rank and habit naturally occasions.   These tables in
Sparta were supplied by private contributions; each head
of a family was obliged to send a certain portion at his own
cost, and according to the number of his children.   If his
fortune did not allow him to do this, he was excluded from
the public tables.   Hence, a certain fortune was indispensa-
ble to the pure Spartan, and this was one reason why it
was permitted to expose infants, if the family threatened to
be too large for the father's means.   The general arrange-
ments were divided into syssitia, according, perhaps, to the
number of families, and correspondent to the divisions, or
obes, acknowledged by the state.   But these larger sections
were again subdivided into companies or clubs of fifteen,

vacancies being filled up by ballot; but one vote could exclude. And since, as we have said, the companies were marshaled in the field according to their association at the table, it is clear that fathers of grave years and of high station (station in Sparta increased with years) could not have belonged to the same table as the young men, their sons. Their boys under a certain age they took to their own pheiditia, where the children sat upon a lower bench, and partook of the simplest dishes of the fare.

Though the cheer at these public tables was habitually plain, yet upon occasion it was enriched by presents to the after-course, of game and fruit.

Lysander was received by his old comrades with that cordiality in which was mingled for the first time a certain manly respect, due to feats in battle, and so flattering to the young.

The prayer to the gods, correspondent to the modern grace, and the pious libations being concluded, the attendant Helots served the black broth, and the party fell to, with the appetite produced by hardy exercise and mountain air.

" What do the allies say to the black broth ?" asked a young Spartan.

" They do not comprehend its merits," answered Lysander.

CHAPTER VI.

EVERY thing in the familiar life to which he had returned delighted the young Lysander. But for anxious thoughts about Pausanias, he would have been supremely blessed. To him the various scenes of his early years brought no associations of the restraint and harshness which revolted the more luxurious nature and the fiercer genius of Pausanias. The plunge into the frigid waters of Eurotas— the sole bath permitted to the Spartans* at a time when the rest of Greece had already carried the art of bathing into voluptuous refinement; the sight of the vehement contests of the boys, drawn up as in battle, at the game of foot-ball, or in detached engagements, sparing each other so little that the popular belief out of Sparta was that they were permitted to tear out each other's eyes,† but subjecting strength to every skillful art that gymnastics could teach; the mimic war on the island, near the antique trees of the Plane Gar

---

* Except occasionally the dry sudorific bath, all warm bathing was strictly forbidden, as enervating.

† An evident exaggeration. The Spartans had too great a regard for the physical gifts as essential to warlike uses, to permit cruelties that would have blinded their young warriors. And they even forbade the practice of the paucratium as ferocious and needlessly dangerous to life.

den, waged with weapons of wood and blunted iron, and the march regulated to the music of flutes and lyres; nay, even the sight of the stern altar, at which boys had learned to bear the anguish of stripes without a murmur—all produced in this primitive and intensely national intelligence an increased admiration for the ancestral laws, which, carrying patience, fortitude, address, and strength to the utmost perfection, had formed a handful of men into the calm lords of a fierce population, and placed the fenceless villages of Sparta beyond a fear of the external assaults and the civil revolutions which perpetually stormed the citadels and agitated the market-places of Hellenic cities.   His was not the mind to perceive that much was relinquished for the sake of that which was gained, or to comprehend that there was more which consecrates humanity in one stormy day of Athens than in a serene century of iron Lacedæmon.   But there is ever beauty of soul where there is enthusiastic love of country; and the young Spartan was wise in his own Dorian way.

The religious festival which had provided the Ephors with an excuse for delaying their answer to the Ionian envoys occupied the city.   The youths and the maidens met in the sacred chorus; and Lysander, standing by amidst the gazers, suddenly felt his heart beat.   A boy pulled him by the skirt of his mantle.

"Lysander, hast thou yet scolded Percalus?" said the boy's voice, archly.

"My young friend," answered Lysander, coloring high, "Percalus hath vouchsafed me as yet no occasion; and, indeed, she alone, of all the friends whom I left behind, does not seem to recognize me."

His eyes, as he spoke, rested with a mute reproach in their gaze on the form of a virgin who had just paused in the choral dance, and whose looks were bent obdurately on the ground. Her luxuriant hair was drawn upward from cheek and brow, braided into a knot at the crown of the head, in the fashion so trying to those who have neither bloom nor beauty, so exquisitely becoming to those who have both; and the maiden, even amidst Spartan girls, was pre-eminently lovely. It is true that the sun had somewhat embrowned the smooth cheek; but the stately throat and the rounded arms were admirably fair—not, indeed, with the pale and dead whiteness which the Ionian women sought to obtain by art, but with the delicate rose-hue of Hebe's youth. Her garment of snow-white wool, fastened over both shoulders with large golden clasps, was without sleeves, fitting not too tightly to the harmonious form, and leaving more than the ankle free to the easy glide of the dance. Taller than Hellenic women usually were, but about the average height of her Spartan companions, her shape was that which the sculptors give to Artemis. Light and feminine and virgin-like, but with all the rich vitality of a divine youth, with a force, not indeed of a man, but such as art would give to the goddess whose step bounds over the mountain-top, and whose arm can launch the shaft from the silver bow—yet was there something in the mien and face of Percalus more subdued and bashful than in those of most of the girls around her; and, as if her ear had caught Lysander's words, a smile just now played round her lips, and gave to all the countenance a wonderful sweetness. Then, as it became her turn once more to join in the circling measure, she lifted her eyes, directed them full upon the young Spartan, and the eyes said plainly, " Ungrateful ! I forget thee ! I !"

It was but one glance, and she seemed again wholly intent upon the dance ; but Lysander felt as if he had tasted the nectar and caught a glimpse of the courts of the gods. No further approach was made by either, although intervals in the evening permitted it.   But if, on the one hand, there was in Sparta an intercourse between the youth of both sexes wholly unknown in most of the Grecian States, and if that intercourse made marriages of love especially more common there than elsewhere, yet, when love did actually exist, and was acknowledged by some young pair, they shunned public notice ; the passion became a secret, or confidants to it were few. Then came the charm of stealth : to woo and to win, as if the treasure were to be robbed by a lover from the heaven unknown to man.   Accordingly, Lysander now mixed with the spectators, conversed cheerfully, only at distant intervals permitted his eyes to turn to Percalus, and when her part in the chorus had concluded, a sigh, undetected by others, seemed to have been exchanged between them, and, a little while after, Lysander had disappeared from the assembly.

He wandered down the street called the Aphetais, and after a little while the way became perfectly still and lonely, for the inhabitants had crowded to the sacred festival, and the houses lay quiet and scattered. So he went on, passing the ancient temple in which Ulysses is said to have dedicated a statue in honor of his victory in the race over the suitors of Penelope, and paused where the ground lay bare and rugged around many a monument to the fabled chiefs of the heroic age. Upon a crag that jutted over a silent hollow, covered with oleander and arbute, and here and there the wild rose, the young lover sat down, waiting patiently; for the eyes of Percalus had told him he should not wait in vain. Afar he saw, in the exceeding clearness of the atmosphere, the Tænarium, or Temple of Neptune, unprophetic of the dark connection that shrine would here-after have with him whom he then honored as a chief wor-thy, after death, of a monument amidst those heroes; and the gale that cooled his forehead wandered to him from the field of the Hellanium in which the envoys of Greece had taken council how to oppose the march of Xerxes, when his myriads first poured into Europe.

Alas! all the great passions that distinguish race from race pass away in the tide of generations. The enthusi-asm of soul which gives us heroes and demi-gods for ances-tors, and hallows their empty tombs; the vigor of thought-ful freedom which guards the soil from invasion, and shivers force upon the edge of intelligence. The heroic age and the civilized alike depart; and he who wanders through the glens of Laconia can scarcely guess where was the mon-ument of Lelex, or the field of the Hellanium. And yet on the same spot where sat the young Spartan warrior, waiting for the steps of the beloved one, may, at this very hour, some rustic lover be seated, with a heart beating with like emotions, and an ear listening for as light a tread. Love alone never passes away from the spot where its footstep hath once pressed the earth, and reclaimed the savage. Traditions, freedom, the thirst for glory, art, laws, creeds, vanish; but the eye thrills the breast, and hand warms to hand, as before the name of Lycurgus was heard, or Helen was borne a bride to the home of Menelaus. Under the influence of this power, then, something of youth is still retained by nations the most worn with time. But the power thus eternal in nations is short-lived for the individual being. Brief, indeed, in the life of each is that season which lasts forever in the life of all. From the old age of nations glory fades away; but in their utmost decrepitude there is still a generation young enough to love. To the individual man, however, glory alone remains when the snows of ages have fallen, and love is but the memory of a boyish dream. No wonder that the Greek genius, half incredulous of the soul, clung with such tenacity to youth. What a sigh from the heart of the old sensuous world breathes in the strain of Mimnermus, bewailing with so fierce and so deep a sorrow the advent of the years in which man is loved no more!

Lysander's eye was still along the solitary road, when he heard a low, musical laugh behind him. He started in surprise, and beheld Percalus. Her mirth was increased by his astonished gaze, till, in revenge, he caught both her hands, and, drawing her toward him, kissed, not without a struggle, the lips into serious gravity.

Extricating herself from him, the maiden put on an air

of offended dignity, and Lysander, abashed at his own audacity, muttered some broken words of penitence.

"But, indeed," he added, as he saw the cloud vanishing
from her brow, "indeed thou wert so provoking, and so
irresistibly beauteous. And how camest thou here, as if
thou hadst dropped from the heavens?"

"Didst thou think," answered Percalus, demurely, "that
I could be suspected of following thee? Nay; I tarried till
I could accompany Euryclea to her home yonder, and then,
slipping from her by her door, I came across the grass and
the glen to search for the arrow shot yesterday in the hollow below thee." So saying, she tripped from the crag by
his side into the nooked recess below, which was all out of
sight, in case some passenger should pass the road, and
where, stooping down, she seemed to busy herself in searching for the shaft amidst the odorous shrubs.

Lysander was not slow in following her footstep.

"Thine arrow is here," said he, placing his hand to his
heart.

"Fie! The Ionian poets teach thee these compliments."

"Not so. Who hath sung more of Love and his arrows
than our own Alcman?"

"Mean you the Regent's favorite brother?"

"Oh no! The ancient Alcman; the poet whom even
the Ephors sanction."

Percalus ceased to seek for the arrow, and they seated
themselves on a little knoll in the hollow, side by side, and
frankly she gave him her hand, and listened, with rosy
cheek and rising bosom, to his honest wooing. He told her

truly how her image had been with him in the strange
lands; how faithful he had been to the absent, amidst all
the beauties of the Isles and of the East. He reminded her
of their early days—how, even as children, each had sought
the other. He spoke of his doubts, his fears, lest he should
find himself forgotten or replaced; and how overjoyed he
had been when at last her eye replied to his.

"And we understood each other so well, did we not, Percalus? Here we have so often met before; here we parted last; here thou knewest I should go; here I knew that I
might await thee."

Percalus did not answer at much length, but what she
said sufficed to enchant her lover. For the education of
a Spartan maid did not favor the affected concealment of
real feelings. It could not, indeed, banish what Nature pre-
scribes to women—the modest self-esteem, the difficulty to
utter by word what eye and blush reveal — nor, perhaps,
something of that arch and innocent malice which enjoys
to taste the power which beauty exercises before the warm
heart will freely acknowledge the power which sways itself.
But the girl, though a little willful and high-spirited, was a
candid, pure, and noble creature, and too proud of being
loved by Lysander to feel more than a maiden's shame to
confess her own.

"And when I return," said the Spartan, "ah! then, look
out and take care; for I shall speak to thy father, gain his
consent to our betrothal, and then carry thee away despite
all thy struggles, to the brides-maid, and these long locks,
alas! will fall."

"I thank thee for thy warning, and will find my arrow in time to guard myself," said Percalus, turning away her face, but holding up her hand in pretty menace; "but where is the arrow? I must make haste and find it."

"Thou wilt have time enough, courteous Amazon, in mine absence, for I must soon return to Byzantium."

Percalus. "Art thou so sure of that?"

Lysander. "Why—dost thou doubt it?"

Percalus (rising and moving the arbute boughs aside with the tip of her sandal). "And unless thou wouldst wait very long for my father's consent, perchance thou mayst have to ask for it very soon—too soon to prepare thy courage for so great a peril."

Lysander (perplexed). "What canst thou mean? By all the gods, I pray thee speak plain!"

Percalus. "If Pausanias be recalled, wouldst thou still go to Byzantium?"

Lysander. "No; but I think the Ephors have decided not so to discredit their General."

Percalus (shaking her head incredulously). "Count not on their decision so surely, valiant warrior. And suppose that Pausanias is recalled, and that some one else is sent in his place whose absence would prevent thy obtaining that consent thou covetest, and so frustrate thy designs on—on—" (she added, blushing scarlet)—"on these poor locks of mine."

Lysander (starting). "Oh, Percalus, do I conceive thee aright? Hast thou any reason to think that thy father Dorcis will be sent to replace Pausanias — the great Pausanias?"

23●

Percalus (a little offended at a tone of expression which seemed to slight her father's pretensions). "Dorcis, my father, is a warrior whom Sparta reckons second to none; a most brave captain, and every inch a Spartan; but—but—"

Lysander. "Percalus, do not trifle with me. Thou knowest how my fate has been linked to the Regent's. Thou must have intelligence not shared even by my father, himself an Ephor. What is it?"

Percalus. "Thou wilt be secret, my Lysander, for what I may tell thee I can only learn at the hearth-stone."

Lysander. "Fear me not. Is not all between us a secret?"

Percalus. "Well, then, Periclides and my father, as thou art aware, are near kinsmen. And when the Ionian envoys first arrived, it was my father who was specially appointed to see to their fitting entertainment. And that same night I overheard Dorcis say to my mother, 'If I could succeed Pausanias, and conclude this war, I should be consoled for not having commanded at Platæa.' And my mother, who is proud for her husband's glory, as a woman should be, said, 'Why not strain every nerve as for a crown in Olympia? Periclides will aid thee—thou wilt win.'"

Lysander. "But that was the first night of the Ionians' arrival."

Percalus. "Since then I believe that thy father and others of the Ephors overruled Periclides and Zeuxidamus, for I have heard all that passed between my father and mother on the subject. But early this morning, while my mother

was assisting to attire me for the festival, Periclides himself called at our house, and before I came from home, my
mother, after a short conference with Dorcis, said to me, in
the exuberance of her joy, 'Go, child, and call here all the
maidens, as thy father ere long will go to outshine all the
Grecian chiefs.' So that if my father does go, thou wilt
remain in Sparta. Then, my beloved Lysander—and—and
—but what ails thee? Is that thought so sorrowful?"

Lysander. "Pardon me, pardon; thou art a Spartan
maid; thou must comprehend what should be felt by a
Spartan soldier when he thinks of humiliation and ingrati-
tude to his chief. Gods! the man who rolled back the
storm of the Mede to be insulted in the face of Hellas by
the government of his native city! The blush of shame
upon his cheek burns my own."

The warrior bowed his face in his clasped hands.

Not a resentful thought natural to female vanity and ex-
acting affection then crossed the mind of the Spartan girl.
She felt at once, by the sympathy of kindred nurture, all
that was torturing her lover. She was even prouder of him
that he forgot her for the moment to be so truthful to his
chief; and, abandoning the innocent coyness she had before shown, she put her arm round his neck with a pure
and sisterly fondness, and, kissing his brow, whispered,
soothingly, "It is for me to ask pardon, that I did not
think of this — that I spoke so foolishly; but comfort —
thy chief is not disgraced even by recall. Let them recall
Pausanias, they can not recall his glory. When, in Sparta,
did we ever hold a brave man discredited by obedience to

the government? None are disgraced who do not disgrace themselves."

"Ah! my Percalus, so I should say; but so will not think Pausanias, nor the allies; and in this slight to him I see the shadow of the Erinnys. But it may not be true yet; nor can Periclides of himself dispose thus of the Lacedæmonian armies."

"We will hope so, dear Lysander," said Percalus, who, born to be man's helpmate, then only thought of consoling and cheering him. "And if thou dost return to the camp, tarry as long as thou wilt, thou wilt find Percalus the same."

"The gods bless thee, maiden!" said Lysander, with grateful passion, "and blessed be the state that rears such women! Elsewhere Greece knows them not."

"And does Greece elsewhere know such men?" asked Percalus, raising her graceful head. "But so late—is it possible? See where the shadows are falling! Thou wilt but be in time for thy pheidition. Farewell."

"But when to meet again?"

"Alas! when we can." She sprung lightly away; then, turning her face as she fled, added, "Look out! thou wert taught to steal in thy boyhood—steal an interview. I will be thy accomplice."

CHAPTER VII.

THAT night, as Agesilaus was leaving the public table at which he supped, Periclides, who was one of the same company, but who had been unusually silent during the entertainment, approached him, and said, "Let us walk toward thy home together; the moon is up, and will betray listeners to our converse, should there be any."

"And in default of the moon, thy years, if not yet mine, permit thee a lantern, Periclides."

"I have not drunk enough to need it," answered the chief of the Ephors, with unusual pleasantry; "but as thou art the younger man, I will lean on thine arm, so as to be closer to thine ear."

"Thou hast something secret and grave to say, then?"

Periclides nodded.

As they ascended the rugged acclivity, different groups, equally returning home from the public tables, passed them. Though the sacred festival had given excuse for prolonging the evening meal, and the wine-cup had been replenished beyond the abstemious wont, still each little knot of revelers passed and dispersed in a sober and decorous quiet which, perhaps, no other eminent city in Greece could have exhibited; young and old equally grave and noiseless. For the Spartan youth, no fair Hetæræ then opened homes adorn-

12*   S

ed with flowers, and gay with wit, no less than alluring with beauty; but as the streets grew more deserted, there stood in the thick shadow of some angle, or glided furtively by some winding wall, a bridegroom lover, tarrying till all was still, to steal to the arms of the lawful wife, whom for years perhaps he might not openly acknowledge and carry in triumph to his home.

But not of such young adventurers thought the sage Periclides, though his voice was as low as a lover's "hist!" and his step as stealthy as a bridegroom's tread.

"My friend," said he, "with the faint gray of the dawn there comes to my house a new messenger from the camp, and the tidings he brings change all our decisions. The Festival does not permit us as Ephors to meet in public, or, at least, I think thou wilt agree with me, it is more prudent not to do so. All we should do now should be in strict privacy."

"But, hush! from whom the message—Pausanias?"

"No—from Aristides the Athenian."

"And to what effect?"

"The Ionians have revolted from the Spartan hegemony, and ranged themselves under the Athenian flag."

"Gods! what I feared has already come to pass."

"And Aristides writes to me, with whom you remember that he has the hospitable ties, that the Athenians can not abandon their Ionian allies and kindred who thus appeal to them; and that if Pausanias remain, open war may break out between the two divisions into which the fleet of Hellas is now rent."

"This must not be, for it would be war at sea; we and the Peloponnesians have far the fewer vessels, the less able seamen. Sparta would be conquered."

"Rather than Sparta should be conquered, must we not recall her General?"

"I would give all my lands, and sink out of the rank of Equal, that this had not chanced," said Agesilaus, bitterly.

"Hist! hist! not so loud."

"I had hoped we might induce the Regent himself to resign the command, and so have been spared the shame and the pain of an act that affects the hero-blood of our kings. Could not that be done yet?"

"Dost thou think so? Pausanias resign in the midst of a mutiny! Thou canst not know the man."

"Thou art right—impossible. I see no option now. He must be recalled. But the Spartan hegemony is, then, gone —gone forever—gone to Athens."

"Not so. Sparta hath many a worthy son besides this too arrogant Heracleid."

"Yes; but where his genius of command?—where his immense renown?—where a man, I say, not in Sparta, but in all Greece, fit to cope with Aristides and Cimon in the camp, with Themistocles in the city of our rivals? If Pausanias fails, who succeeds?"

"Be not deceived. What must be, must; it is but a little time earlier than necessity would have fixed. Wouldst thou take the command?"

"I? The gods forbid!"

"Then, if thou wilt not, I know but one man."

"And who is he?"

"Dorcis."

Agesilaus started, and, by the light of the moon, gazed full upon the face of the chief Ephor.

"Thy kinsman, Dorcis! Ah, Periclides, hast thou schemed this from the first?"

Periclides changed color at finding himself thus abruptly detected, and as abruptly charged; however, he answered with laconic dryness:

"Friend, did I scheme the revolt of the Ionians? But if thou knowest a better man than Dorcis, speak. Is he not brave?"

"Yes."

"Skillful?"

"No. Tut! thou art as conscious as I am that thou mightest as well compare the hat on thy brow to the brain it hides, as liken the stolid Dorcis to the fiery but profound Heracleid."

"Ay, ay. But there is one merit the hat has which the brow has not—it can do no harm. Shall we send our chiefs to be made worse men by Eastern manners? Dorcis has dull wit, granted; no arts can corrupt it. He may not save the hegemony, but he will return as he went, a Spartan."

"Thou art right again, and a wise man, Periclides. I submit. Thou hast my vote for Dorcis. What else hast thou designed? for I see now that whatever thou designest that wilt thou accomplish; and our meeting on the Archeion is but an idle form."

"Nay, nay," said Periclides, with his austere smile, "thou givest me a wit and a will that I have not. But as chief of the Ephors I watch over the state. And though I design nothing, this I would counsel: On the day we answer the Ionians, we shall tell them, 'What ye ask, we long since proposed to do.' And Dorcis is already on the seas as successor to Pausanias."

"When will Dorcis leave?" said Agesilaus, curtly.

"If the other Ephors concur, to-morrow night."

"Here we are at my doors; wilt thou not enter?"

"No. I have others yet to see. I knew we should be of the same mind."

Agesilaus made no reply; but as he entered the court-yard of his house, he muttered uneasily,

"And if Lysander is right, and Sparta is too small for Pausanias, do not we bring back a giant who will widen it to his own girth, and raze the old foundations to make room for the buildings he would add?"

* * * * * * *

(UNFINISHED.)

[The pages covered by the manuscript of this uncompleted story of "Pausanias" are scarcely more numerous than those which its author has filled with the notes made by him from works consulted with special reference to the subject of it. Those notes (upon Greek and Persian antiquities) are wholly without interest for the general public. They illustrate the author's conscientious industry, but they afford no clue to the plot of his romance. Under

24

the sawdust, however, thus fallen in the industrial process of an imaginative work, unhappily unfinished, I have found two specimens of original composition.   They are rough sketches of songs expressly composed for "Pausanias;" and, since they are not included in the foregoing portion of it, I think they may properly be added here.   The un-rhymed lyrics introduced by my father into some of the opening chapters of this romance appear to have been sug-gested by some fragments of Mimnermus, and composed about the same time as "The Lost Tales of Miletus."   In-deed, one of them has been already printed in that work. The following verses, however, which are rhymed, bear evi-dence of having been composed at a much earlier period. I know not whether it was my father's intention to discard them altogether, or to alter them materially, or to insert them without alteration in some later portion of the ro-mance.   But I print them here precisely as they are writ-ten.—L.]

FOR PAUSANIAS.

[Partially borrowed from Aristophanes's "Peace," v. 1127, etc.]

Away, away, with the helm and greaves,
　　Away with the leeks and cheese!*
I have conquer'd my passion for wounds and blows,
And the worst that I wish to the worst of my foes
　　　　Is the glory and gain
　　　　Of a year's campaign
　　On a diet of leeks and cheese.

---

* Τυροῦ τε καὶ κρομμύων.   Cheese and onions, the rations fur-nished to soldiers in campaign.

I love to drink by my own warm hearth,
Nourisht with logs from the pine-clad heights,
   Which were hewn in the blaze of the summer sun
To treasure his rays for the winter nights
   On the hearth where my grandam spun.

I love to drink of the grape I press,
   And to drink with a friend of yore;
Quick! bring me a bough from the myrtle-tree
   Which is budding afresh by Nicander's door.
Tell Nicander himself he must sup with me,
And along with the bough from his myrtle-tree
We will circle the lute, in a choral glee
   To the goddess of corn and peace.
For Nicander and I were fast friends at school.
Here he comes! We are boys once more.

When the grasshopper chants in the bells of thyme,
I love to watch if the Lemnian grape*
Is donning the purple that decks its prime;
And, as I sit at my porch to see,
With my little one trying to scale my knee,
To join in the grasshopper's chant, and sing
To Apollo and Pan from the heart of Spring.†
        Listen, O list!

Hear ye not, neighbors, the voice of Peace?
"The swallow I hear in the household eaves."
      Io Ægien! Peace!
"And the skylark at poise o'er the bended sheaves,"
      Io Ægien! Peace!

---

* It ripened earlier than the others. The words of the Chorus are, τὰς Λημνίας ἀμπέλους εἰ πεπαίνουσιν ἤδη.

† Variation—

   "What a blessing is life in a noon of Spring."

Here and there, everywhere, hear we Peace,
Hear her, and see her, and clasp her—Peace!
The grasshopper chants in the bells of thyme,
And the halcyon is back to her nest in Greece!

IN PRAISE OF THE ATHENIAN KNIGHTS.

[Imitated from the "Knights" of Aristophanes, v. 565, etc.]

Chant the fame of the Knights, or in war or in peace,
Chant the darlings of Athens,* the bulwarks of Greece,
Pressing foremost to glory, on wave and on shore,
Where the steed has no footing they win with the oar.†

On their bosoms the battle splits, wasting its shock.
If they charge like the whirlwind, they stand like the rock.
Ha! they count not the numbers, they scan not the ground;
When a foe comes in sight, on his lances they bound.

Fails a foot in its speed? heed it not.   One and all‡
Spurn the earth that they spring from, and own not a fall.
O the darlings of Athens, the bulwarks of Greece,
Wherefore envy the love-locks they perfume in peace!

---

* Variation—

    "The adorners of Athens, the bulwarks of Greece."

† Variation—

    "Keenest racers to glory, on wave or on shore,
      By the rush of the steed or the stroke of the oar!"

‡ Variation—

"Falls there one? never help him!   Our knights one and all."

Wherefore scowl if they fondle a quail or a dove,
Or inscribe on a myrtle the names that they love?
Does Alcides not teach us how valor is mild?
Lo, at rest from his labors he plays with a child.

When the slayer of Python has put down his bow,
By his lute and his love-locks Apollo we know.
Fear'd, O rowers, those gallants their beauty to spoil
When they sat on your benches, and shared in your toil?

When with laughter they row'd to your cry "Hippopai,"
"On, ye coursers of wood, for the palm wreath, away!"
Did those dainty youths ask you to store in your holds
Or a cask from their crypt or a lamb from their folds?

No, they cried, "We are here both to fight and to fast,
Place us first in the fight, at the board serve us last!
Wheresoever is peril, we knights lead the way,
Wheresoever is hardship, we claim it as pay.

Call us proud, O Athenians, we know it full well,
And we give you the life we're too haughty to sell."
Hail the stoutest in war, hail the mildest in peace,
Hail the darlings of Athens, the bulwarks of Greece!

24*